THE VOICE OF REASON

BOOK 3: THE POISON GARDEN SERIES

MARY OLDHAM

Copyright 2025 Mary Oldham
First Printing 2025

All rights reserved. This book or any portion thereof may not be reproduced or used in any manner whatsoever without the express written permission of the publisher except for the use of brief quotations in a book review.

Print: ISBN: 979-8-9985766-3-8
Kindle: ISBN: 979-8-9985766-1-4
Ebook: ISBN: 979-8-9985766-2-1

Any references to historical events, real people, or real places are used fictitiously. Names, characters, and places are products of the author's imagination. None of this book was created using AI.

Line and Grammatical Editor: Arleigh Rodgers
Cover Design: Lynn Andreozzi Interior Book Design
Interior Book Design: Teri Barnett/Indie Book Designer
Author Photo: Tanith Hawthorne

Printed in United States of America
By-Creek-Ity Publishing
Portland, Oregon

www.maryoldham.com

For Mom:

*Thank you for reading the first version of this, my first book in 2000.
You will always be my first and best Beta reader.*

*I miss you every day.
Love,
~MGO*

CONTENTS

Author's Note	vii
Prologue	1
Chapter 1	5
Chapter 2	15
Chapter 3	23
Chapter 4	29
Chapter 5	45
Chapter 6	49
Chapter 7	55
Chapter 8	65
Chapter 9	73
Chapter 10	81
Chapter 11	85
Chapter 12	87
Chapter 13	95
Chapter 14	103
Chapter 15	109
Chapter 16	115
Chapter 17	119
Chapter 18	129
Chapter 19	133
Chapter 20	139
Chapter 21	143
Chapter 22	149
Chapter 23	161
Chapter 24	167
Chapter 25	169
Chapter 26	185
Chapter 27	189
Chapter 28	193
Chapter 29	207
Chapter 30	209
Chapter 31	213
Chapter 32	217

Chapter 33	221
Chapter 34	225
Chapter 35	231
Chapter 36	237
Chapter 37	243
Chapter 38	247
Chapter 39	251
Chapter 40	259
Chapter 41	263
Chapter 42	267
Chapter 43	273
Chapter 44	275
Chapter 45	279
Chapter 46	283
Chapter 47	291
Chapter 48	295
Chapter 49	299
Chapter 50	301
Chapter 51	305
Chapter 52	309
Epilogue	313
Acknowledgments	319
About the Author	321
Also by Mary Oldham	323

Author's Note

When I had the relationship that motivated this story, a lot of people had a hard time believing it. I remember one person actually saying to me, "Come on, Mary, that really didn't happen." Enough happened that it took me over twenty years and three attempts to write this book. Women do not lie about abuse. We are embarrassed and scared.

Did this person only let me have four pairs of shoes in the closet at one time? Yes, he did.

Did he think my lipstick was whore red? Yes, he did.

Did the green silk robe belt go missing? Yes, it did. (That was the same night I was threatened with strangling until I was dead.)

Did he forbid a garbage can in the kitchen? Yes, he did.

Did he call himself *"The Voice of Reason"*? Yes, he did.

Did he consider me "loud and obnoxious" when I laughed too loud? Yes.

Did he take polaroids of me crying to show me how I looked when I was "overwrought and out of control"? Yes.

Did I get a new BMW after I left him? Yes, and it was candy apple red. Because he told me I looked horrible in red.

Did he say I wasn't smart and probably didn't know the meaning of the words like "obtuse and pejorative"? Yes. I replied that girls like me only knew words like bastard and asshole.

Fun fact, version two of this book beat 82 other entries to win a writing contest based on the best opening chapter. It was

AUTHOR'S NOTE

the true story of how I ran around the house and threw things into luggage that was laying open on the master bedroom floor. Only, in the true story, he came home right after I'd scrambled into the car, and he dove for the door handle. Thankfully, it was locked.

And lastly, life is short. If any of these little statements resonate with you, get out.

PROLOGUE

(Three years earlier)

"I like the greenhouse," Amber Daniels commented as she stepped off the brick patio onto a lush lawn bordered by mature trees. She and her husband had just toured a beautiful American Craftsman style home, which had just finished a full renovation. And their Realtor just happened to be her husband's little sister, Maggie. They walked into the deep backyard toward a cute little A-frame glass structure. The little greenhouse was small, but big enough for what Amber had in mind. And the spacious yard would be perfect for the children they hoped to have one day—private, yet open enough that it looked like a well-manicured golf course.

Amber and Jack had been looking for a home for about a month, but there was something about this house that felt good. The greenhouse all but sealed the deal. She could picture snow gently gracing the trees in winter and twinkling lights decorating the backyard in lacy fashion on hot summer evenings.

This would be Amber's first home. And it was a heck of a lot better than the Las Vegas first-floor apartment she'd grown up in, which looked out on baking dirt and desolation. At different times in her life, her living conditions had improved. Heck, even when she was Dr. Kelan Smith in Kansas, there had been a little house she was planning on buying in the small town she lived in. Then, well…she'd accidentally killed her boss and had to leave. Quickly. Now, years later, she was living the life she had only dreamt of as Amber Daniels, the wife of a successful attorney and the love of her life, Jack Daniels. It was a little different life than she imagined when she was Dr. Kelan Smith, but loving Jack was the most wonderful surprise she hadn't seen coming.

Jack had come into her life twice, first in Saint Barts, and then he was the out-of-town guest at one of her friend's dinner parties. Both times were so uncanny, she realized that the feminine hand of fate was playing matchmaker. They fell in love quickly, and now life without him wasn't imaginable. Now they were going to buy a house and have children. All things she'd never thought were possible for her.

It was almost like she was normal. That was a loose term. Maybe normal, with a touch of vigilante serial killer added in. Well, when life gave you lemons, you made lemonade. And she had one mean recipe for lemonade.

"I knew you would like it," Maggie Drake replied, her smile beaming. "That is why I had to show you this house. It is a gem and has only been on the market for about five hours."

"I'm glad you got us in to see it so fast. And bonus points for the greenhouse. Amber does have a green thumb," Jack answered with a knowing wink. He knew almost all of her secrets. And truth be told, she could grow a mean hemlock flower when needed.

"It is good for my business," Amber explained. "You know, with the lotions and things. When I can grow the plants myself, there is a certain added integrity. I know where everything came from and can assure people the products are one hundred percent organic." She had a little side business with organic lotions and cosmetics. People seemed to like them, and they explained away her obsessive need to garden. However, the greenhouse was very intriguing for another idea she had long wanted to put into fruition—one that had to do with greenhouses, rhododendrons, and bees. She liked honeybees and tried to use their honey and wax in her cosmetics and lotions. But in this case, what the honeybees would be forced to make would have a darker end goal than hand lotion. It should be a lovely red color and quite poisonous. In Nepal, they called it Mad Honey.

"I love my violet hand lotion," Maggie said. "I think it is wonderful."

"I'm so glad," Amber said, thinking of how the lotion was only Jergens with a little bit of crushed dried violet and a scant amount of Xanthan gum added in to create a little bit of texture that could fool even the smartest people. "You let me know when you need more, and I will make sure you never run out. Family should never suffer from dry skin."

"Sometimes I like you better than I like my brother," Maggie said with a sincere smile that almost made Amber feel a little guilty, but she got over it.

Amber liked cute Maggie and her sweet way the moment Jack introduced her when she also met his parents. Maggie offered a sincere smile in an ocean of speculative, judging looks. Amber always wanted a sister, and Maggie fit the bill perfectly, even if Amber couldn't be completely honest with the other woman. Well, she was about as honest as Amber ever got, which was saying something.

Despite the fact Maggie was a low-pressure salesperson, which was exactly what they needed, she was family, and she knew the kind of house they were looking for. And by chance, they'd found it, or more accurately, Maggie found it.

Maggie was married to the famous Dr. Michael Allan Drake, marriage counselor and relationship guru extraordinaire. Amber would never have thought they would go together, but what did she know? They made a handsome couple. The fact he was a bit of a celebrity took all the potential limelight away from the rest of the family, including Amber, which was fantastic. It was possible her brother-in-aw and sister-in-law had a wonderful marriage. Amber was happy for Maggie, yet she also sensed there was occasionally trouble in paradise. It was probably just paranoia from Amber's unique past, but Amber hadn't been able to shake it, and she had been watching people from the sidelines for a very long time.

Several months earlier, when Maggie confided that she didn't think she wanted children, Amber felt sorry for her because Maggie would be a wonderful mother. She just wondered if it was that Maggie didn't want children or didn't want them with Dr. Drake. If Amber were a betting woman—and, well, she was from Las Vegas—she'd bet on the latter. She had a feeling Dr. Michael wanted all the limelight. Children might get in the way of that.

"This is a great price. Heck, I wouldn't let you make a mistake," Maggie said. "And if we were to make an offer, I'd probably start right at full price, maybe consider a little over, but not much. It is so new on the market, but I don't think it will be on for long. I've already heard whisperings of other interested parties and possibly a time when all offers will be presented at once. Then, in order to get it, we have to decide how badly you want it. The price could increase quickly in this market."

"I really like this house. What do you think, darling?" Jack asked.

"I think we may be home. I love it," Amber said, smiling first at Jack and then at Maggie.

"Make them an offer that will get my darling wife the house she wants," Jack said.

"Then I've got some work to do," Maggie said with a nod and a smile.

CHAPTER ONE
*(Margaret Daniels Drake
Present Day)*

Maggie Drake entered the home where she had lived for the last six of her twenty-eight years. She slipped off her shoes and put them in a specially designed cubby by the front door. It was habit and second nature to her by now. It hadn't always been that way, but she learned, and she had learned quickly, that *he* wouldn't tolerate scuff marks from her heels on the pristine cherry hardwoods. The floors were expensive and perfect. They needed to stay that way. That is why they would never have a cat —or a dog, for that matter. Their claws would be murder on the highly polished floors. In fact, Michael spent the better part of a Saturday afternoon putting felt footies on everything that had legs until the furniture slid around silently. Maggie learned to be like the furniture. *Silent.* Had Maggie wondered if he would put those little pieces on her someday? Yes. As it was, he didn't like her to be barefoot on the hardwoods; she had to wear slippers.

As for the pets she'd always wanted, Maggie assumed Michael liked animals when they were dating, but she hadn't thought of asking to get a definite answer before they got married. It was a costly error that would prevent her from having a fur baby as long as she was married to Michael. She cried when he told her, but her tears weren't tolerated either, and she was threatened with equal and opposite reactions if she didn't stop. So, she stopped and suffered silently.

Never forget what might set him off.

It was something new each day.

Now, for example, if she forgot and accidentally wore her shoes inside and stepped on the hardwoods, a blatant oversight, she would retrace her steps with a rapidly beating heart and look for scuff marks that, more often than not, did not exist. Not that he would ever see any of the marks if she saw them first, but even one little infringement would be an issue, and the resulting punishment, well, she couldn't think about that. It was too humiliating. After all, he never left marks that could be seen and questioned by other people. Why did she have a memory issue when it came to her shoes? Oh, right, she wasn't that smart. Not like him.

There were a lot of rules to remember inside the pristine home of Dr. and Mrs. Drake, but not wearing shoes in the house was by far one of the more basic, a foundation rule, as he called it, so it was well worth remembering. Heck, she had his top ten rules burned into her head and memorized, word for word. She could recite them when asked. And just to be clear, he had asked. More than once. For a while, it was a daily exercise. Then he got bored with this humiliation and moved on to something else.

She took a moment and relived every action she'd taken, from the time she parked perfectly on her side of the garage to the removal of her shoes. This forethought saved a lot of punishment. She didn't do a lot of wool gathering to reflect on her stressful day. No, this was not the time for that. Besides, her day was a picnic compared to the night she had ahead. She needed to make sure she was alert and remembered the rules. And sometimes, the fear of the punishment made her forget her daily routine. She would cringe at the very thought. She knew the rules inside and out, for shit's sake. She recited them in her car. She no longer listened to music while driving. She listened to the sound of her voice reciting rules. She had to remember what was expected of her.

She stepped away from the shoes in the cubby hole and gave them one last glance over her shoulder. They would have to go back to the basement this evening. She couldn't forget. He only allowed her to have four pairs of shoes at a time in the master bedroom closet. This pair of Ferragamo's wasn't one of her usual "go-tos." They were a metallic plum. They would be considered overflow, as he liked to call them. The rest, or overflow, were relegated to the moldy, dark basement. And there was only a two-hour grace period before they would be thrown away after he'd done a count.

Down in the basement, they probably only had a shelf life of three months before they became too saturated with mold to wear. If they weren't covered with green spots outlined with a yellow crust, they smelled like something that had died several months earlier. It broke her heart to lose so many lovely things because, besides shoes, he had similar rules for handbags. She took to hiding them in her car's trunk until he caught her. That had been a bad day. She took to hiding them at work, but she had to be careful because sometimes he stopped by to check on her. She quietly added two chairs to her office with hidden storage underneath their cushions. It still made her nervous. What if he stopped by and chose to look there?

She absently touched a spot on her arm where the skin was thicker. It was a scar, small, but still a scar to remind her of what happened when she got "creative" with the rules of their marriage. It was small. She had a much larger scar on her leg. She didn't like to think about that one.

The basement itself was a setting for any horror movie just waiting to happen. One of her darkest fears was that the basement, that foul-smelling hole in the ground, would be her home one day. He threatened it often enough. She pictured her husband erecting a cage, something that was intended for something else from a helpful Home Depot do-it-yourself aisle. Then, he'd drug her, maybe during her morning coffee or the one cocktail he allowed her to consume on a daily basis as they discussed their day during what he deemed "their civilized cocktail hour." She liked the cocktail hour in the beginning. Before she knew what was expected of her. One could not forget that he was known to drink an entire bottle of Southern Comfort in one sitting. Meanwhile, she had to have cocktail skills. He'd insisted on it. Once she mastered the twenty most popular cocktails of the day, she discovered that he only drank his Southern Comfort neat. She just knew that when she least suspected it, she would wake up behind bars or just be locked away.

She thought about writing a letter and sending it to her brother Jack with a warning on the outside of the envelope. *Only open if I disappear...*

If she gave something like that to Jack, he would be curious. It would be like dangling chum before a shark. He would want to know more. And the bottom line, Maggie was embarrassed. She wasn't supposed to fail. She was supposed to have the perfect marriage. Everyone believed it, and she had done a lot to keep that belief alive. She didn't want to disappoint anyone.

She thought again of the basement. Michael would tell people she'd left him, but all the while, she would be right there. A prisoner in her own home. She'd scream, but he'd have thought of that and would erect soundproofing so she could scream to her heart's content. He was very sensitive to sound. If she spoke too loudly, she was "loud and obnoxious," which resulted in punishment. She learned to whisper. To her horror, the whispering crept into her work life a time or two. People noticed with narrowing eyes and curious glances. She had to watch that.

More than once, she thought about hiding objects around the basement that could one day help her to escape: a screwdriver here, a set of pliers there, heck, even a nail or paperclip...it was paranoid to think this way, but there was some necessity to her actions as well. He wouldn't show her any mercy. Heck, he hadn't in the past. Well, in the beginning, there had been hope for her, so he'd said. Now, all he could do was tell her what a disappointment she was. Besides, he was smart enough to look in every nook and cranny of the basement to make sure there wasn't anything that could help her.

She didn't call out that she had arrived home because he didn't like that kind of jocularity. Besides, she didn't use her voice anymore. Not to mention, she might disturb his hard-fought concentration. He might be in the middle of something, like typing an amusing line of text for his new book or articulating a line of prose that had taken years to populate in his brain for one of his wildly popular podcasts. If she called out, she could ruin his train of thought. She might rob the world of his amazing and profound insight. It had happened before. She wouldn't let it happen again because remaining quiet was much easier than enduring the resulting punishment. In the case of her loud greeting in the past, it resulted in three hours locked in the dark basement or as she liked to think of it, dress rehearsal.

Hadn't he explained that she didn't possess the intellect he had to share such insightful wisdom with the world? He'd locked her in the basement to think about it. The scary thing was she was starting to believe he was right. She had messed up, but that wasn't right. He was starting to get under her skin. His logic was starting to make sense, and hers was starting to dwindle. This was what captives started to believe, she realized. Heck, she was falling under his spell as if she were a kidnap victim. Stockholm syndrome.

A few more months and there would be nothing left of her. His words were already under her skin, but just how deep would they go?

How much longer would it take before she was a complete zombie at his mercy? Or was she already there?

As she passed through the living room, silent as a cat burglar in the night, she automatically glanced toward the bowl where he left messages that he wanted her to "read immediately and take seriously." They usually involved a recipe he wanted that evening or dry cleaning—more likely one of her flaws, like a complaint about her housekeeping. To overlook such a clear request would prove she was as intellectually inferior as he always told her she was. It was his expectation that she would look in the bowl, so she'd better obey.

A page from his personalized notepad, the heavy velum paper that was headed with *"From the desk of..."* His mother gave her favorite and only child the notepad last Christmas before her dementia had really taken hold, and she'd had to be put in memory care. The note was in the bowl where she was also supposed to leave her keys. It was odd he would grace her with the special notepad paper. He made it clear that this notepaper was for special occasions. It wasn't for her. Something was up.

She picked up the paper by the edge and noticed that her hand was already shaking as she wondered what fresh hell awaited her. She glanced down at the printing that he had perfected with a fountain pen that was perfectly etched into the fine vellum of the paper.

From the desk of Dr. Michael Allan Drake...
The message was succinct.
Margaret, Back at 4:15. -MAD

No "love you." No "see you soon." No surprise.
Love hadn't been part of their dialogue for years. Well, he liked to remind her that she loved him, but she didn't. And despite his declarations to the contrary, he didn't love her. If you loved someone, you didn't abuse them, not the way he abused her. He was incapable of loving anyone but his cold mother and

himself. Maggie hadn't loved him. Not since the day he'd picked up her body and thrown her through a door for breaking one of his rules. She had a few bruises on the outside from that one. On the inside, something much worse had taken hold. She believed she was forever broken from that experience and would never be repaired. He'd left a scar on her soul.

Still holding the paper by the edges, she glanced at her fake Cartier watch, a present from him after a very bad argument, which was meant to buy back her affection. The bribe hadn't worked even though he liked to show the watch to guests and brag that he'd bought it for her. She had it checked. It wasn't a real Cartier.

It was 3:50 p.m. Where had he gone? He always worked from home. This absence was odd. Occasionally, he had an outside appointment, but it had been a while. How long had it been since she'd been alone in the little prison known as their home? She couldn't remember the last time. Was he setting her up or planning something?

And did she have enough time to execute the plan she'd been perfecting in her mind for months?

It didn't matter. She had to try. *Try or die.* That would make a great quote for her tombstone.

She didn't take longer than three heartbeats to contemplate what she had rehearsed.

She ran through the perfect and tidy house in her stocking feet, which occasionally would slip on the highly polished hardwood floors. She scarcely noticed, and she didn't go down. She had other things on her mind.

Within ninety seconds, two suitcases lay open on the floor of the master suite. She didn't take things off hangers, and it wasn't like she'd need the wardrobe he'd insisted on, "...*skirts and blouses that make you look like a chaste woman worthy of being married to a doctor of my status...*" Skirts and blouses by the same designer that his mother wore made her feel matronly and old.

She called the clothing *The Uniform*. The same boxy design over and over again in a wide variety of knit pastels. No, she needed her jeans and tee shirts, a few oversized sweaters, things that he had forbidden because they weren't feminine enough. Thankfully, she had almost packed one suitcase already. The fireproof document case that he hadn't noticed. It had the things she would need the most: important papers, contact information, and her passport. She checked to make sure they were all there, and then she added a couple of her photo albums from BM, *Before Michael*.

His words, his personal mantra, echoed in her head, "I'm *The Voice of Reason*. You listen to me. No one will ever believe you…"

She shouldn't have been silent. She should have spoken up. It happened so gradually. No one would suspect what happened behind closed doors. She tried to tell someone once. Only once. The people around her were a genuinely positive group. They thought the best. The one time she had spoken up to another agent in her office about why she was putting her shoes in her office, she could see the doubt in the woman's eyes. Maybe she thought Maggie bought too many shoes or was hiding the fact from her husband. Anyway, the woman had really avoided Maggie since the conversation, and Maggie took it as a warning as to what people would think and assume, so she had stayed silent.

Crossing to the closet, she reached into the pocket of one of her evening gowns that was toward the back of her closet. It was worn rarely and usually only to charity functions where Michael could be praised. The gown had a hidden pocket where she stashed cash. Each week for the last two years, she had put at least $100 in that pocket. She felt the familiar lump and pulled out a wad of bills and tossed it into one of the two suitcases.

She had family, but the thought of being a burden, well, the very thought of having to own what she had hidden, admit to what a sham she was living, how dangerous the one person who was supposed to love her beyond reproach was...they would be so disappointed. It was beyond embarrassing.

A distant noise penetrated the silence. She paused and listened. Was that the garage door? It was definitely mechanical. If it was the garage...

RUN.

CHAPTER TWO
(Jack Daniels)

Jack looked again at the dark blue velvet box he had picked up on his lunch hour from Amber's favorite jeweler. Amber was going to go crazy for the diamond earrings he'd picked out to celebrate their wedding anniversary. It was such an odd thing. She was independently wealthy. She could have anything she wanted, but it was the gifts he gave her that seemed to mean the most to her. He couldn't blame her. He felt the same way. He valued her above everything. They knew each other's darkest secrets, but they were still together and always would be. They had unconditional love. He never thought he'd find the female equivalent of himself, but he had.

He was going to take her out tonight to dinner at their favorite restaurant, La Serre. In the beginning, La Serre had been a joke. It was French for "greenhouse," but it quickly became their favorite spot. It was French chic and reminded him of one magical month they'd spent traveling through France, where their children were conceived.

Tonight, they would sit in the candlelit atrium space and look up at the skylights, maybe seeing the last of the season's snow. They would be surrounded by lots of lush greenery and plaster walls finished with straw. Authentically French.

He would order a bottle of Veuve Clicquot and then give her the diamonds. He was second-guessing himself already. It was hardly equal. She had given him their adorable twins, a boy and a girl, a little over a year earlier. He couldn't top that kind of gift. But at least the diamonds had a lovely sparkle. And they would look lovely on her. He just wished he could give her something a little more like the children...an event...a situation? Something to ponder. Too bad he didn't have a despicable spouse for her to take care of. Maybe someone they could kill together. That was kind of romantic. Well, their kind of romance...

His desk phone buzzed. It was his assistant, Judy.

"Mr. Daniels, there is a woman on the line. Her name is Margaret Drake. She said it was urgent. Do you know a Margaret Drake? Is that Maggie? She sure doesn't sound like herself."

His sister? She rarely called him because since he'd married Amber, most of the communication happened between the two women. He and Maggie still chatted, but not as often.

"Yes, that's my Maggie."

"Sweet little Maggie? Why didn't she say so? She doesn't sound like herself. And well, it has been ages."

"Please put her through," he said, sitting up a bit straighter in his chair as he looked at his watch. 4:30 p.m.

He answered with a smile, "Maggie, is that you?"

"Jack, I'm so sorry to bother you. I just need to talk. I'm in trouble. I need help, and I didn't know where to go..."

Immediately, he could pick up the terror in her voice. She was crying, sobbing, actually. He didn't like it one bit. He wouldn't have recognized her voice if he didn't know it was her.

"I'm here. It is okay. Were you in an accident? Are you safe? Are you okay?" he asked.

"I'm sitting in the lobby of your building. I'm scared to go anywhere."

"I'll come down—"

"I'd rather just get in the elevator and come to you before he figures out where I am and shows up," she said, her voice strained, edgy. "Which floor again? I forgot."

THE VOICE OF REASON

She had been there many times. How could she forget?

"11th floor," he said. "Hang on," he held his hand over the phone and called to Judy, who appeared in the doorway, having never been summoned in this way before.

"Maggie is on her way up. Bring her in immediately. Cancel anything on my schedule for the rest of the day."

Judy nodded at his words. She was efficient, and with the tone Jack used, he didn't have to elaborate.

"Jack—" Maggie said, interjecting over the phone.

"Maggie, it is fine. You're my sister, and it is past 4 p.m. It is no big deal. I'm far more worried about you."

"If Michael shows up or calls, don't believe a word he says... promise me!" That would not be hard. He didn't like Michael, the blowhard.

"Okay, I promise."

Thirty seconds later, she was there, looking terrified, her eyes large, her usually tidy hair disheveled as she crossed the threshold to his office. He held his arms open, and she collapsed into them. He could hear her sobs as he held her and felt her body rise and fall with the effort of the painful exhalations. What had happened? Should he call an ambulance? He never liked Michael, but if he'd hurt Maggie...

Jack moved with her and eventually sat, pulling her down onto the oversized couch in his office, and waited. He wanted to ask her if she was alright, but he couldn't, not now. Judy discreetly put several bottles of cold water on the coffee table and then silently left.

In a few minutes, Maggie had gone through a dozen tissues and drank some water with trembling hands, causing the water to slosh on the table. Finally, she seemed calm enough to talk.

"Is the door locked?" Maggie asked.

"No, but I can—"

"Do it, please, Jack," she begged.

Different scenarios went through Jack's mind. Amber had

told him that she long suspected that all that glittered was not gold behind the front door of the Dr. & Mrs. Michael Allan Drake residence. He hadn't considered it until Amber brought it to his attention. Then it bothered him, and he had never quite forgotten Amber's concern. He had never seen such fear on his sister's face. There was a lot to unpack here, but he would first make sure she was safe.

He went through scenarios, hanging on to the extremes. Had Michael hurt her? Had she hurt him? He'd seen worse. And it wasn't like he ever really bonded with the great Dr. Michael Allan Drake. The guy was a prick with a huge ego. Jack was more than a little relieved when Maggie said they weren't going to have children until she was in her mid-thirties. Lately, she'd even mentioned to Amber that, perchance, children weren't even in the realm of possibility.

He knew something bad had happened. It took a lot to upset Maggie. She had always been his easy-going little sister, with a ready smile on her face and love in her heart for everyone. She was also tough as nails.

Had she injured her husband? Maybe she'd hurt him, left him for dead? Was he bleeding out somewhere? Amber was right; guns and knives were messy. They left a lot of organic material behind. Okay, Jack could admit that he had a vivid imagination. His wife's and, heck, his own past, left him a bit paranoid. But he wondered if he had the right equipment to take care of any cleanup if it was as bad as he thought. He had a tarp, shovel, and gloves in the trunk of his Land Rover. He also had a few assorted chemicals to clean up a mess. Amber had given him a list. She always leaned on the side of caution. He'd have to get her to help with this. Ironically, it would probably excite Amber to kill off this loser. Jack's wife, the love of his life, was a beautifully complex woman who liked to meter out her own justice.

. . .

THE VOICE OF REASON

Maggie knew that once she told Jack her story, there would be no going back. A couple of years ago, that really would have bothered her. She'd been trying to keep a tight hold on the façade that was her 'happy' marriage. She had always been competitive. She thought she could change him. Damn, she had been so naïve.

She played the good little wife well, maybe too well. Trying to be successful. Trying not to anger her husband. Being the sweet wife who was always everything she could be. Perfect. The perfect house, the perfect food, the perfect wife with the perfect clothes. Yet, he still found fault with her. It was only in the last couple of years that she realized it wouldn't matter. She would never be good enough for him. She could follow all his rules. There would always be something else, something more that she wasn't doing or needed to do. He would always find a reason to punish her as if he enjoyed it. It left her tired. Tired of playing the game she could never win.

She had been so in love with him once, but not anymore. And it was that sweet memory that was so intoxicating. But in the last few years of escalating violence and fear, she was starting to forget that there had ever been love.

She was numb to the feelings of grief and shame today. She had taken action that could not be undone.

It no longer mattered. Living was the only thing that mattered. And hadn't his threats gotten a bit more serious in the last few weeks? She didn't need to ask the question. She knew the answer. She just wanted to be free and safe. She just wasn't sure if it was an option.

If she stayed, he'd kill her one day. He was probably already planning it. Knowing him, he probably had already written her suicide note and planned her funeral. He was sick like that, the bastard.

Now that she had left, would she ever be safe?

One of the bottles of water fell over on the coffee table, the base uneven. It made her jump.

Jack put his hand on hers and said, "It is okay. Whatever happened, you aren't alone. I'm right here with you. I'm not going anywhere."

"I'm not sure I feel safe."

Jack shook his head. "I also have a concealed weapon permit and a gun in the desk drawer. You are safe."

"Yeah, but it is in the desk, not with you. And could you pull the trigger on someone you knew?" she asked.

"Who? Michael?"

"Yes," she said, and she wondered if he could really do it.

"To protect you? Yes, there is a lot I wouldn't do. Don't worry. I could kill him if I had to."

Taking him at face value, she looked at a painting on the wall and focused on it. She felt his eyes on her, but she couldn't meet them. Not yet.

She turned to him, her voice flat as she ordered, "Get the gun."

He did as she asked, putting on a harness so that he could wear it under his suit coat.

She was ashamed and embarrassed that it had come to this. What if he didn't believe her? He had to believe her. What if he wanted Michael's side of the story? What if he called Michael? Could she run before he arrived? But where would she go? She thought that least her brother had to believe her a little bit. He'd gotten the gun.

If she needed to protect herself alone, she had a bit of money, but seriously, it wasn't enough. It wouldn't last forever. She couldn't go to their parents. She didn't want to put them in danger. And anyone between her and Michael would be in danger. Maybe she should not have even come to see Jack. Maybe that was a huge mistake. What if she put him in danger, too?

THE VOICE OF REASON

She should have gotten in the car and driven. But how far away would be safe?

Looking back at the painting, she said, "I left him. I couldn't take it anymore. So, this afternoon, when I saw that he wouldn't be back until 4:30, I realized that I had forty minutes to escape, so I left him. I've tried to leave before, but he wouldn't let me go. He's known to lock me in the basement. Even at my office, he has a friend, a disciple, watching me."

"The basement? What the fuck? A disciple?" Jack asked, his voice sounding unnatural.

She faced him and then grabbed his hand. "I'm sorry. I know it sounds crazy, but he has this other life. There are men following him like he is their unofficial leader. Men who think like he does. They call themselves *The T Society*, short for *The Traditionalists of Society*. They believe in old-school shit. Women obedient to men. Women chaste and do not work outside the home. He's got all this crap on the dark web. It is so much larger than anyone thinks. He has started to align with like-minded politicians. It is getting serious. He turned from being a disciple to an admired voice in the organization. He tries out ways to discipline me and then posts the results online. I can't take it anymore."

"Holy shit. How long has this been going on?"

"The abuse started on the honeymoon, but it is so much worse in the last three years since he got involved with *The T Society*. His book, which is about to come out, is just meant to help fund his real cause. He's working on another book, something much darker. I know it sounds crazy, but you have to believe me. He is thinking of taking his messages off the dark web and sharing them with the population. I hope he does. They will think he is crazy, but I don't know it will be enough people to make a difference."

Her cell phone buzzed inside her purse. She glanced at the handbag as if it was a snake. It had a specific chime for Michael.

He wanted her to answer in three rings. If she didn't, she'd better have a damn good reason. Well, she wasn't even going to open her purse.

Her voice sounded high even to her own ear. "Promise me, whatever he says, don't believe him. I do not want to go back. He'll come for me and try to tell you I'm imbalanced or something. I'm not. Don't leave me alone with him. He'll hurt me. I can't go back. Promise me."

A knock on Jack's office door had Maggie jumping a foot off the couch. Jack put a reassuring hand on her arm.

"It's okay. It is just Judy," Jack said, then he called, "Judy?"

The door opened, and Judy stuck her head through the door, smiling. She said, "Dr. Drake is in the lobby. He wants to talk to you, Maggie, privately. I cannot believe it is really him. After seeing him on television, I cannot believe he is in our lobby."

"For god's sake, don't let him in," Maggie said in a whisper at first that became a shriek.

"Tell him I'm in a meeting. You don't know with whom. Make sure he knows it's with a man," Jack said. Then he shook his head and pointed at Maggie. Judy understood. She was a quick study and loved anything that inferred cloak and dagger.

"Okay, boss," Judy replied.

"And tell him I'm busy for the rest of the day. Let me know when he leaves. If he doesn't, we are going to call security and get him thrown out of the building. Got it?"

"Yes, boss."

CHAPTER THREE
(Jack)

It was so much worse in some ways than Jack anticipated. At least Michael was still alive. Jack didn't have to dispose of a body or, in the worst case scenario, defend his sister in court for murder. Okay, getting rid of Michael would not be that hard. Making it look like he had simply run away or decided to disappear, well, that was the hard part. And damn it, the guy was popular. He was the Dr. Phil of marriage counseling. And now, there was this added wrinkle that Maggie was telling him about, *The T Society*. His wife kept a lookout for these kinds of things. And recently, Amber mentioned she was watching an organization of men called *The T Society*. It bothered him on many levels, more than anything he was worried for the women in his life.

For the first few minutes before Michael showed up in his lobby, Jack was sure that Maggie killed him or at least seriously injured him. He had looked for telltale blood stains or signs of a struggle, but she was in an aubergine silk suit and looked like a young lawyer. Well, now that he knew that Michael had been abusive to Maggie, Jack was facing the reality that he might really have to kill him. He could ask Amber if she'd do it. She got off on that kind of thing, and it had been a while. He should know. He'd been the recipient of her post-elimination celebrations. It was like good sex after a bad fight. She basked in the feeling of making the planet a better place for humanity. Thankfully, they didn't fight. It was probably why he was still alive.

Amber needed a good anniversary present. And was it wrong

that he was selfishly thinking of his wife when his sister needed him? Heck, if he knew his wife, she'd smile at the thought of making the brother-in-law a permanent ex. She probably already had a plan on how to do it. She was prepared in that kind of way. He couldn't wait to tell her. She'd never liked Dr. Michael Allan Drake. And now that they knew he had a connection to *The T Society*, Amber would be chomping at the bit to take care of business. But he needed to take care of the woman trembling in his office first.

He gently took hold of Maggie's hand and asked, "Can you tell me what happened?"

"I couldn't take it anymore," she said. "I didn't want anyone to judge, so I stayed silent. It was the wrong decision, and I know it. Basically, I was embarrassed, so embarrassed…"

"I'm sorry. You should never feel embarrassed. It was a reflection on him, not you. I've never liked him. Tell me everything," he said.

"You didn't?" She looked surprised, as if the idea never crossed her mind.

"No, he's a pompous dick who has only gotten more pompous with time. I put up with him because he seemed to treat you well, and I thought you loved him, but he was a dick."

"I haven't loved him for years. And you have to promise me that you won't tell Mom and Dad," she said. "They would be so disappointed in me. I just can't face that with everything else."

"They would want to know. They would be upset, but they'd just be glad you got out. I'll be honest with you. They have been hit and miss on your husband, too. I'm pretty sure they didn't love him like a son. They love Amber like a long-lost daughter, but it just isn't the same with Michael," Jack said, and Maggie raised her head to meet his eyes. He continued, "Dad thinks he's a prick. We've had a few conversations."

Maggie wore a look of surprise that broke him as she whispered, "Really?"

THE VOICE OF REASON

"I'm kind of hurt that you sound so surprised. They thought you've changed since you married him, and I have to agree. You were always so happy...heck, Mag, you were joyful. You were this pixie who was always looking at the glass being half full. You used to laugh and were carefree. I thought he saw that in you and liked it. But then something happened. You seemed less confident, more...I don't know, you doubted yourself. Sometimes, I thought you were scared of your own shadow. We were talking that maybe we needed to take you out someplace without Michael and have a frank discussion with you."

"Really? Wow..."

"Well...you were downtrodden, especially in the last few months. Like he is sucking the life out of you. You didn't laugh. I did not know how to talk to you about it, but it was coming. I just didn't know how to start the conversation. I've even talked to Amber about it. She wanted to be part of the conversation."

Maggie nodded and looked down. Then, she said, "I think he would have killed me if I stayed. It was getting more toxic. It started off...well, in the beginning, it was just little things. I thought he was joking. But now, it is just different. I think he thinks that he is untouchable as he gets more famous and that I'm expendable. When someone wants you dead, you just know it. I just wasn't sure if it would be him or one of his people."

Jack sat back. It was hard to think that mild-mannered, self-absorbed Michael was capable of violence. But he knew, he knew, without her saying a word, that Michael had hurt her. It had gotten violent, and she escaped. Jack would have to make sure Michael knew there were consequences for hurting his sister. But having *The T Society* involved made it so much worse.

Thankfully, Jack didn't have to look too far to have the perfect weapon at his disposal. His wife had an impressive body count that had reached double digits. She was the last person he'd ever suspected of being able to kill, but she had, and she was good at it. When he told her about this, Michael and any of his *T* friends that she could uncover would be in her crosshairs, then god help them. She was relentless.

Jack didn't want to know, but he had to ask.

"Did he ever tell you that he wanted to kill you?"

"Many times, but last week…I started thinking he was planning it. Okay, let me be more direct. I know he was planning it. I just didn't know what to do, and then today, well, I took the opportunity, but now I don't know what to do. I guess I never planned beyond escaping. Frankly, I'm surprised I was able to make it this far."

Jack let out a breath he'd been holding inside, closed his eyes as he pinched the bridge of his nose, and said, "Forget that I'm your brother. I'm your lawyer, and I need to get you to safety. Tell me everything."

"I'll tell you one story. If you can handle it, I'll tell you more."

He nodded in encouragement. She didn't quite trust him, not beyond running to him. She needed to work with him, to trust him.

"Promise you won't hold back. Please, Mag. And I need you to tell me everything, even if you know it will be hard for me to hear."

"Okay," she said reluctantly.

"Okay," he repeated.

"Okay, but try not to react," she said, having made a decision. "You know that green silk robe Mom gave me for Christmas two years ago?"

"Vaguely," Jack said. Keeping track of his sister's lingerie wasn't high on his list of priorities.

"I love that robe. I wear it almost every day," she said.

"Okay," he prompted.

"Last Thursday, the belt went missing."

Jack's immediate conclusion was that it must have fallen in the closet or bathroom. So what?

"I'm not following," he said.

"You will. That evening, I was reading in the den. He walked into the room and leaned down next to me," she began. "He whispered in my ear, 'Sometimes I fantasize about strangling you until you are dead.'"

Jack's eyes widened as he searched for his words and finally asked, "Holy shit, Maggie! Why didn't you tell us? Why didn't you call me? I would have come for you. Hell, I might have called the police."

"I was ashamed and assumed it was my fault," she said.

"Why would he say that? Did you two have a fight? Why didn't you leave then?" Jack would never, ever consider saying anything like that to his wife. First, she would take care of business long before he had a chance to do so, and he didn't want to be dead. Second, he loved Amber more than anything else in the world. Ironically, he felt a little more at ease now that they'd had children together. Well, until the day that no longer mattered and she silently snapped and went all black widow on him.

"He wouldn't have let me leave. Do you understand? What can I say? We didn't fight. Not anymore. Not after I knew the ramifications. Our fights weren't normal. We didn't apologize. It was always my fault. And toward the end, apologies weren't enough. I think he just decided to hate me. If I fought with him, there would be punishment, especially if I'd broken a rule he'd set. I didn't tell you because I didn't want the questions. I wasn't ready to face it. And he'd have told you I made it up. Who would you have believed?"

"You," he said. "What do you mean rules?"

"Well, we will never really know because I didn't give you a chance to help me until now."

"Okay...okay...We can't recreate that moment, thank god. Rule? What rules? What kind of punishment?"

"We will get there. Just know that I dirtied too many dishes in the kitchen when I'd made dinner that night. He said I'd done it on purpose. So, I apologized, but he didn't accept it."

Jack was speechless. "Let me get this straight. You might have used a lot of dishes to cook dinner for the two of you, and he threatened to kill you?"

"Well, when you say it like that, it sounds really stupid. But it was a serious infraction to him, and he wasn't taking my apology," she said. "So I decided that since he was mad at me, I'd better sleep in the guest room that night. Remember, the robe had a missing belt."

"Okay, I remember. I don't want to interrupt your story, but we must come back to all of this."

"I know," she said, resolved. "So I slept in one of the guest rooms. Only none of our doors have locks, so I wedged a chair up under the doorknob. I heard nothing from him. He stopped speaking to me the moment after he told me he told me he didn't accept my apology."

Jack let out a frustrated breath, and Maggie continued.

"The next morning, I opened the door, and there on the floor outside the room was the belt to my robe. He'd wound it into a little rosette. It hadn't been there the night before. I would have seen it. I would have stepped on it. No, sometime in the night, he'd stopped outside my door and left it. It was like he was thinking about it and decided not to do it. But he thought about it. He wanted me to know how close he had come."

Jack's heart was pounding in his chest. The implication of her words was terrifying. He was scared for his sister, angry that she had felt the fear of living in her own house and realized she hadn't even told him all of it yet. He thought there was probably much worse. And he was right.

CHAPTER FOUR

(Dr. Michael Allan Drake)

Afternoon talk shows tried Michael's patience, but he'd been told they were good for book sales. And heck, the female talk show host wanted him in a carnal way. It was like she was in heat or something. He wondered if she'd present her nether region to him in a come-hither gesture, the slut. It was easy to see the lust in her dull brown eyes, framed by a botoxed, almost plastic face, which looked so puffed and stretched he was worried she might explode. She had the typical bleach blonde hair and displayed her too-large ass in a tight pencil skirt that had to be three inches too short. He'd bet money that she had an ex-husband she'd emasculated and a cat she dressed up in costumes and treated like a baby. He also wondered what she spent on makeup with all that she was wearing. Geez, what a mess. He thought he could probably scrape it off with a putty knife. It would take a lot of work to fix her. He shuttered at the thought. It was almost beyond him.

But heck, what was she up to? He was a married man. He was wearing a wedding ring. A thick gold band, a shackle his wife picked out. Was this woman blind to it, or did she just like the challenge of married men? Hell, maybe she didn't care.

Did she like forbidden fruit? Would it be worth a shot to flirt with him? Ignoring social norms and traditions? Maybe she just wanted a roll in the hay. Why did it surprise him? It shouldn't. Women tended to be all like in this regard. They wondered how a man might make love to them. Especially a celebrity like him.

Heck, some of these little slutty women had some pretty good little fantasies. He could take her after the show. Throw her against the nearest wall in her dressing room, pull her panties down and her skirt up. Make it a little rough, a little memorable for her. No one would find out. He bet she'd like it. He'd scratch her itch.

Reality check. Chicks like this liked to tell people of their sexual conquests, and he did not feel like having his personal life shared with the masses. Not yet anyway.

He didn't need the scandal, so he knew what to do: smile respectfully, then wait for whatever she had planned. If only she was a bit more attractive. He might risk the scandal, and they would be having a completely different discussion.

"Do I have a treat for you today," Greta Grace said into the microphone to her large mid-western audience as she glanced at Michael and batted her flat eyes with the fake eyelashes in a gesture she probably thought of as playful. He bet nothing about her was playful. He'd bet money that she liked to be spanked or degraded. Well, he didn't have enough of him to go around for that kind of therapy.

Had she called him a treat? Or was she referring to herself? He hadn't heard women refer to themselves in that way, but he was game.

"You've heard about him. You've probably listened to one of his radio shows that used to be on daily from 2 to 4 p.m. And if you are anything like me, you've missed him for the last few months, but ladies, the wait is over. We are in for a treat. My guest, Dr. Michael Allan Drake, is about to come to your city. That's right, he's written a book on marriage, and he is making a tour to share it with all of you. And for those of you lucky enough, he will meet you and sign it in person, so remember, you're married, ladies. I've got my hands on the sexy new book entitled Rules of the Marital Bond. *It will be out two weeks from today. And we can question him about his return to radio. But why am I talking about all*

these insignificant details? Well, Dr. Drake is our guest in the studio today...Let's let him talk..."

As if on cue, there was canned applause, and the phone panel lit up.

"Welcome, Dr. Drake. How are you today?" Greta Grace asked, her whore red lips curving into a fake smile. He bet that warpaint stained her after she wiped it off. Not to mention what it would do to him or his underwear. He wondered if old Margaret would even notice. Well, even if she did, it was none of her business.

His hostess was looking at him expectantly.

Two could play at that game. He told himself to smile, to put on the dog. Assume the role you want to play. You don't have to feel it. You just have to look at it.

"I'm great, Greta. Thank you for that warm welcome," Michael said. "Thank you for having me here. I'm glad to know I was missed, as I took a little time to write down a few of my thoughts." He added a light-hearted chuckle. He worked hard not to have it sound artificial. It still did, but maybe to his ears only.

"Thoughts? Oh, my goodness, just by thumbing through your book, I can tell it will soon be the bible that good, traditional married women will live by. Or they will give it to their husbands and ask them to live by it. Goodness knows they need it in these trying political times."

Look humble; he thought as he said, "Well, the book isn't all that, but I tried to make it a roadmap for my friends, my friends who I don't know but seem to like what I have to say. Who struggle with trying to figure out what to do when the initial passion of their marriage wears off. It is my hope that husbands and wives read it together and that it brings about an understanding of their roles in the marriage. A counselor in book form, as it were."

"I absolutely love that. Now, I'm sure you get asked this a lot because, let's face it, you are one tall drink of a handsome man. Are you married, Dr. Drake?"

He looked away and tried to look a little embarrassed. He wished he could blush on cue. He never had, but Margaret had when they first started dating.

"Yes, I've been happily married for almost six years to my lovely wife. I never divulge her name because of safety concerns, which I'm sure you can appreciate. It is amazing how quickly time has passed."

"How lucky is she? And how nice of you to be so protective," Greta Grace said with a laugh.

What a bunch of bullshit. The only person he needed to protect from his wife was herself. His own wife had so many flaws he didn't know where to start. She struggled. Oh, how she struggled... He tried for so long and in so many ways to get her to be what she should be, his loving, dutiful wife, beyond reproach. He was starting to think it was too late for her. He had not chosen wisely when it came to picking out a wife.

Lovely? He would never use that word to honestly describe her. Maybe a *Stupid Fucking Bitch*. Yeah, he liked to call her that to her face. It summed Margaret up so perfectly. When he first said it, she seemed really offended and hurt. Now, she just accepted it.

"Do you have children?"

"Not yet, Greta, but hopefully soon."

He and Greta Grace discussed some of the highlights of the book. He laughed on queue and tried not to think of how the book was a fraud to his real feelings. Heck, this book was the PG version of marriage, safe for all to read, very traditional, but not very realistic. But was he really doing the world the best service he could? He'd wanted to write something dynamic, but his agent and his editor mansplained to him how the book needed to be. *Something appealing to women*. Why he'd let them influence him, he still didn't know. Oh yeah, money. They were all about the sales. His thoughts went to end results. If this book was well regarded, it would be a green light to what he really wanted to do. His next book would be epic. But for now, he'd play by the rules and spew praise about the prose he'd written. Believe it? Believe all that love-y shit he'd written? Yeah, sure. It made him want to vomit.

He wrapped up the interview strongly, of course, because hell, he liked money, and this was an easy way to make it. The woman shook his hand, lingering a bit too long. He could tell that she wanted to do more, but she'd settle for what she could get. He'd been right all along. She wanted him. He thought of those red nailed claws of hers, those talons touching more intimate parts of his anatomy, and cringed. It wasn't going to happen.

Seriously, if it wasn't a dressing room romp, what did she expect? A clandestine offer of a meet-up at a hotel that rented rooms by the hour? Well, it wasn't like his wife would know if he chose to make or take such an offer. Heck, he'd spent a few long lunch hours with an ex-girlfriend that first year he'd been married, and Margaret, as stupid as she was, had never figured it out. Not that it was any of her business. It hadn't ended well, either, for Lisa, the ex, but that was then, and this was now. Then, right around his third wedding anniversary, there was the cocktail waitress he met one night when Margaret was out showing property instead of being home cooking a nutritional meal for them both. He and the waitress had gone at it in his car. It had been quick and easy. Hell, he didn't know her name, and she didn't know his...well, to be honest, he'd given her a fake name. No further contact was made. No guilt was felt.

Margaret had been so disrespectful lately. It would serve her right if he looked for comfort in the arms of someone else. Especially a woman who was so wanton that she needed to be broken. He was the man to do it. He craved that feeling of controlling another so completely that he held their life in his hands. It was a rush. However, it always led to a certain obedience that became tiresome quickly, i.e. *LISA*. She had started to make assumptions he had to change. That had been messy. Had he learned anything? Nope. He was married and vowed not to be entrapped by another woman, not again. Yet the pull, *the need* called to him. It was such a conundrum!

Leaving the studio, he got into his car, an immaculately clean black Cadillac Escalade with a black interior and pearl black paint. When he got home tonight, he was going to have to tell old Margaret about the other woman who wanted him. Aside from fornicating with the bleach blonde, letting Margaret know he could have, well, that would at least make him happy. He had to remind Margaret of how lucky she was and all that she would lose if she kept up with the wild thoughts of independence. If he made her cry, well then, he'd achieved his goal. He paused to look inside the glove box at the stack of polaroids that he kept locked in there. Photos of Margaret looking out of control and overwrought as she cried. It used to upset him, the noise of her crying. But that was in the beginning. Now, he knew it for what it was, the sound of breaking her. He needed to celebrate the noise, not be annoyed by it. Hell, maybe he should laugh at her. That would be a whole other level. Yeah, he liked that idea. And didn't she need to be reminded of her place?

She'd been slacking lately on the rules. She dirtied fourteen pots, pans, and dishes last week over one simple dinner. She should be able to cook anything with at most seven pots, pans, lids, and dishes. She was getting spoiled. That had to stop. And if it didn't, he had some new ideas about how to punish her.

He was a patient man, but there was only so much he could do. Had he found five pairs of shoes in the closet just that morning? She knew better. She was only allowed to have four pairs of shoes at the most at one time.

There had been talk of a child. Well, he talked. She listened. However, she hadn't really said anything. Truthfully, he didn't know if he really wanted a child. Yet, he felt a responsibility to pass on his superior DNA to another living soul, someone who could take over for him when he was too old to continue. So there was value in the idea of reproducing, but what if he had a girl instead of a boy? How would he handle that?

He needed boys who would grow into strong men. This line of thought always gave him too much to think about. Maybe he should get a few surrogates, get them pregnant, and only keep the boys. And by using intellectually smart women, he wouldn't have to deal with Margaret's weaknesses. He could breed weaknesses out of his children. The only woman who had been strong was Mother. She was a pillar of strength. She warned him not only not to marry Margaret but not to marry *any* woman. He should have listened. He thought he loved Margaret. He thought she was perfect. He thought she was beautiful, smart, and, best of all, worshiped the ground he walked on. But he held that belief for exactly two days into their marriage. She was loud and obnoxious at a restaurant on their honeymoon after half a bottle of wine. His mother had been right. And the laugh, the damn laugh. At least he'd found a way to stop her from doing that.

Could he trust her to have his babies? He couldn't keep a female baby. That was the bottom line. He didn't want another weak woman like his wife. It was impossible to predict if a female would be more like his mother or his wife. If she was like his mother, if that was the case, he'd be happy with a female, but no, he couldn't risk it. His mother was one in a million. He was sad to think of her now, rotting in the memory care. She was too perfect a woman to have been cursed in this way.

It was what started his interest in *The T Society*. He'd quickly ascended the ranks and was now one of their most valued leaders. When he made a selfless vow to help the women in his life and maybe offer guidance to a few men who wanted to learn what he had to offer, it had finally given his life purpose. These men privately basked under his tutelage, became better men, and were really starting to flourish. His numbers increased each week. They were who he really wanted to impress. Not some horny housewife, like Greta Grace or her disciples.

He'd made a lot of money being Dr. Drake, the famous marriage counselor. He had to keep up the façade because it offered him a certain lifestyle. This first book would more than help with that.

He was just glad he didn't see patients anymore. That had been a grind. Thankfully, he'd gotten his own radio gig and then the book deal. Did he want to go back to radio? Not really, but if they paid him well, then yes, he'd do radio.

But again, he was haunted by the idea of the second book. There were times he just wished he could break free and help his fellow brothers in *The T Society* in the way he wanted to, but it just wasn't easy because too many people on the outside judged. With his guidance to other men, he could better the world. He shook his head. There was so much he wanted to give and so little time for others to embrace his teachings. He only hoped the membership of *The T Society* would continue.

He flashed again on the idea of a baby. How nasty. Ugh. A drooling, shitting baby that might be a girl. Yeah, he'd have to make sure a daughter was never recognized. And didn't people want healthy babies? He could probably sell it on the open market. Heck, it might be another way to make money. Margaret might protest, but the idea didn't bother him. He could handle her.

He'd have to write a whole new set of rules regarding a child for Margaret to learn and abide by. And babies, they could be so obstinate. They cried all the time. What if the child didn't obey him? It was a fear. Okay, so what if he impregnated Margaret? Her family was too close. She'd get all emotional. They'd get all emotional. And the rules would go to hell. It wasn't like he could discipline her if she was carrying his child. He might hurt his son. And she'd figure that out. She could go off the deep end. She might regress.

And what if the boy was soft like his mother? Babies were not the delicate things that people wanted them to be. They were little humans and needed to be treated as such. And then there was Margaret. What if she liked the baby more than him? And what if something happened to her during the birth, and he was left having to deal with a baby? Or what if she could no longer perform her wifely duties? He should not be expected to stay with her then! He'd have to farm out the child or get married again. Ugh. He hated being married. It was so much work. It was all too much for him to think about.

Okay, okay, he needed to calm down. This was all the worst-case scenario stuff. It wouldn't happen.

He clutched the steering wheel a little tighter in frustration. As for the drivers this evening, my goodness, did they have no place to be? Didn't they understand that some people had places to be? It hadn't rained in a few weeks, but welcome to spring showers. Maybe that was what caused their stupidity. These were snow drivers! After all, what were they scared of, a little rain? A little liquid snow? Anyway, he was going to be late getting home. Five to seven minutes. He'd left her a note, and he liked to be precise to the minute. He didn't care that he was breaking a promise to her. He was breaking more of a promise to himself. When he said he was going to be somewhere at a certain time, he was there. He didn't like letting himself down.

He parked in the garage, as was his habit. But he noticed right off the bat that Margaret's car, a three-year-old gray Honda the color of soiled doves, was not parked in her designated spot. She should have been home by now. She should be baking the beef bourguignon that they discussed earlier. He liked to set the menu out a week or so in advance so that she would know his expectations. Tonight was beef bourguignon night. He knew the preparation and cooking took one hour and fifty-five minutes.

This was not like her. She knew how worried he became when she wasn't following the schedule. She said she would be home by 4:00 PM. It was now close to 4:22 PM. Where was she?

At the very least, she was behind on dinner preparation. It should have gone in the oven five minutes ago to accommodate for plating and serving. He was generous to only allow for ten minutes of preparation.

He couldn't believe she was purposely breaking the rules so soon after the last rule infringement. Wasn't it just a day or two ago that she dirtied too many dishes? Had she set out to purposefully make him angry? She had done that in the beginning, and he quickly adjusted her behavior. Then, she had fallen into line.

But then there was the shoe issue they hadn't begun to discuss.

This felt concerning. It wasn't like her to break multiple rules in multiple days. Something was different this time. And different was bad. He couldn't even think of a punishment to meet this latest infringement.

He tried her on her cell phone, but she did not pick up, which was the height of disrespect. That really did it. Yet another rule was broken.

He pulled up the app he had installed on her phone earlier that showed the phone was in downtown Minneapolis. On further examination, he was able to determine that she was visiting her brother. She had not told him she was going to visit sleazy divorce attorney Jack Daniels today. She always told him who she was visiting. It was a rule. This felt wrong, and there was only one thing to do about it. Correct the behavior before it led to chaos.

Reluctantly, he got back behind the wheel of the Escalade. Rush hour traffic was just starting, but he knew he could be at his brother-in-law's office in 20 mins.

With each mile, his anger grew. He had to be careful. He

didn't show his anger in person, but when he got Margaret home, it would be a whole other story.

Once inside the lobby of *Smith, Bellows & Daniels, Attorneys at Law*, he was swiftly ignored by some low-level receptionist. After wasted prose with the minimum wage gatekeeper, he was passed along to Judy, Jack's personal assistant, who emerged from some side panel hidden door like a vampire out of a coffin. She was one of those holier-than-thou chicks who thought she was so self-important, wearing a structured suit that was meant to make her look like a man, but he could see her weakness. She had low self-esteem. She thought she could be a lawyer, but look at her. She was a glorified secretary.

He could break her in a matter of days, but she was an old chick, and he had other things to think about, like dealing with his dear wife. She was close. He could almost smell her. There were hints of her perfume in the air. Chanel No. 5, like his mother wore. He bought it for Margaret every Christmas with instructions to make the bottle last for a year. The woman often ran out by September because she wasn't smart enough to budget. It was a bone of contention for him.

Now, the woman before him, Jack's little helper, looked a little starstruck. Of course, she was a fan, and Hollywood was standing before her. He was famous, and everyone who was anyone knew it. God, he hoped she didn't flirt. He really couldn't fake it with the old chicks. The very thought of dried-up prunes in their fifties had his manhood shriveling. Maybe for a thrill, he'd give her an autograph. He'd make her ask for it. He didn't give those things away for free. Besides, it would give her a thrill to speak to him.

"I'm so sorry, Dr. Drake, but Mr. Daniels is in a meeting for the rest of the day. May I leave him a message for you? Or if you'd like, you can leave him a note." She held out a pen and paper as if she was oh-so-helpful. The twat.

"Is he with my wife?" he asked sharply, making sure his tone had some bite behind it.

"I'm not sure who he's with, sir. The meeting is private. I believe it is a gentleman."

"I know she is in the building. If I find out later that he was having a meeting with my wife, there will be hell to pay. And I will start with you."

She was taken aback, as if he'd slapped her. Damn, his words were powerful, but he didn't like this kind of reaction unless he got something out of it, like the satisfaction of an actual slap.

"Excuse me, sir. Are you threatening me?" she asked. He could almost see her fear.

"No. I'm merely explaining my displeasure and the consequences of those actions."

"If you continue to threaten me, sir, I'll call security." Oh, now she was all self-important.

"Whatever, you officious twat, I'm done with you." He turned on his heel and stomped out of the office. When Margaret got home, not only would there be hell to pay..., but he didn't know how he would stop himself from layering on one punishment after another.

How dare Margaret meet with someone without him? It didn't matter that it was her brother. How dare she not tell him what she was planning to do? He hadn't approved of this. Margaret would have to understand what happened when she broke multiple rules at once. The punishment would have to be something new, something unique. It was enough to make his head spin.

He briefly heard the Judy woman talking to another fembot, threatening to alert security. She was nothing but a little peon to Margaret's brother Jack. He hoped she felt so powerful now. It probably made her day, if not her week, to speak to him in that way.

As he drove home, he wondered what this disobedience, this fresh hell, was about, but he chose not to think about it too long. He had an upcoming book tour. He had things to do. He was an important man. Leave it to Margaret to go sideways when he needed her the most. This little distraction today could not and would not be overlooked. He could just see her reappearing as if everything was all right. Well, surprise, surprise, it wasn't.

He parked in the garage at the home he purchased shortly after he'd married Margaret and carefully walked inside, placing his shoes in the little cubicle that he had designed especially for space by the front door. He slipped into his crocs and sighed. Margaret's shoes should be there because she should be there. Again, he tried to make sense of it. How dare she not be home? What was wrong with her? If she were the perfect mate he deserved, things like this would not happen. He had selected badly. He didn't think so at the time, but with time had come perspective. And now he knew.

Going to the bar in the dining room, he opened one of the finely carved cherry wood doors to the liquor cabinet and pulled down a Waterford crystal lowball glass, one of six that had been a wedding gift from one of his mother's friends. Once in hand, he looked at the liquor before him and selected something mellow. It was arranged alphabetically, of course. He passed over the Bullet Bourbon, the Jack Daniels, which always made him think of his sleazy brother-in-law, the Maker's Mark, the Pendelton, and finally settled on the Southern Comfort. He poured three fingers of the golden amber liquid into the glass and gulped it down in a way he would never do in front of company. Not like he'd have to worry about that tonight.

He shook his head, trying to shake off this feeling. Margaret really irritated him today. What little game was she playing? Was she jealous, jealous of his success? Maybe that was it. Of course, that was it. He was outgrowing her, and she could see it. After all, he let her do her little Realtor thing, but wasn't it time for her to dedicate herself to the real breadwinner in the family? That she stopped with all the nonsense of trying her own little career? Wasn't it time that she respected his job, his career, his motivations? He casually started to mention this. Heck, he wasn't even sure that she'd listened to him. He was going to let her keep the job for a few more months. He'd been generous with her, and what had she done? She disrespected him. Always talking about her career. She was never taking the kind of interest she should in his career. She had thrown it away.

He was tired of being subtle. When she came home, which should be any moment, he would tell her the way it was going to be moving forward. No, he wasn't about to get distracted by her acting out. No, he would not be distracted by her childish rule breaking. She would be punished, of course, but he knew what the end goal would be. It was time for her to stop playing at her little job and dedicate herself to him. He'd given her too much time to play. He saw that now. It made her think she was independent.

He glanced up from the bar and through a doorway to the front parlor where the baby grand piano with its fine, dustless polish waited to be played. As usual, there were five photos aligned on the piano. Margaret needed to resume her lessons. She wasn't trying hard enough to learn. Yet another frustration. He wanted his wife to play a musical instrument. It was becoming a mandatory requirement—

What was wrong with the piano? He recounted the framed detritus on top of the elegant instrument. Only four framed photos decorated the piano. That couldn't be right, but it was. The one that was missing was that of Margaret's grandparents. How long had it been gone? He thought back to his near photographic memory and remembered seeing that photo just yesterday. It was missing, which raised a tendril of new unease.

He looked around and really took in his surroundings for the first time in several days. The equilibrium that was his home was off. Some things were missing... little things. Things that he wouldn't necessarily notice unless he was looking for them, like the framed photo of her grandparents. The tiny crystal vase that her mother had given her, which had been her grandparents' vase, no longer resided in the China cabinet. Where it should have been behind the neatly polished glass doors, it was just gone.

Realization settled deep within his bones.

He picked up the Waterford crystal glass and threw it hard against the opposite wall of the dining room. The resulting melody the glass played as it shattered was sorrowful music to his soul, calming him.

He left the broken glass where it lay. Heck, Margaret caused it. She could clean it up. He searched through the rest of the house and noticed little things. Margaret's makeup bag was missing from their master bathroom. The most telling sign was that her wedding band sat atop the nightstand next to the bed. She hadn't removed it in the six years they'd been married. It was a request he had made, and she respected it until now. The room was washed in a red haze of his anger. He didn't understand, but on some very dark level, he did, but he didn't want to vocalize it because to vocalize it would make it true.

He reached down and touched his own wedding ring. He only took it off when he knew he had a therapy session with a particularly fragile, attractive female. The ex-girlfriend he had spent so many lunch hours with requested that he leave it on. She enjoyed pulling the wool over Margaret's eyes as much as he had.

Margaret's clothing was all there, which made no sense. But several pieces of their matched luggage were missing. Had the bitch left? She was too meek, too scared of her own shadow to do such a thing...

But she had been at her brother's office, and he was a divorce attorney. How dare she think she could leave *The Voice of Reason?*

CHAPTER FIVE
(Amber)

Amber looked at her little boy and little girl and marveled. They were a perfect mix of her and Jack. She liked to think they had the best traits of both of them. Time would tell on some of those little personality traits, but they were both destined to be beautiful children and stunning adults. Okay, maybe she was a little biased...but who could blame her?

She couldn't believe that she was a mother. Clayton and Libby were now a little over a year old. Libby started walking at eleven months, which annoyed Clayton. Not wanting to be left behind, he started walking three days later. That determination would serve him well in life. They were starting to entertain themselves, playing together with made-up games that brought them a lot of joy. They even communicated in their own language. She had heard of it happening and felt her children were more than a little special for picking up the trait. As she watched, they were in the family room on a blue gingham blanket that their grandmother had made for them. Stuffed animals were holding court in their made-up game.

Amber took stock. Her life had taken such a different turn than where she had been four years ago. She realized something at that moment. She liked herself a lot better now than she ever had. Four years ago, she was going from neighborhood to neighborhood, making sense of things that were out of balance and putting them right again. It was only in reflection that she realized how each time she took matters into her own hands, she lost a part of herself.

She was so incredibly lucky to have met Jack the first time and then the second time when they decided they could not be apart. She was also lucky to have never been caught. More than once, after a bad dream, she'd awakened happy that she wasn't in a jail cell for murder. She wondered how close she'd gotten. Perchance, the fear would never fully leave her.

She'd never believed in soul mates. She didn't believe in true love, forever after happiness, until she met Jack. And for the first year they were together, she'd probably been waiting for the other shoe to drop, wondering if he would decide that he couldn't be with her or accept the things that she had done. But on the contrary, he had done a few bad things himself. As a team, they helped each other out, and together, they were stronger. They finally had that other person to confide in, to share with all their deepest and darkest secrets. She was no longer alone. And with the birth of Clayton and Libby, they were now a family. If you had told the poor kid that was Kelan Deluca that she would be a mother and a wife someday, she wouldn't have believed it to be true. Heck, they even had a copper-colored Vizsla dog named Pumpkin, and a black cat named Wicca.

After she had her last season as Madame Emma, she vowed never to return to that transient life. With Jack's love and support, she'd settled into being a wife and mother. That wasn't to say that her friend Miss Violet from Yachats didn't call every now and then, needing something. Amber would like to say that she turned down Miss Violet when Miss Violet had an interesting project that needed help because she was a different person now, but she wasn't. Amber hadn't turned down any of the opportunities that Miss Violet presented. Well, Amber didn't want to get rusty with her skills. The only difference was that Amber didn't know the person, but Miss Violet did. Amber trusted Miss Violet to vet well. This is something else that surprised Amber. She now trusted a few select people. Jack and Miss Violet knew her darkness. Kelan Deluca had come a long way. And Miss Violet, true to form, sent the best baby gifts and couldn't wait to meet Clayton and Libby. They were going to meet up in Puerto Vallarta in the fall.

Her cell phone vibrated in her pocket, and with one glance, she smiled. *Jack.* It was their anniversary today, and she was already excited about what the evening would entail. Jack's parents were going to babysit and would be arriving in about an hour.

The thought of how they'd end the evening in each other's arms already had her tingling. She loved the feel of him and how he could do things to her and bring out emotions that no other human on the planet could. She picked up Jack's call immediately and greeted him in her standard way.

"Hello darling," she said.

He responded in kind, "Hello, my darling. I just wanted to let you know that we've had a bit of excitement around the office today. Maggie will be coming home with me tonight and staying for a bit."

She could tell by his tone that there was a lot he was not saying. He must have an audience. He sounded sad as he was sorry for canceling their evening plans. It didn't matter. They could go out for their anniversary any night. Just spending time together was all they required.

"Good, she left him. I'll make sure the guest room is ready," she said.

"Exactly. About our reservations—"

"No worries, darling," she replied. She could hear Maggie in the background trying to backpedal, telling them to keep their reservation. But there was no way they could do that, nor would she want Maggie to be alone.

"If Michael should call, or more frighteningly, show up at our house, call the police. Don't let him in."

"That's no fun," she said ominously.

He knew her well enough to know she could take care of herself, but there were children to think of now, so she had to consider all that she had before doing anything rash.

"I know, but he is dangerous. He's been abusive to Maggie," Jack said, lowering his voice. Something in his voice bothered her, and although she was used to taking care of such situations herself, she would respect his wishes.

"Is Maggie all right? I always said I thought Michael was an asshole. I have a feeling that we'll need to take care of evening the score on that."

"You were right. I think she will be fine, but there is a lot to unpack here, and a lot of it isn't good. I think in the coming few days she'll have a lot of stories to share with us."

"That bastard. Maggie is a sweet person. I'll make something nice for dinner. We'll drink some wine and solve all the problems of the world."

"I'll call my parents. I need to tell them that Maggie has split from Michael, but I don't want to get too detailed. It would only upset them."

"That is probably a good idea."

"Thank you, darling. See you soon."

CHAPTER SIX
(Maggie)

Maggie didn't want her parents to know, and therefore it was hard to even tell her brother Jack. There was no going back, but he didn't seem to have an issue once he volunteered to be her attorney, and she handed him a requested $1 bill to represent her. But she knew that, unlike most problems, this one—her horrible marriage to Michael, *The Voice of Reason*—was not going to go away. She needed to strategize. She needed to plan. She needed to escape *The Voice of Reason* once and for all.

But she was in so deep. She still didn't know how she would get away. If she moved to another country, would she be safe? Not bloody likely. At least she had taken the first step.

Jack told her that she could stay at his and Amber's house for as long as she wanted. She loved him for that offer because she never felt more lost in her life. At least he had a security system with cameras, and she remembered him saying he had a concealed weapon permit and carried a gun. She didn't think Amber was a shrinking violet either. No, her sister-in-law had steel in her soul. Jack had once said that Amber had a difficult childhood, but he hadn't elaborated and hadn't needed to. Maggie could feel it. And if there was any time she needed some of that strength to rub off, it was now.

"We have the space, and Amber loves you. Besides, the children would like to get to see more of their Aunt Maggie."

Maggie smiled, and then she said, "The children are too young to even know me." *The Voice of Reason* hadn't let her visit as much as she wanted to. And when she visited, he insisted on coming with her. He not only wanted to hear the conversation, but he also wanted to guide it.

"Well, our children aren't like other children. They are exceptional. My guess is that within a week, they'll be calling you by your full name, Aunt Maggie."

By mutual agreement, Maggie left her car in Jack's parking garage and rode home with him. They didn't want to encounter Michael lurking around her car. It was highly unlikely that he remembered what Jack drove because he was a narcissist, and Jack had just gotten a new Land Rover a month earlier. While they waited in the safety of his office, security men from his law firm moved everything from her car to his, making sure that they were not observed by someone who matched Michael's description.

And when it was time to go home, those same security men gave Maggie and Jack an escort to Jack's car.

Maggie was tired and had a hard time keeping her eyes open as Jack drove home. How long had she slept with one eye open, fearing every sound in the night? How long had it been since she'd had a decent night's sleep? How long had she been running on a tightrope waiting for her opportunity to leave *The Voice of Reason*?

Her mind went to all the dark places that scared her. Was she safe with Jack? Had he checked the car? She glanced over her shoulder more than once. She had the paranoid feeling that maybe Michael was hiding in the back amongst her boxes. She didn't want Michael to hurt Jack. Was she doing the right thing by going to Jack's house, or was she bringing evil into his home? He had a wife and children. That was a lot to lose.

The whole thing made her tired, and even though the fight had not even begun yet, she had made the big first move. She had declared war. She hoped. Fallout would happen, and it would happen soon. But for the moment, she was safe.

She liked her sister-in-law Amber, but she didn't want to just drop in like this. Maggie felt horribly guilty and hated to burden her family in this way. And seriously, what if she was putting them in harm's way?

Jack's words pulled her away from her musings.

"Please tell me you'll never go back."

"I don't think that would be a good idea. If I went back, he'd kill me."

"I don't even know what to say to that," Jack said. "You are so calm. You sound absolutely matter of fact."

"I'm not overreacting," she murmured.

"I know you aren't. I'm in the business of calming people down who feel they have been mistreated. I know you are serious. I can smell bullshit, and there isn't any bullshit here. You're calm but resolved and a little terrified. That is why you can never, ever go back," Jack said as they pulled onto his street, and he hit the button for his garage door.

Maggie checked in all directions. She looked for anything out of place. She didn't see Michael's car and didn't see anyone lurking behind any bushes or trying not to be seen. The street was deadly quiet.

"Don't get out until the garage door is completely shut," Jack advised as he drove into his driveway, pulled into the garage, and then stopped, hitting the garage button as he did so.

"Good idea," Maggie said as the door quietly rolled down and thudded against the concrete floor of the garage.

Amber opened the door that led from the garage to the kitchen and looked to Jack as he secured the space. Then Amber nodded, unspoken words between them. Maggie was used to seeing an easy smile on her sister-in-law's face, but tonight, she looked serious, and Maggie felt guilty for being the reason why. And it was their anniversary. For the hundredth time, she wondered if she should have gone to a hotel and called Jack tomorrow. She had really shaken the calm of their evening.

Maggie got out of the car and stopped before Amber, who held out her arms. Maggie fell into them.

"I'm so sorry about ruining your anniversary," Maggie said as she started to cry.

Amber said the words that Maggie needed to hear: "You know, your brother and I, we don't need to go out to dinner to remind us about things like our anniversary. We are so glad we can be here for you when you need us."

"I still feel bad," Maggie said.

"Well, stop it," Amber said, stepping just far enough away to look Maggie in the eye. "Listen to me. We are here for you. It's going to take a while, but you're going to be okay. I just don't want you to go back, and I haven't even heard the full story. Look at it like this. You might have given us the best anniversary present imaginable. I never liked Michael. Knowing you left him makes me happy. Come inside. We'll get you some chocolate or cheese and definitely something with alcohol in it."

"I'll bring in her stuff," Jack said.

"Thank you, darling," Amber replied as she opened the door and ushered Maggie inside their beautiful home.

Amber and Maggie moved into the living room, where they sat on the floor and played with the children.

Jack moved the few boxes she'd managed to leave with into their guest room along with her meager luggage.

Maggie tried not to think that these might be all the possessions she had left in the world. But if she knew Michael on any level, she knew he was probably systematically destroying all her belongings as they spoke. He liked to destroy when he was angry.

Maggie sipped the beverage that Amber put in her hand without questioning what it might be. Did it have alcohol? Had it been laced with something to make her tired? She had no idea. She was numb, and she did what Amber told her to do. She drank it. It tasted good, but later, when asked, she could not recall what it tasted like. She moved to the couch where Pumpkin and Wicca joined her, bookending her body.

Amber stayed on the floor and played with the twins, who seemed curious about Maggie but also involved in their game.

When Jack reappeared in the living room, Amber stood with the excuse that she wanted to check on dinner.

"Mags, you've got a run in your stocking," Jack observed as he sat on the floor and took the space vacated by his wife. The children immediately started crawling all over him, and he smiled and made funny faces at them, which they seemed to love.

"I left in a hurry," Maggie said with a nod.

"Do you want to take a shower, maybe change into something more comfortable before dinner?"

"That's a good idea. Do you mind?" Maggie asked Jack.

"Take your time," Amber answered from the door. "Dinner is a pasta bake, kind of a cross between pasta primavera, chicken breasts, and mac and cheese. It can hang in the oven as long as you need. It just gets better with time."

"Thank you," Maggie said, feeling she overused the phrase as she stood, earning a sigh from the dog, who was leaning up against her and demanded pets and a harsh meow from the cat as she walked toward the stairs. She paused and looked over her shoulder.

"Third door on the left. Lots of fresh towels in the attached bathroom," Amber said. "Take your time."

She nodded her thanks instead of saying it. What she really wanted to say was, "Thank you. I think you have helped to save my life."

"I'm just glad you came to Jack," Amber said.

Amber waited until she heard the door upstairs close, and then she looked at Jack.

"Worst fears realized," Jack said, standing and crossing to Amber, who he pulled into his arms and kissed before continuing. "Sorry, I meant to do that earlier, but my routine is a bit off."

"No worries," Amber said as she sunk into her husband's arms and watched their children play.

After a moment, Jack said, "So. Michael is everything you ever thought he was and more. You should have seen him today. Judy said you could see the rage in his face. He is incredibly dangerous. At Maggie's insistence, I put on my gun from the desk."

Amber looked up at him. "I thought you were packing," she said with a smile.

"I decided to wear it home," he said.

"It doesn't sound like you would've had an issue eliminating the problem," Amber said as she leaned into Jack's chest.

"I wouldn't have, but by the same token, I think you could do a better job of it."

"Aw, thank you, honey," she said and kissed him. "I'm already thinking of how I'd like to do it."

"He's in your crosshairs," Jack stated.

"Well, he has racked up a few pages in my little black book, if that is what you mean."

Her little black book was as close to anyone in her crosshairs as she got to a judge and jury. Once they were in the little black book, their fate was as good as sealed.

"I'll leave it to you. Tell me when you need my help, and I'll be there for you."

"Best anniversary gift ever," Amber said with a smile that could freeze any surface quicker than liquid nitrogen. "I've never liked that bastard."

CHAPTER SEVEN
(Maggie)

For the first time in several years, Maggie enjoyed a shower in quiet peace. More times than she could count, when Michael was angry about something, he would wait until she was in the shower, then he would silently glide into the bathroom, pull back the curtain, and threaten her. He liked the way she would cower, vulnerable, in her nakedness. It was a game for him. It was also very psychotic.

Now, in this bath with Amber's bath products that were unfamiliar but lovely, Maggie not only felt safe, but she could also relax. Well, relax as much as she could. Demons of her past continued to tap her on the shoulder in fearful memory. She might have escaped, but the fear would take a while to disappear.

After the shower, she sat on the edge of the bed in the attached bedroom in a comfy bathrobe with her hair wrapped in a towel. Her body shook as she gently rocked herself.

She had done it. She had really done it. She was safe. She had survived. Well, she thought, for now.

This was a horrible day—like international travel, hours and hours of discomfort—but it was the first step toward getting her life back. Freedom had a price, and she was very willing to pay it. She felt tired, both physically and emotionally.

Michael was probably drunk, angry, and raging around their house...well, correction, she wasn't on the deed...his house. He probably scrambled an egg, which was the extent of his culinary expertise. Too bad there were some eggs in the fridge. If she could go back, she'd have cracked all of them.

Her phone sat on the nightstand. At Jack's office she disabled her location setting so he couldn't track her. He probably figured out where she was anyways. He tried to call her thirty-four times in the last three hours. Her voicemail was full. She would listen to the messages with her brother. She wanted a witness. She only hoped Michael had shown his real personality. No one would believe it. That was always her biggest fear. But maybe, just maybe, the façade had finally fallen away.

Jack put her luggage on a little bench against one of the walls so she could open the cases easily. She found her jeans, a soft old sweatshirt, and a pair of tennis shoes—all the things Michael forbade her to wear. She felt younger, lighter than she had in years. Her love of jeans hadn't disappeared. She slipped into them, and they felt wonderful.

Pulling her wet hair back in a ponytail, she removed mascara smudges from under her eyes and put on a shade of bright red lipstick, "Passion" by Chanel, which Michael hated and she had taken great pains to hide. She could admit that on her pale white skin, it was a bit shocking, but then it also screamed independence. She gave a hesitant smile to the mirror. It was a small start.

Opening her bedroom door, she heard Amber and Jack in the hall bath with their children. Clearly, it was bath time in their home. Pushing open the door slightly, Maggie watched from the doorway, feeling a bit like an intruder. They were singing some sort of children's song that delighted the children. This was obviously something they had done often, and they made it fun. The children were smiling and laughing as they splish-splashed in the water. She enjoyed watching them until bath time was over. It didn't last long enough for her to see how the family's unadulterated joy reminded her of all the reasons why she'd left

The Voice of Reason. Before long, Jack and Amber had the kids all wrapped up in their pajamas and blankets, ready for bed.

They had matching rocking chairs in the babies' room. Jack took one chair, Amber took the other, and each took a baby. Within a couple of minutes, the babies were asleep.

After placing each baby in their cribs, they walked out of the room and quietly shut the door. Then, they smiled at each other.

Jack said, "Believe it or not, it was easy tonight."

"It did not look easy," Maggie said.

"I think they were just tired," Amber said as Jack wrapped an arm around her. "And thank goodness they are down. I'm starving. Come on, Mags, let's get some pasta."

They sat at a large table in the dining room under a gorgeous Art Deco chandelier they had bought on a trip to Paris, drinking wine and eating pasta. Maggie had more of an appetite than she would have thought possible. She had fought off cravings for cheese and pasta many times over her marriage, and now she was enjoying each bite despite her desperate circumstances. But maybe what made it taste so good was that there was freedom to enjoy the food when someone wasn't watching, monitoring her calorie intake.

Amber broke the silence by asking, "How bad did it get? I surmised there were issues, but I need to hear it from you."

Maggie suddenly lost the appetite that had fueled a second serving of the pasta.

"I don't know exactly how it began," she said, laying her silverware at a perfect ten-to-four position on her plate.

Jack immediately began clearing and managed to refill her wine glass. When she looked up at him, he said, "You're with family. Partake."

Amber said, "Take your time. The only thing I'm going to do is grab the cake and coffee." She stood, joining Jack, and they stepped into the kitchen together. Amber returned a moment later with her aunt's famous chocolate cake, which Maggie always loved. Jack followed with a silver French coffee plunge and cups.

"Oh, is that what I think it is? When did you have time to make a cake?" Maggie asked.

"The pasta bake was already assembled and just in the freezer. I slipped it in the oven. I had already made the cakes. They were in the freezer, too. I just frosted them. It is good to be prepared," Amber said. "I always have a quick dinner ready, just in case."

"You are kind of amazing," Maggie said with admiration. Amber waved her off as she sat with the cake on a green milk glass stand before her.

"I think she is," Jack said, kissing Amber's cheek.

"Both of you, stop it. I want to hear Maggie's story," Amber said as she distributed large slices of her aunt's cake onto a plate and placed it before Maggie.

Jack poured the coffee from a French silver coffee press and placed a cup and saucer in front of his sister. He did the same for himself and Amber.

Maggie took a bite of cake and shut her eyes, sighing before she began. Then, she set her fork on the edge of the plate and then, reluctantly, started to speak.

"The signs were there, but I didn't see them for a long time. Maybe it started on the honeymoon. I thought we would have a wonderful honeymoon, but he didn't like how I arranged my cosmetics in the bathroom. He didn't like how many pairs of shoes I brought with me. I wondered if he was having second thoughts about marrying me. I actually asked him, and he said he just liked things to be neat and orderly. That was day two.

"When we got home, these nervous little tics, like the shoes, became rules for the inside of our house. At first, I thought he was kidding, but he wasn't kidding. He was serious."

"Shoes?" Jack asked, sipping from his coffee.

"He only allowed me to have four pairs of shoes in the closet at one time."

"Controlling. Demeaning. What else besides the shoes?" Amber asked, abandoning her cake in favor of holding her coffee cup as she listened to Maggie.

"There were rules about things like garbage cans in the kitchen. He didn't want garbage cans in the kitchen because garbage is filth and should be removed immediately, so that is why we never had a garbage can in our kitchen."

"I think I noticed that when I was at your house one Sunday afternoon. I wanted to throw something away, but I couldn't find a garbage can. What he said, that barely makes sense," Jack said.

"More control," Amber muttered and nodded as she set her cup gently in the saucer.

"None of it made sense. No matter how much I tried to reason with him and talk to him, nothing changed. There was no compromise. And it got worse the longer we were married and the more famous he became. He started drinking, and he started finding fault with everything that I did. I tried to change. But nothing I ever did was good enough for him. There was nothing I could say or do that didn't come with a reprimand. And believe me, I tried. I spoke with a harsh voice, a soft voice, I whispered. I was contrite. I was angry. Nothing mattered. He got just as mad when I whispered as when I screamed."

There was so much she didn't say, so much she wanted to say, but she knew that once the words were uttered, they would change the situation to a point where her brother might do something. She couldn't have him risk his family, his freedom, his job for her. She had to figure out how to deal with this herself.

"Was he ever physical with you?" Her brother asked.

She couldn't take too long to answer, but it was a complicated question. The first time it happened, he'd been apologetic.

The second time, not as much. The third time, he blamed her. *She needed to stop making him so angry. Why did she do that? Did she enjoy irritating him? Was it a game to her to bait him?*

How could she explain that the violence had escalated? How could she explain that she didn't think it would stop? How could she explain that this person that she loved, who she married in front of them, in front of three hundred people, was now the person she feared more than anyone else in the entire world? She felt like a fraud.

She thought of the threats. She thought of the name-calling. She thought of the scar on her leg. What could she say now?

"That bad, huh?" Amber asked.

"I didn't say anything else," Maggie said.

"Sometimes you don't have to," Amber replied.

"My concern is that when I file for divorce, he will be the angriest I've ever seen him. I don't know what he's capable of. Look at what he does for a living. His book is coming out in a few days. He isn't going to forgive me for leaving. He's going to want to punish me. And if this hurts his career at all, he is going to come after me."

"I know the way he got today," Jack said. "Judy was scared."

"That? That was nothing," Maggie said. "He was irritated but keeping it together. I bet he is going crazy tonight."

"Jesus, Maggie, he acted crazy *today*," Jack countered.

"You haven't seen him really mad. *The Voice of Reason* becomes inconsolable and completely unreasonable," Maggie said, realizing she'd disclosed something she didn't want to disclose.

"Why do you call him *The Voice of Reason?*" Amber asked, scrunching up her nose.

Maggie took another bite of cake and chewed it, enjoying the sweetness and the acrid bite of chocolate. Then she took a deep breath and answered. "He used to say to me that he was the only one in the conversation who was reasonable. I was overwrought, obtuse, and pejorative.

"It was early then in the marriage. I said something like, 'Oh please.' He then said he thought I was smarter when he married me. I was a big disappointment, so it should come as no surprise that I didn't know words like overwrought, obtuse, and pejorative. I said that he was right, 'Girls like me only know words like bastard and asshole.' That was a mistake, as you can imagine. In the end, he said, 'I'm *The Voice of Reason*. If only you'd listen to me, we could be happy.' I never contradicted him again."

Jack muttered something derogatory under his breath but didn't say it loud enough for anyone to know exactly what he'd said. He stood, went to their liquor cabinet, and pulled out a bottle of brandy. He added a shot of the liquor to Amber's cup of coffee and then his own. He looked at Maggie, who reluctantly nodded.

"I'm having a hard time because I want to hurt him," Jack murmured.

Amber smiled, "Patience is key, darling. We don't act rashly...never rashly."

"If he tries to hurt you again, I will hurt him back," Jack murmured.

"We need to make sure he doesn't hurt you," Amber said to Maggie.

"You can't watch me 24/7, and I don't feel safe in Minneapolis."

Jack seemed to understand as he looked at Amber and said, "Maybe Maggie should leave town for a while. And I'll take care of business on this end. Like getting her divorced."

Amber nodded, "I think it might be best if Maggie is out of town while business is taken care of."

"I think that might be a good idea. How soon could I get a

divorce?" Maggie asked. "I don't want the house. I don't want any of his money. I just want freedom. I want my name back."

"I want you to have fairness. That means that he will be paying you something because you should look at what he makes compared to what you make. It will probably take four to six months for a divorce. Even if he fights it, we'll get you out of this in six months."

"When can you start the paperwork?"

"Tomorrow morning. I'll get everything ready from my home office, so you don't have to come downtown."

"Almost not soon enough."

"And we have a few other things to do tomorrow," he said.

"Like what?"

"I'll get a restraining order. It won't matter, but it might help us get more in the divorce if they know he is hostile. Also, we will look for any insurance policies, and we will make sure he doesn't benefit from your death. I will talk to the court about getting time for you to get your things out of the house. Once we know that you have no other business with him, then we will get you a different car. Something he won't recognize. Possibly, we have it in Amber's name, so he can't find it. When he is no longer bothering you, Amber can sell it to you for a dollar. Next, we get your name back so you can be Maggie Daniels again."

"Good, but what if he doesn't stop?" Maggie asked. "This is going to affect his career."

"That is why we need you to hide for a bit. Think of someplace he wouldn't think of finding you. Meanwhile, I'll have him served tomorrow."

"More than anything, you have to know that you are not alone," Amber said, taking her hand. "We are here for you."

"I hate to bring this to you."

Amber shook her head and then said, "Don't be. We all have our stories. I'll share one with you. Many moons ago, there was this man I liked. When he asked me out, I thought that, finally, something was going my way. I liked him more than he liked me. We dated long enough that I thought he might be the one. He was actually my boss at some coffee shop.

"But then, one sunny afternoon, he broke it off with me. I was shocked, and then I found out he wanted to date another girl from the coffee shop we all worked at, who happened to be my roommate. I found out they started dating a month earlier. He was hooking up with her every chance he had. So now all the weird schedules that left me working while they weren't, well, they now made sense.

"And she didn't mind when he'd stay over with me because she was a bit twisted and contemplated how all of us might end up together. *His little harem.* They laughed that I was a hick and prude and would never get with it. And, of course, when they shared all this with me, I was horrified. He told everyone at the coffee shop that I was a prude. There was a lot of sick and twisted right there. It was embarrassing.

"I ended up leaving the apartment, getting my own place, and finding a new job. I heard they moved in together, and about three months later, I was driving downtown, going to my new job, and I stopped at a four-way stop. This man stepped into the intersection. Immediately, I knew it was him. I was so angry, so embarrassed, so enraged that he'd made a fool of me and was having a good time while I was suffering. Moving was expensive. The new job didn't pay as much. This was my first time on my own, and I wasn't doing a great job.

"My foot was on the brake, and it wavered. I thought of how easy it would be to hit the gas. Allow my car to plow into him. How good it would feel to have his body crumple."

Maggie had set down her coffee cup and was looking strangely at Amber.

"But I didn't. He wasn't worth the jail time, and I realized that fact at that exact moment. I believe that's what expensive therapists call a turning point. And thank goodness I didn't because I'd have never met your brother or had the children."

"Wow," Maggie said, looking a little shocked.

"I wouldn't worry about bringing anything to us. Between Jack's line of work as a divorce attorney and my life of hard knocks, we've got you covered. The most important thing is that you don't go back. Because you might be scared of him tonight, but someday he might have a reason to be scared of you."

CHAPTER EIGHT
(Maggie)

The next few days felt like a month.

Relenting and telling her parents some but not all of the details had been hard, but Maggie managed to do it. Her mother cried. Her father wanted to kill Michael, but it was Jack who was with her and piped in, "Join the club. I'm handling it." She didn't like showing any weakness or failure. Something like this would never happen to Jack. She should have left earlier. That was clear. And she listened to them as they reiterated that point. Well, easier said than done.

Her parents offered to help her any way they could, but Jack and Amber beat them to the punch, and she was happily still in their guest room. Her parents were about to take their yearly spring trip to Sedona, and Maggie was happy they would be out of town for a few weeks. Jack encouraged them to move up the trip.

It was hard to believe that she had escaped exactly six days ago. It felt like it was six months ago.

Michael had gone, as predicted, ballistic. Jack related that Michael punched the poor process server, who was there to serve divorce papers. Michael ended up spending a little time as a guest of the Minneapolis Police Department until his lawyer bailed him out. He was a free man until his trial in a few months for assault.

Jack was pleased. Michael was acting out. That helped their case.

She was glad he was showing his anger to another, although she felt bad for the process server. It also was a warning about what he might do to Maggie.

Michael had shown up at Jack's office, and Jack simply called the police and filed a restraining order.

Maggie now had a new cell phone with a number she only gave to her family and a few friends. Even her office didn't have it. Any real estate-related calls still came in on the old phone, along with Michael's multiple, demanding, ranting phone calls. Michael sent her over one hundred emails that first day to her personal and to her work email, which led to her creating a new personal email account. With her work email, she didn't want to tell the IT department what was happening, so she had to label his email as spam. He would then go automatically into his own file. Jack had her keep a log of the unwanted calls and emails from Michael, and if he left either, she forwarded them to Jack to add to his already thick file.

Eventually, Michael calmed down enough to finally figure out that she wouldn't pick up his call. He started to call her from a burner phone, but she learned how to block his calls, and by the end of the week, she had blocked seventeen numbers he called her from already. He could call all he wanted; she wasn't going to pick up. She also discovered that using the basic settings to make sure he wasn't able to track her phone wasn't enough. She suspected he was tracking her old phone through several different pieces of software that he downloaded onto the device without her knowledge. It helped that Jack had a friend at Apple. They wiped her phone and started over again. So, they had to assume that Michael knew she was at Jack's. It was interesting to her that he hadn't stopped by. It put them all on high alert.

In case they missed something, it was decided that when she left town, she would leave the phone with Jack. If any business came up, he could call her. A lot of details needed to happen before she left, but Jack was working on an idea he had.

Meanwhile, her three-year-old gray Honda was a thing of the past. She now had a two-year-old pearl white BMW sedan with a sand interior, which was parked a few streets away from Jack and Amber's house. When Jack went with her to the dealer to get rid of the Honda, they placed the Apple AirTag, which they discovered Michael had hidden in her trunk as they cleaned it out, under the carpet in the trunk of a Mini Cooper fleet rental at the dealership.

They still remained on guard that Michael could appear. A calm Amber confided that she hoped he would stop by for a visit as she showed Maggie her concealed weapon permit. She told Maggie she was a very good markswoman. Sometimes, Maggie's sister-in-law scared her a bit because nothing bothered her. Maggie was just glad Amber was on her side of this war.

Jack found a way to fast-track her name change, and she was Maggie Daniels once again.

When Michael assaulted the process server, at least twenty media outlets descended on him, and public scrutiny of Michael began.

Maggie went into a local Target to get some additional supplies for the trip she was planning and saw Michael's photo on several of the national tabloids. The headlines alluded to trouble in paradise:

Publisher Set to Dump Doctor Love's Contract for Future Books Amid Divorce Rumor.

America's Marriage Counselor's Marriage -- Trouble in Paradise?

She could almost feel his anger. And it was only just beginning.

Maggie kept her gaze low and purchased the shampoo and toothpaste she needed. The clear glasses and scarf she wore were Amber's suggestions, and she was glad she had listened. No one recognized her. Michael wasn't stalking her. She didn't want to think of how easily Amber pulled together the disguise. She was a damn near professional about it.

Still, Maggie was glad she had let the other woman dress her up. She made her purchases at a self-serve kiosk and then walked carefully to her car, watching, hyper-aware of her surroundings. How long would it take Michael to figure out that she had ditched her car? All the better that she was about to leave town—heck, the state and the country.

For the first time in years, she was sleeping. She was keenly aware of everything around her and scared of fast movements, loud noises, and anyone who was bigger than she was, but the fear was starting to be manageable. And by that, she meant a part of her brain was starting to rationalize that she had escaped. Jumping and taking a defensive stance 24/7 was not necessary, but, when in public, she needed to remain aware.

Amber explained her perception over tea one afternoon, and what she said made sense. "He has gotten under your skin. Even though he isn't around you, you still can hear the words in your mind because he beat you down for years. In time, that will fade. You will find your voice again. It is just going to take a while. And don't you worry, if he comes here, I'll take care of him, or Jack will."

Maggie had no doubt that Amber would. Her smile held a flash of something dark, now covered by a sweet façade. It was like having a pet jaguar at your disposal. Maggie had seen it rarely in the time Amber had been married to Jack, but now she saw it every time they talked about Michael. Call her crazy, but she thought Amber actually hoped Michael would show up and cause trouble.

On her way back to Jack and Amber's after Target, Maggie drove around a bit, as they suggested to make sure Michael wasn't following her.

Her new phone, attached to the car's Bluetooth, rang.

She glanced at the dash and saw it was from *Graystone*,

Hudson, and Fields, her new employer in Vancouver, B.C. She took the call.

"Hello, this is Maggie Daniels."

"Good afternoon, Maggie, I'm Rick Fields. I'll be your advisor at G, H, and F."

"It is very nice to meet you," Maggie said, meaning it. Jack had gone to school with one of the principles of G, H, and F fifteen years earlier. With Maggie's marketing degree, Jack was able to call his buddy, Henry Hudson, and get her a three-month internship. She was too old to be an intern, but it would serve its purpose and get her out of town for a few months.

She had a fleeting memory of Henry when she visited her brother one time at school. She remembered that she thought he was handsome, but when she mentioned it to her brother, he told her that Henry had a steady girlfriend at the time and any thoughts she'd had fell by the wayside.

Aside from this being a generous favor from one of Jack's friends, there was one little problem she kept pushing to the back of her mind. Henry Hudson's business was in Vancouver, BC. It was in the same city where she and Michael had gone for their first anniversary. It was Michael's idea, and she hoped it might rekindle some of the love they had once felt for each other. It didn't, and she had forever hated the city. She needed to put those memories on the back burner. She needed to get out of town. She remembered the first conversation she had with her brother and now felt it in her bones. She needed to leave town, the sooner the better.

"*You don't have to do this, but getting out of town might be a good idea,*" Jack had said.

"*I think I need it,*" Maggie said.

"*It will be nice for you to have a break. And I know Henry. He's a good guy. I trust him.*"

Maggie tried to pay a little better attention to the man talking to her now.

"We are looking forward to meeting you next Monday."

"I'm looking forward to it too," Maggie said, trying to sound enthusiastic. Henry obviously passed her off immediately, but she didn't care. Her escape from Minneapolis was one week away. She could not believe it.

"Do you have everything you need?"

"Yes, I leave Minneapolis tomorrow. It's going to take me a few days of driving to get there, but I'm not pushing it."

"That's good. Try to enjoy the drive."

"Thank you, I will. I've rented a little place near the office, so let's hope it is half as nice as the photos online. I think I'm all set."

"Well, if it isn't what you want, I've lived here all my life and can steer you in the direction of a good neighborhood."

"I might take you up on that. Thank you."

"I look forward to meeting you on Monday."

Maggie thanked him again, figured she had thanked him almost too much, and got off the call, her next adventure coming together.

"I think we can all agree on one thing," Maggie said as she looked at the plate Amber set before her, shut her eyes, and savored the smell of cheese and garlic. "You have completely spoiled me."

"This kind of thing makes me very happy," Amber said as she sat down to her own lasagna.

"She gets tired of spoiling just me. And the twins are too young to care," Jack said with a smile as he reached out and grabbed Amber's hand. "It is nice for her to have a fresh person to spoil."

"We will miss you, but I think what you are doing is a good idea," Amber said.

"What if he starts bothering you?" Maggie asked. "I know we have a restraining order, but I just don't trust it."

"Don't worry, we will take care of him," Amber said. "You just watch yourself up in BC. It is hard to think of you so far away."

"It actually makes me happy to have you out of town for a bit," Jack said.

"Thank you for all you've done."

"It has been fun to have you around regardless of the circumstances. Now, how about some peach cobbler?" Amber asked.

"You made peach cobbler?" Maggie asked.

"I did," Amber said with a smile.

"It has been years since I've had that."

"I know. You said it was one of your favorites," Amber said with a nod. "I think you've earned it."

CHAPTER NINE
(Dr. Michael Allan Drake)

What was Margaret playing at?

First, she took her wedding ring off and left it where he would see it. If that wasn't the ultimate sign of disrespect, he didn't know what it was.

Second, she just thought she could leave. Was she kidding? Was she having memory loss? She had proclaimed her love for him. Promised before God and witnesses to stay married once their bond was formed. They were a mated pair. He had molded her in his image. Well, he had tried, but she had been unwilling to be molded.

Third, he might have been able to forgive and eventually forget if she had come back immediately and begged for forgiveness. Now, she'd been gone for a week. Boy, when she came home, he was going to have to teach her that running away was not only wrong, but she also needed to be punished for it. She wasn't a five-year-old who had been denied access to cartoons. No, she was his wife, and she was throwing an adult temper tantrum. Well, two could play at that. He had warned her time and again—what would happen if she made him angry? And he was definitely angry, which was her fault. The legal pad in front of him had page after page of notes on things he would address with her when she returned. He needed to organize them. Have all his lessons in simple, achievable stages for her to learn. He would get there. Heck, it would make a wonderful outline for a book for like-minded males: hell-bent on order and keeping their family intact.

Damn her! She had done this to him. And his hand was now cramping with all the writing he'd done. He had a lot going on, and the result was that he was just a bit distracted at the moment.

The damn book tour for his Pollyanna views on marriage was looming. What if he came home from the tour and found Margaret here as if nothing had happened? If she thought she could just sneak back while he was away and everything would be fine, that he would just accept what she had done, she had another thing coming. Hadn't they agreed to do the book tour together? Well, he told her she would be going because he needed someone to make sure he was happy and well-fed. Now who was going to do that? It was just another embarrassment caused by her that he would have to deal with.

He tossed the pen down, stood, and left his office.

He went to the liquor cabinet and found another Waterford crystal glass. He shook his head. These were sold in sets of two, and he used to have three complete sets. Thanks to Margaret, he now only had two and a half sets. He was bothered by the unevenness.

Pouring three fingers of Southern Comfort into the fine crystal, he drank it quickly to calm his nerves. He needed the intervention after how angry Margaret had made him that morning.

As he drank, he looked at the remains of the glass shards that Margaret's disrespect resulted in when he threw the tumbler against the wall that first night. He glanced down at the now-empty glass in his hand. With might, he tossed it to where the shards of the previous glass still lay. He smiled at the sound as it bounced off the wall and, like a fine chime, shattered and fell upon the remains of its partner. One couple had been destroyed, dying together. It felt like balance had been restored.

His little chore done, it was time to reflect a little more on his wayward wife. He'd never taken Margaret to be one of those feminist chicks. He supposed that letting her go to work as a Realtor had brought this on. Well, that little act of freedom had been a mistake, but it was over now. When she came home again, and she would, the little "working outside of the home" gig was over. She was going to know her place as his wife. He was the breadwinner. She was there to make his life easier. And she would. Dinner would be at six p.m. sharp. This 6:01, 6:03 p.m. late business was bullshit. There was no need to dirty extra dishes either. Moving forward, the responsibility would shift, and she would be taking the dishes in and out of the dishwasher. He'd tried to be a nice guy, the helping husband by helping and loading the dishwasher. A fat lot of good it had done him to suggest he help her with that chore! It made her lazy. And she wasn't grateful as she should have been, but that would change.

He had been so kind to her, so accommodating. Sometimes the guidance that came with a gentle hand needed to have a little more bite than bark.

He sighed. He had been so lenient. A couple of times, not so much. The problem was in being consistent. That would be new for him. Now, he'd have to write new rules about the laundry, the house in general, their bedroom, and the bathroom. He had a lot to regulate when it came to the bathroom counter and the medicine cabinet. In the kitchen, he thought of his rules about dishes, but there was the fridge to think about and how the dishes, silverware, and cooking implements were arranged.

And hadn't his white glove test proven that she wasn't dusting or keeping the home to the level he required? It was all going to change.

He grimaced. This caused him such stress.

There were so many things to think about. He was only one man.

His cell phone started to play *Jamming* by Bob Marley.

Just what he needed. It was his agent.

He'd assigned the song as a ringtone to Benjamin because he suspected Benjamin of being a pothead. At least he hoped Benjamin's lack of attention to detail and basic lax attitude was chemically induced. If it was his personality...well...Benjamin was a waste of space, not to mention a special kind of stupid.

Michael remembered to smile and then answered, "Hello, Benjamin."

"Hey Michael. It's Ben," Benjamin said and then realized his faux pas with a giggle. "Jinx!"

"Ha, ha. What can I do for you?" Michael asked dryly.

"Sorry man, listen, I'm hearing rumors. I'm sure they aren't true, but what they're saying—we got to talk some words, bro."

"What are they saying?" Michael asked, thinking that people loved to gossip, making nothing into something. They were obviously bored in their lives.

"There is no easy way to ask this. Did your wife leave you, file a restraining order, and then file for divorce?"

Michael let the silence bloom between them. He needed a moment of composure. Maybe Benjamin would feel uncomfortable as he should. *Breathe in, breathe out. Calm...*

"We had a minor misunderstanding. It will be resolved shortly. It is no one's business but ours," Michael said, adding another item to Margaret's list of punishment. She had embarrassed him with this uneducated stoner hick. That had to be a new low.

"Well, your publisher, Paula, is freaking out with *Forming the Marital Bond* coming out in a week. It doesn't look good to have one of the premier authorities on marriage have his wife leave. Feel me, bro?"

"Paula? She's so weak, a typical female. It might be time to take back what is ours as men."

There was a pause.

"See? When you say shit like that...that's the stuff that gets you into trouble," Benjamin said. "Keep to the formula that works. You are the kind, big brother. The reasonable man. Every woman wants to marry you. Well, unless the abuse rumor is true. Nah, keep thinking that you are the most excellent husband that ever lived."

"Well, that is true. The fault does not lie with me. Margaret caused this. Margaret's disrespect for our marriage vows has brought my enlightened thinking to the forefront. Here's the deal. I have the strength and guts to say it. Most people won't, but I think it is time for men to be men and take back control of these power-hungry women who think they are equal to men," he said. "It was about time someone put irrational women like Margaret in their place."

"Um...well, I'd remind you that most of your audience is women. So, please don't say stuff like that. Keep it the way it has been. Women love you. Don't go off the fucking deep end, Michael. Feminists will rip you apart. Hell, my mother loves you, but if you spewed this male domination stuff, she'd skewer you on the nearest sharp object. And she will do it with a smile on her face. She's mean like that," Benjamin cautioned.

"Women are weak. They want guidance. If I talked to your mother for ten minutes, she'd know her place."

"Actually, I think you'd be dead. Mom doesn't take shit from anyone. Dad once pissed her off, and she said if he did it again, she'd take his house, his family, his dog, and our family business. Then she'd leave him a pot to piss in."

No wonder Benjamin was such a weak sperm. His mother had cut his balls off, not that they'd ever descended.

Benjamin continued, "Man, listen to me. Women will revolt. They are stronger than they look. My mother is one of those strong ones. But enough about that. Remember, we want sales. Your presales for this book are good. Let's go with that for a bit."

"You are so tiresome with all your pedantic rules about feminism. Hell, you sound like Margaret."

His agent was the one having a mental meltdown. He was trying to manage Michael. Well, Benjamin was a complete idiot. Michael was starting to lose his patience with Benjamin too. He hated having to repeat himself, yet that seemed to be all he did during the back-and-forth of this phone call. If he told Benjamin once, he'd have said it twenty times. Margaret had brought this on. She'd get over it, and he, ultimately, had nothing to do with it. Once she was back where she was supposed to be, all the press would die down.

It was like the parasitic media were always looking for something, some minor crack in his façade. Didn't they get it? They should be applauding his generosity for taking on someone so damaged as Margaret. Heck, this latest stunt was proof positive that she was a mess forever but that the sanctity of their marriage had whipped her into shape. Well, he had done a lot to get her there at great personal sacrifice. She challenged him in ways he hadn't thought were possible. He often told her that if she had to look at herself in the mirror, really look at herself, she wouldn't be able to. She was the problem. She was a mess. Only he could fix her.

"Okay, agree to disagree. One last thing I have to ask. Did you punch the process server?" Benjamin asked.

"His side of the story is wrong. The process server thing was a misunderstanding. I never would have lashed out physically. But I should add that such a person should not be responsible for such sensitive documents, even if they are a joke. I'm thinking of a countersuit. After all, it is all hearsay. What happened between us was really anyone's guess. And the fact that the man was now saying that I reached out and did something to him was just bullshit. He slipped into me, and I tried to steady him, but it makes for better press to say I punched him."

"This is such a mess," Benjamin whispered. Michael still

heard him because Benjamin was bad at this. He'd have to explain the facts of life to the little stoned creature. *Please let it not be today.* Michael already had a slight headache.

"Well, I wouldn't be surprised if the man now claimed that he was hurt," Michael said. "Let's be clear. He hurt himself and claimed that I had done it to him. That is probably his angle. He wants money. Benjamin, this is what happens when you are famous. People came out of the woodwork. They want a piece of you. We have to be strong and say no to this kind of injustice. Are you the man for the job?"

"Yes, Michael, I can handle it. I just don't know if I can handle you."

Michael took that as a compliment. He wondered if maybe that was Margaret's goal all along. He'd gotten just famous enough that she thought she could push him around. Well, the joke was about to be on her. He wasn't going to put up with that kind of mockery.

Now, her worthless, sleazy divorce attorney—who also happened to be her brother—had served him with divorce papers. He couldn't even take it seriously. It was so disrespectful. What business was it of Jack Daniels to get in the way of his marriage? He had no right. Michael surmised that's what happened when you were an ambulance-chasing-sleazeball. Heck, Jack had even gone beyond that by filing restraining orders for himself and Margaret. They were laughable. It wouldn't keep Michael away from his own wife. He never liked Jack Daniels, never trusted the slick lawyer. Maggie seemed to worship the ground Jack walked on before they got married. Michael thought he had broken her of the unconditional love she had for her brother.

"Can you just do one thing for me?" Benjamin asked, interrupting his thoughts.

"I'm not going to promise to do anything. I need to know

what you are asking first," Michal said with a deep sigh. He needed a new agent.

"I'm going to move up the book tour and get advanced copies. I want you to go out and make nice with the world to get ahead of the bad press. Think of what they are paying you. None of this male domination talk. Can you do that for me?"

"I'll think about it," Michael said and hung up on Benjamin.

CHAPTER TEN
(Maggie)

Maggie felt lighter the moment she left Minneapolis city limits, listening to satellite radio and letting her thoughts wander. Just to get further away from Michael felt good. Yes, she was going into the unknown, in another country, away from her family. But living with Michael meant facing the unknown every day, and her family could have been hundreds of miles away, but they were right there. They hadn't kept her safe, but she hadn't been honest with them when she should have been. Because it wasn't like she was able to see them that often. It was hard to say goodbye to Jack and Amber because she had become so close to them in the last week and a half, but it was necessary and a leap of faith into a better future.

Her first stop was Bismarck, North Dakota, which took her a little over seven hours with lunch. She stayed at a Marriott and had dinner at a nearby chain restaurant. Not knowing why exactly, she wore the clear glasses and scarf she had worn to Target. There was no way Michael had followed her, but the fear was real. Her next stop was Missoula, Montana. She wanted to drive straight through or make the trip in two days, but Jack and Amber wanted her to be safe and take her time. Her third night was in Everett, Washington, not too far from Seattle. Although she was only a few hours from her destination, she was tired and settled for room service and a rom-com movie. If only life and love were as simple as it was portrayed in the movies. But her life had been more of a horror movie, where the heroine barely escapes. Maggie had gone over every significant detail of the last six years of her life. She only wished she could hit some hidden delete button and have all the memories go away.

On the fourth day of her journey, she drove the final two hours and crossed the border into Canada. She visited the condo rental company and got a key and then settled into her furnished condo with a view of Stanley Harbor in Vancouver. It was cozy and had a fireplace for those last cool days of spring. She had groceries delivered without worrying about the meals she would create with the ingredients she purchased. She vowed to gorge on potato chips and dip one night without guilt. Heck, maybe she'd follow it up with a pint of chocolate and peanut butter ice cream. Michael's rules no longer pertained to her, but her rebellion was still delicious.

The condo was quiet when she wanted it to be or filled with music. It was her choice.

Within a couple of hours of arriving, she settled in by unpacking and fighting the urge to smile. The drama of her old life felt far away.

As she watched the sky darken and the lights come on from the floor-to-ceiling windows in her temporary home, she drank a glass of crisp, white wine and listened to Billie Eilish on her stereo system that connected to her cell phone. Dinner was a little overcooked as she learned the oven. Panic filled her. Then she remembered that the only person who would notice was her. And she didn't mind overcooking anything because it meant freedom. Her life had taken a 180-degree turn in a matter of days, and she was so thankful. But even as the thought entered her mind, she felt a trickle of fear.

There was no reason for Michael to look for her here. She was safe for the first time in months. She needed to let her body believe it.

How long would it take for her to feel normal again? Before she married Michael, she had been a strong, happy person. Now, she was scared of her own shadow. She didn't remember what it had been like to laugh as loudly as she wanted. To not censor each word out of her mouth. He'd taken her strength, and he had no right to do that. She wanted it back. She wanted her life back.

Sometime in the last few days, Michael figured out that she had ditched her cell phone. He had taken to increasing his threatening emails. He wasn't thinking clearly because the emails were filled with hate, phrases like *You will be so punished when you get home.* Sarcastically, she thought that really was a great invitation to return to the life she had just escaped. As promised, she sent each and every communication to Jack. He mentioned that it would be quite damaging if one of those emails got leaked to the press. But, by the way he said it, she knew he hoped one just might. Heck, she wouldn't put it past him to leak one himself. Actually, she hoped Jack would.

Such a thing would be career-ending for Michael. She wondered if any of the twenty news agencies had read the email that had been anonymously sent from an email that had no connection to her. The thought made her smile. If the email wasn't so bad, if there was nothing wrong with it, it wouldn't be damaging. Right?

The song that was playing in the background abruptly paused. She had an incoming phone call. Placing her wine on the coffee table, she snatched her phone, recognized the caller ID, took a breath of relief, and answered.

"Hey!"

"I'm sorry to bother you," Jack said. "I know you're getting settled in."

"If there is any bright spot in this, it is that we are talking a lot. I've missed you." This wasn't the first time they had talked today. He wanted to know when she had arrived and was settled in. It was nice to have someone care. For years, she thought Michael cared, but he didn't. He was obsessed with controlling her. There was a very real distinction, and it had nothing to do with care.

"I've missed you too, Magpie."

"I'm glad. Thank you. What is up?" she asked.

"Michael sent you what appears to be a card. It was sent to my office to you in care of me. I haven't opened it yet."

"Open it," she said.

"Are you sure?"

"Yes," she said and grew silent, waiting for him to open the envelope. "It isn't thick or anything, is it?"

"No, it is a flat envelope, like a card. Okay," he said, "I used my letter opener. Now, I'm looking at a card that is a crude drawing of the Earth with a black background and stars."

"Subliminal. *Where in the world are you, Margaret?*" Maggie said sarcastically.

"Could be. Opening the card. He's written: *Margaret, please come back. If you would stop involving others, we could be happy again. – MAD.*"

"Let me guess, no, *I love you?*"

"No. Did I know his initials spell out M-A-D? That feels like something I should have remembered."

"I did," she said.

"He is kind of delusional. Do you want the card, or can I just put it in the file?"

"File, please."

After they hung up, Maggie moved to the window and looked out at the harbor. Staving off a chill, she shut the blinds so that no one could see in.

Then she walked around the condo and made sure all the doors and windows were locked up tight.

CHAPTER ELEVEN
(*Amber*)

Once the children were bathed and in bed, Jack and Amber retired to their living room filled with candlelight and shared glasses of wine to discuss their day. Amber tried very hard to make the house kid-safe but elegant. Jack had given her free rein to do anything she wanted to make their house a home. She jumped at the chance.

It was the first time she had the money and ability to really create something that truly expressed who she was, or the person she was trying to be. She wanted it to be a sanctuary for both Jack and her where they could feel comfortable. She settled on oversized and overstuffed living room furniture made out of rich, expensive fabrics. The effect led to a very comfortable space that was worthy of an interior design magazine.

"Penny for your thoughts," Amber said as they sat close to each other on the couch, and Jack's fingertips made slow circles on her leg.

"A quarter for yours. They tend to be more interesting," Jack replied.

"Touché," Amber said and took a sip of wine.

"I just know you. What are you thinking?" Jack said, and his tone was serious.

"If he was my neighbor, if this were a season, I'd have already taken care of business. He can't be left alone and given the opportunity to repeat his behavior on another person. I'm no expert, but it would appear he's got all the signs of a sociopath. If not exactly that, he falls into the patterns of someone who has some very deep issues living in society. His narcissism is off the chart. He should be away from people. Left alone, he will harm more violently each time he is given the opportunity."

"Can he be fixed?"

"Sure. Two bullets to his brain would take care of him."

"It is going to be tricky because we are related to him. We never, pardon the term, shit where we eat."

She waved away his concern with a hand and said, "For every rule, there is an exception. Maybe we should deliver a care package to his house. You know, *I'm so sorry this happened…*"

"He's got cameras."

"Shazbot," she said and took a sip of wine.

"I had a crazy idea," Jack said.

"No idea is too crazy," Amber said.

"Well, Maggie said he was about to be on a book tour. Couldn't we be preemptive? One of our favorite cities, Portland, is always a popular stop on any book signing tour. We just need to figure out where he is staying. Miss Violet is always up for a little adventure. And if we knew when she was going to make a move, we could have enough time for a solid alibi."

Amber smiled, "Hire it out. Kind of a reverse of what she does with me. Very *Strangers on a Train*. Intriguing. But where is the fun in that? I like to see my results. Maybe a team effort."

"However, I can help," Jack said.

Amber thought for a moment and smiled. "Like any true villain, he has something that is his personal Kryptonite. I know what Michael's is. It can be used…creatively…against him. I keep circling back to it. Well, to be honest, I've wanted to do this since the day I met him."

"Whatever makes you happy, darling."

She smiled, running her index finger along his jaw. Then she moved a little closer and said, "You, you make me very happy."

CHAPTER TWELVE
(Maggie)

Maggie dressed in one of the new suits she purchased in Minneapolis the week before. Amber had taken her shopping, and she had procured a dozen new outfits for her new job and at least six pairs of shoes. It was the same day she had drained one-half of her joint bank account with Michael. The account she paid into monthly for her share of expenses. She wondered if he'd noticed yet. She also had a personal account that was the recipient of her real estate earnings direct deposit. Several months earlier, she changed that account to a bank that Michael wasn't aware of.

The suits, with all the new shoes and several pairs she brought from Minnesota, were in the closet at the condo. There had to be at least ten pairs in the closet at the same time! The little rebellion was a thrill.

Maggie and Amber had a lot of fun during their day of shopping. It was nice to visit other areas of the store than the designers Michael insisted she buy. She felt ten years younger. Hell, she looked ten years younger. Her normal dark blonde hair had been cut and colored to a pretty honey blonde, and she had a makeover at the Chanel cosmetics counter. Her only real opinion had to do with lipstick. She looked like a different person. Someone she thought she might never see again.

Michael liked the red lipstick she wore before they were married, but after the honeymoon, that had changed. Still on the heels of the shoe fiasco, she was incredulous. However, she didn't know what would happen if she broke a rule. She still seethed at the memory, which she hoped she would forget one day.

"I need you to change something," Michael said shortly after their honeymoon.

She defiantly asked, "What is it this time?"

"We need to talk about your lipstick."

"My lipstick?" she asked incredulously.

"Your whore-red lipstick."

"What are you talking about? You loved my lipstick when we were dating."

"Well, that was then, and this is now. First, I will probably die of lipstick poisoning, or I'll just stop kissing you, but the color really doesn't portray the message you think that it does. It is time that you know the truth."

"I highly doubt you will die of lipstick poisoning. That isn't a thing," she replied, starting to feel repulsed at the idea of his touch and wondering if he would stay true to his word and stop touching her. That would not be so bad. Quite the opposite, it would be her optimal wish to never have him touch her again. "And just what message do you think my lipstick is portraying?"

"It is the color of whores, Margaret. It is what whores wear. It isn't what my wife would wear," he said seriously, just like he'd stopped calling her Maggie and now called her Margaret.

"Are you kidding? It's Chanel."

"It is garbage and makes you look like trash. Stop wearing it immediately," he said. Then he held out his hand. "Surrender the lipstick."

"Surrender? You have got to be kidding me," she said, slapping his hand away.

He didn't speak to her for four days. Unfamiliar with this kind of conflict and not able to handle it anymore, she thought changing her lipstick was a small price to pay for peace. And she had always been the peacemaker growing up, so what was the big deal?

THE VOICE OF REASON

She gave *The Voice of Reason* six of her seven tubes of lipstick, and peace reigned again in their home, well, for a few weeks. He'd won, and she started wearing some nude gloss that did nothing to brighten her pale skin. It was one mistake in a list of mistakes. It was the beginning of the end. She not only lost the lipstick battle, but she'd already lost the war. She just didn't know it yet.

"Stop it. You're going to look great in that lipstick," she said to herself, enjoying the image that looked back at her in the mirror of her condo in Vancouver.

Today, the lipstick was a cloudy memory from her past. It was Maggie's first day at the advertising agency as a paid intern. It was something she might have really wanted when she was in college, but as a woman about to be in her thirties, it was humbling to have an entry-level job. How the mighty had fallen. She didn't want to think about the pay. She could sell one house and make triple what this job would pay over the next three months. But she was mindful. This wasn't about furthering her career or adding something to her resume. It wasn't about making money. This was about taking a break and escaping from something that was very unpleasant. This was a reset. A life reset. And there were other, much less pleasant places she could be.

And it was a lot about hiding. She was hiding for a very good reason. And wasn't a few months worth it in the scheme of a lifetime?

No one but Jack and Amber knew where she was. Not even her parents knew. All they were told was that she was going somewhere safe for a couple of months. Her real estate office was shocked when she said she was taking a three-month leave and put her real estate license on referral status, but that had been necessary. And she might make at least 25% of her commission if she was lucky and if the person who agreed to cover her desk was diligent.

Carefully, Maggie outlined her lips with a darker red pencil that was the color "Sierra," then she filled it in with a new red Chanel she purchased called "Passion." The effect was wonderful. Her lips had a sharp outline, and the difference in color blended to a lovely contrast, making the edges slightly darker.

She bought four different tubes of bright red lipstick, but Chanel's "Passion" was her favorite. It went smoothly and brightly. To deny herself such pleasure for so long had been much more difficult than she'd imagined.

She wore a navy suit from a designer she did not know. It cost about a fifth of what she used to spend on suits. And the lingerie. How fun was it to buy colorful lingerie when she didn't need to think about pleasing Michael but only pleasing herself?

Under her suit, she wore a matching Chantelle bra and panties in hot pink. Definitely what a high-priced whore would wear, according to Michael. Well, screw him and his white cotton undies without lace.

It was okay to wear sexy lingerie. It was okay to buy it for just herself. It had been a long time since she bought things that made her happy. And how lovely was that?

It had been fun to pack all the new stuff in her new suitcases. A new adventure, well, that was a better way to think of it than an escape from her marriage. The horror her life had become was never too far away, but buying clothing he'd never seen her in, wearing things that didn't look like her old life or what he approved of, was a great start.

She was so incredibly lucky. The way she lied about what was really going on behind closed doors for so long. How long had *The Voice of Reason* been abusing her? The Daniels were strong people. They didn't fear anything, but without the support of her family, Maggie feared Michael. Despite how much she had admitted to her family, there was so much more.

When any particularly disturbing incident rose its head to remind her of something that was ugly, she had buried it away.

She simply wrote an email to her brother with the pertinent details, the date of the event, what had started it, and how it ended. But there were a couple of things she didn't want to talk about. The scar on her leg was one of those things.

She wanted him to have enough to never doubt her. It was overkill but necessary. The abuse in the marriage was like layers of an onion. And the more she peeled away, the more she remembered.

It wasn't an exaggeration to say that Michael would have killed her. When she looked at the full picture of what she'd been through and what she ignored, it was not only the predicted outcome, but it was also the eventual outcome. She had almost waited too long. The thought of how close she had come made her shiver. She wasn't cold. She was terrified.

This divorce, when word of it came out, would be devastating to Michael's career. When people knew what kind of monster Michael was, it would destroy him. She felt bad for five seconds, which was five seconds too long. He had done this to himself. She was just collateral damage. But what if people didn't believe her? Some of them wouldn't. She knew that. If his mother wasn't in memory care for dementia, she would be campaigning for Michael. Probably painting Maggie as mentally unbalanced.

Even Jack told her that not everyone would believe her. It would get worse before it got better, but no one would ever control her the way he had, never again.

Just the night before, she talked to her cousin, Logan. He was now married to Gingie, a cute Realtor from Eugene, Oregon. Gingie introduced Amber and Jack when Jack went to visit Logan. Maggie should have a lot in common with the other woman, considering they were both real estate agents. But it all ended there. Logan loved, if not worshipped, Gingie. The places she walked were hallowed ground to Logan.

Maggie laughed bitterly at the empty space of her condo. She barely recognized the sound as coming from her. She had been quiet for a long time, but she was starting to find her voice again.

Michael never worshipped her. He'd faked it in the beginning. He acted protectively, as if she were fragile. She liked it, just for the fact he was so much larger than she was. At the time, she didn't fear his physicality, but she came to realize it. That warmth and compassion ended after the honeymoon. He thought she should worship him, and he told her so repeatedly.

During the phone call, she opened up to Logan. She thought it would be hard, but it was easier than telling her brother.

Logan was all too familiar with domestic abuse. They were, he said, his saddest cases.

"I'm glad you left," he said.

"I was worried he'd kill me, or maybe I'd start hitting him back."

"And then you might kill him, and we would have to arrest you for murder. No one would care he was an abusive son of a bitch. No, they would go after you. Best to leave. I just wish you'd never gone through it in the first place."

"Me too," she said, her voice unnaturally soft.

Her skewed reality was what really scared her. One day, she thought she might hit him back with something like her iron frying pan or the fireplace poker. She wouldn't stop until she knew he would never hurt her again. She'd kill him. If she fantasized about it ten times, she'd fantasized a thousand times. In her mind, she felt it would be justified. If people knew what kind of a monster he was, they wouldn't convict her. They'd consider her a hero. Hell, they'd throw her a parade.

Reality was a hard pill to swallow. They'd have arrested her for murder, and no one would have believed her.

And people, like his mother, before she ended up in memory care, had sung his praises and made him sound ethereal. *Mother* would have told anyone who wanted to listen just how horrible

Maggie was to her long-suffering son. The day that horrible woman had to go to the care facility had been the best day in Maggie's marriage.

Maggie escaped with her life and so had Michael. She just wondered if he ever knew how close he came to dying at her hand.

One last look in the bedroom mirror, and she was ready to go. Now, Maggie just wanted to do well at her job and blend in. She didn't need to be a standout.

Maggie practiced the drive to the office and added a half hour onto the time for traffic, not wanting to be late on her first day.

She approached the parking garage cautiously, with pepper gel in her hand, and pointed in the direction it would be most effective.

Caving to her new second nature, she looked all around her parking garage, both at the condo and the new office, just looking for Michael. He couldn't find her. She'd been careful, but the fear never left. Maybe it never would. Maybe that was a good thing. She didn't know if she would ever let her guard down. He had taken that innocence from her, but it wouldn't weaken her. She would find a way to be herself again.

CHAPTER THIRTEEN
(Amber)

Amber didn't like the doorbell. Maybe it was her old habits checking back in with her, thoughts flooding her memory... *Cover the body in the living room. Don't cover the body in the living room because a covered body looks like a body with something covering it. If it isn't covered, maybe he is sleeping? Yeah, right. Okay. Okay. Get rid of the person at the door. They can't come in. You want to be polite, but bad things could happen. They might see the body, and then you'd have two bodies to get rid of. That cannot happen. Get rid of the visitor. Do it politely, but do it...*

Where had that memory come from? It was some sort of PTSD. Oh yeah, Yachats, her last season before she and Jack decided to try for a baby. It worked out all right, but then she'd rather be lucky than good any day of the week. And getting rid of that body had not been easy. She'd gotten rid of her car and everything she was wearing. Invisible death cooties were still death cooties, and just because you couldn't see them didn't mean that they weren't there.

Amber cringed at the memory of rolling that body into the Pacific Ocean. Well, he deserved it. And then, a few days later, he rolled in at high tide. Too close for comfort.

But when the doorbell rang this morning, and she wasn't expecting anyone, she intended to ignore it. People who didn't call first were rude. Her neighbors always called her first. Her friends always called her first. Door-to-door bible thumpers did not call first, and she didn't feel like having a theological discussion this morning, probably any more than the visitor needed to meet the most frightening person they would meet in this lifetime.

So, on this Monday morning, when she heard the doorbell, she decided to do the bible thumpers a solid and pretend she wasn't home.

Looking down at the Bulgari watch her husband had given her for one of their anniversaries, she made a note of the time. It was nine in the morning on the dot. Really, it's too early for anything like civilized conversation. She was barely into her second cup of coffee.

She was on the second floor of their home, the nursery, which looked out over the front yard and cul-de-sac and was to her advantage. She slowly moved the edge of the curtain away from the window and gazed down at the caller. It was Dr. Michael Allan Drake. Well, well, she wondered what had taken him so long.

"Ah crap," she muttered.

She told Jack that Dr. Demented would show up around week two. It was hard being right all the time.

She let the curtain fall back into place against the window. Jack asked her to ignore Michael if he were to show up. To pretend she wasn't home. He didn't order her to pretend she wasn't home. They didn't have the kind of marriage where he told her to do anything. It had been a request, or she might even call it a plea to ease his troubled mind. And there were the twins to think about. She couldn't argue with that logic. She'd protect the twins with her life.

But here is the truth. Jack didn't like to dispose of bodies. He could talk the talk, but walking the walk was his problem. She could do both. She just didn't like it.

He was much better at creating solutions with wet work and walking away. With a shot to the head, the person drops dead, and Jack walks away. He turned his back on the lifeless body, and he was done. Amber could relate. She liked to see them alive, hand them something that she'd put together, and walk away. Did they live, or did they die? It was a bit of a random chance, actually. More often, they died. She didn't have to make a body disappear, no, she disappeared. It was like she was never there.

She didn't like having to deal with bodies, but she had, and in the end, she was proud of herself for stepping up when she needed to. And one shower was not enough to rid herself of those damn death cooties. Ten showers helped. To have to move a lifeless body, well, she would do it if she had to, but Jack, he got kind of squeamish. Her sweet boy was so sensitive. That is probably why he was so good in bed.

Focusing back on Michael, she was angry at him for many reasons. Today, however, he was disturbing the twin's morning nap. He was such a tool.

Still, she could invite him in for a cup of tea. Hadn't she mentioned to Jack that she should make up a batch of her *special* tea just in case Michael came by? But Jack reasoned, and rightfully, that he feared the children would somehow find the special tea and eat the ingredients. She couldn't argue with his logic. It was a highly remote chance, but still a chance, nonetheless.

Remember his Kryptonite...

When she thought of all the dried things she had in her personal arsenal and how they were now locked away in a storage unit two miles away, she rethought the wisdom of the decision not to have one or two things at home ready for her use. An emergency kit. What? People stockpiled food and water, so why couldn't she stockpile some of her special plants in their dried form? She could hide them on a high shelf in the garage. The twins were too small to ever find anything out there.

After her chat with Jack, they compromised. She ordered a safe the size of a shoebox from Amazon. Jack had installed it in the garage, among other boxes. It would be the perfect place to store some of her ingredients. She just hadn't gotten around to using it…Yet.

Michael rang the bell a second time. Their dog, Pumpkin, was sitting in front of the door and giving a deep-throated growl. She was a big baby, but she had an impressive voice. Amber would have to give Pumpkin some steak in her bowl for dinner. Good dog!

Amber did nothing to silence the dog. Michael didn't like Pumpkin, and the feeling was mutual. When Pumpkin was a rambunctious little Vizsla puppy, jumping up on the couch next to Michael during one of their many family events, he pushed her off as if she were an annoying throw pillow that was in his way. Pumpkin's feelings had been hurt, and Amber could not blame the dog. She was a highly sensitive creature, and Amber liked that about her and the Vizsla breed in general. Besides, she didn't like anyone that her dog didn't.

It wasn't that Michael disliked only dogs. He didn't like Wicca, their black cat, either. Well, in truth, he seemed a little scared of Wicca, always watching where she was. In general, Michael had no tolerance for animals.

Not for the first time, Amber was thankful that Maggie left town. When you knew someone would be angry with you and might try to kill you, it was the smart thing to do. Amber had learned that lesson the hard way, too.

The landline rang. The bell on their phone could wake the dead. If she answered, he'd know she was home. If she didn't, the babies would start crying, and he'd know she was home.

Taking a deep breath, she answered the phone before it upset the sleeping babies.

"Hello," she answered.

"Good morning, Amber. It is Dr. Michael Allan Drake. I'm standing outside your front door. I'd like to talk to you about Margaret, of course."

THE VOICE OF REASON

No.

"Oh, Michael, I wish you'd called before driving over. We all have a bug. I'm testing this afternoon to see if it is Covid. Jack is the only one who doesn't have it, but we all have got a fever, and the babies just went down for a morning nap, which was no easy task." She was mad at herself for sounding so pleasant.

She did not like saying her babies were sick when they weren't, but letting Michael into her home where her babies innocently slept was not an option.

"You sound fine," he countered as if she wasn't to be believed and she should take his word, the tool.

"It is amazing that I can have a 102-degree fever and a splitting headache that makes me want to vomit but sound normal," she said, putting a little steel into her voice. "You never know how Covid will affect the body. And I am a woman, after all. We know how to suffer in silence."

"You know, I thought you would be the reasonable one," he said, his voice taking on a hint of inflated tone she didn't like. "I want to talk about Margaret. I think she is sick, and not with some made-up Covid. I think she needs help. Lots of help. I need the family to back me on this so we can get Margaret the help she needs. I picked out a facility that is willing to take her for several days. With lots of intense therapy, they might be able to fix her."

Amber was silent for a good ten seconds. He didn't scare her. Few people did. Bullies just made her want to take action. Damn. Why didn't she have some of her tea? She thought she could make him anaphylaxis in three to five sips.

She laughed.

"Seriously?" she asked. "This is the approach you've decided on? Why don't we cut the shit? I'm a direct woman, Michael, so I'm going to say this once." She looked down at him through the curtain, seeing the rage contort his face. "The only person who needs help is you, you sick fuck. If you ever come here again, I'll introduce you to the friends my husband bought me when he taught me to shoot, something I picked up on very easily. My friends Smith and Wesson. My gun will cut through the bullshit you're spewing and, hopefully, your body. I will not hesitate to use force. I will not hesitate to take you down. In fact, I wrote your name on two bullets this morning. Does this scare you? It should. I'm not messing around. Had I known what was happening in your little house of horrors, I'd have already acted. You leave Maggie alone. You leave us alone. If you don't, I'm coming for you. By the way, you're trespassing."

She hung up then, having snapped several photos of him with her cell phone. She then sent the photos to her husband and alerted him to Michael's violation of his restraining order.

Her cell phone rang in her hand within ten seconds.

"I'm sending the police," Jack said when she answered.

"Don't bother. He is leaving, getting in his car."

"You didn't open the door?"

"No, this was all over the phone. I threatened him when he stood at the front door and tried me on the landline."

"The dumb bastard has underestimated you."

"Oh, I hope so. I spoke of Smith and Wesson like some ballsy housewife. Oh, and I called him a sick fuck just to see his reaction. He's found a facility ready for your sister."

"You've got to be kidding me..."

"You know, I should have called him a dumb fuck. I bet that would have really pissed him off. I don't think he likes anyone questioning his intelligence."

Jack let out a long breath and then said, "I'm trying not to be worried because I know you."

Lightening her tone, she asked, "Say, could you stop at our storage unit and bring home the red padlocked box? I need a few supplies. Don't worry, I'll keep them in the new safe my handsome husband installed for me in the garage. But truth be told, I'll just pick up most of what I need at the grocery store. It is never too soon to start planning."

There was a pause, and then Jack laughed as he said, "You sound happy. Do you have a solution in mind?"

"Yep. I fine-tuned it about two minutes ago."

"That poor bastard has no idea what is coming for him."

"Well, you know what they say...*some like it hot.*"

CHAPTER FOURTEEN
(*Maggie*)

Maggie couldn't stop the Realtor inside her from making judgments about each structure she passed as she made her way to the address of *Graystone, Hudson, and Fields Advertising*. The building looked a little old when Maggie looked at it from the street, not dilapidated. Once she set foot inside, she could tell it had been totally redone. It probably had historical status. She would be able to walk to a lot of nearby cafes for lunch, and she spied a Starbucks a couple of blocks down the street. This was going to be alright. Being comfortable in her surroundings and knowing her way around was a big thing. It made her feel comfortable and less vulnerable.

As she walked through the polished lobby of the building that housed *Graystone, Hudson, and Fields*, with its carved totem poles that were so popular in Canada, especially British Columbia, she wondered how the day would unfold. So far, so good. She made her way to the elevator and punched the button for the 6th floor. She stepped inside the elevator and as it climbed to the sixth floor, she gave herself a little internal pep talk.

No one knows you here. No one knows about Michael. You have a fresh start. A clean canvas. Even Jack's friend Henry Hudson doesn't know the real story. Jack just asked for a favor. They had been good friends, and Henry didn't hesitate. It was perfect timing…

Treat everyone well. Work hard. Don't stand out too much. Don't hide in the corner. Just be average.

The elevator door opened, and Maggie stepped out to be faced with a tall reception desk that sat before a wall display that read Graystone, Hudson, and Fields Advertising. It was all blonde wood and silver metal trim. She was in the right place, and she was ten minutes early, which to her was right on time. The office buzzed with high energy. She could hear conversations and laughter happening beyond the lobby.

She stepped up to the smiling receptionist, reminded herself to smile, and said, "Hi, I'm Maggie Daniels, and it is my first day. I'm supposed to report to Rick Fields?"

The woman nodded. She was expecting her, and that made Maggie happy. She was right where she was supposed to be.

"Hi Maggie, I'm Bethany. I'll call Rick. Let me know if you ever have any questions. Here is your parking pass," she said with a smile as she handed over a pass. "It can be challenging being new. I can at least tell you about the best restaurants for lunch or to get a drink after work, etc."

"Thank you, I really appreciate that," Maggie said with a heartfelt smile at the magenta-haired woman.

Before their conversation ended, a man in his fifties appeared in the lobby with a ready smile. He was cute once. Now, he looked comfortable and reliable, like someone's dad. He was probably two inches shorter than Maggie's five feet six-inch-tall frame, and he carried about forty extra pounds. He wore a wedding ring and a ready smile. He didn't appear to have short man's syndrome. Non-threatening, that was good. Maybe it was a Canadian thing.

"Maggie, welcome! We were so glad we could get you here on short notice."

Oh yeah, Henry needed bodies for a special project. Lucky her, she was one of the bodies.

Five minutes later, she was sitting in Rick's impressively large office with a view of Vancouver and hearing about a new project, kitchen utensils, *GreatChef*. She had never heard of them. Michael insisted on Le Creuset and Henckels. Anything else was substandard. When they received an expensive Cuisinart toaster as a wedding gift, it was returned. He replaced it with a Casa Bugatti for ten times the price. She didn't even want to think about what the professional espresso maker he'd insisted on had cost. All she knew was that it intimidated her, and Michael wouldn't allow her to touch it.

Rick talked with his hands in front of him as if he was trying to reason with her. "You see, we have a chance to be their ad agency of choice. They are a huge international company. We have a big pitch in two months. It is worth millions of dollars, so everyone is chipping in and freaking out. We like the idea that you are from the United States and bring a bit different perspective, and we want to use it to our advantage. That is why we haven't told you anything about it until now. We didn't want to influence you or have you thinking about the project. So what you will do for us is look at various products and come up with different advertising ideas. Obviously, you aren't the creative team on this. That is your strength. You'll let us know whatever comes to mind."

Maggie couldn't help but look at the bookcase behind his desk. And there it was, Michael's new book. Considering that it had only been published days ago, it had to be a recent addition. She could not blame him, but she could feel uneasy. If she told him that Michael was her husband, he'd certainly either worship her or hate her. She had to let it go. Lots of normal people didn't know what kind of monster Michael was. There would be people who were not going to believe that she left Michael. They would assume there was something wrong with her. She had to develop a thicker skin. She also had to make sure that no one knew she was divorcing him. For the moment, she had to pretend she'd never seen the book.

"Whatever you come up with. You are like a very specialized focus group of one. We want to keep you away from the creative team. You will be on your own island, thinking of ideas and then sharing them with us. They don't have to be great, they just have to be different, so there is no perfectionist pressure. What we are hoping is that you will offer a spin that we haven't thought of."

"Have you thought of just having focus groups?" she asked.

"We have, but people who participate, how can I say this? If some college kid approached you on the street and asked you to be in a focus group, would you do it?"

Maggie smiled a little. "Say I was too busy."

"Exactly. Because if you are out in downtown Vancouver, you are going somewhere. You don't have time to drop everything and be in a focus group, which might take several hours. Now, for this position, you are technically an intern. But I want you to know, I see a smart woman in her thirties who has money to spend on the right kitchen equipment for her family's kitchen. Those are the women we want to reach. This idea of Henry's, well, is just like Henry himself, out-of-the-box thinking. And in the end, we will ask you to seriously critique the idea we go with. So even if you don't come up with the idea we go with, you will have input. Win-win for both sides."

She was not thirty yet. Strike one, Rick.

And her new position, that wouldn't cause any hard feelings with the creative team. No, not at all. Maybe she was too sensitive. She would have to watch that.

Maggie felt stressed. She was okay with the thought of obeying others, but this idea that she might come up with her own slogans, etc., was way out of her comfort zone and beyond her creativity. Well, she wanted a good distraction. This would work. And how was she supposed to do the storyboards? She wasn't an artist, although she could probably design some slick stuff with online programs like Canva. All in all, it wouldn't be easy. And it sounded like she would just be staring at a bunch of equipment every day, for hours and hours...

THE VOICE OF REASON

Rick was a bit of a blowhard. He was leaning back in his chair now, looking at the ceiling, talking to hear himself talk. He was Michael's perfect target. Maggie was paying attention, but not closely. No, she just listened and waited. His conversation circled around and around. He said she would have her own little office where she could brainstorm and create. Hours and hours just by herself. Just what had Jack said to this Henry guy? Was it wrong that she wanted a bullpen full of people? Isolation wasn't the best for her, but it wasn't her call.

"So, come on, we need to shake some lamb tail if we are going to get to the weekly staff meeting. It is a great group of people. You'll love the team. I should mention that a few of them are jealous of you. They wish they could only have this kind of freedom and responsibility for *GreatChef* on their plates. No, everyone around here works their tails off, but this new campaign has really separated the wheat from the chaff, so to speak. And when they heard about you, they all felt a little threatened."

Great. She was about to spend some time with her firing squad.

Three minutes later, they were in a conference room, and Rick was pointing to an empty chair where he wanted her to sit. No one talked to her, but they all observed her. Finally, a severe young woman with sculpted eyebrows who sat next to her introduced herself as Amanda Payne, the Creative Director of *GreatChef*.

"I suppose we could look at each other as enemies, but I think this little competition of Henry's is all in good fun," Amanda said.

"Competition? I've only heard of *GreatChef* in the last ten minutes. I hope I can be of help to you," Maggie said. "I didn't think we were pitted against each other. I thought we were supposed to help each other out. I'm a collaborator."

"Just stay out of my way, and we will get along fine," Amanda said.

Before she could respond, a good-looking man appeared. She recognized Henry as he stepped to the head of the table, and said, "Okay, team. What frogs are we eating this morning?"

It was a term she often said when there was something unpleasant that she had to do and was dreading. Once the frog had been eaten, the rest of the day was usually smooth sailing.

Rick raised his hand, and the man called on him. "I have an introduction. Miss Maggie Daniels from the United States starts today."

The man at the end of the table said warmly, "Welcome, Maggie. Okay, everyone, let's go around the table and introduce ourselves. I'll start. I'm Henry, the managing partner of G, H, and F. Welcome to our little circus. Let's have you meet the menagerie."

CHAPTER FIFTEEN
(Dr. Michael Allan Drake)

Michael did something uncharacteristic as he entered the home he shared with Margaret. He slammed the door, which rattled the windows. He had been to Changing Waves Nursing Home & Memory Center, to visit Mother, and it had not gone well. This was the third time in a row she had not recognized him. So, it wasn't like he could talk to her and tell her about the upheaval in his life.

He contemplated a cocktail before noon to soothe the rage Margaret had brought out this unfamiliar frustration in him. He wouldn't need a mirror to show that his face was contorted in anger. The bitch had done this to him. When he first introduced her to Mother, Mother had been right. Margaret was too outspoken, too independent. Mother saw the problem before he had. He should have listened to her. She had the intuition of the smartest man. The integrity and class Margaret would never have.

Women.

Every stupid woman on the planet aside from his mother was a hot mess. And wasn't he the lucky one? They seemed to want to share their weaknesses with him. They were drawn to him like a moth to the flame, as if he was some sort of safe space or crash test dummy.

Time to catalogue.

First, it had been his wife who needed more help than he could offer. But rest assured, he was making plans for her return. He would make sure she was modified to the docile being she truly was before bringing her back into his home. Thankfully, his reputation would ensure that he would be able to direct medical personnel to the right course for her intensive treatment. They would not dare to second guess his diagnosis. She obviously had a break from reality, so he was willing to try any treatment he could to bring her back. Who knew what she was saying to people? Well, whatever it was, the lies weren't helping him. He needed to stop her. He heard that mild shock therapy was becoming trendy again. He was a big fan of mind altering drugs. He was all for it. Behavior modification success took many forms. He was willing to have Margaret try it all. So, with the right care, all the lies would be stopped.

Second, his sister-in-law, Amber Daniels. He had to think about her a little more after the way she had treated him that morning. She must have recently taken an assertive female empowerment class or some bullshit like that. He hadn't underestimated her, but it was like she finally found her voice. It is too little too late if you ask him. They had never really communicated, aside from mindless banter at social functions. Everyone always complimented her on some famous chocolate cake she made, so at least she knew how to be domestic. He didn't know what Jack saw in her. She seemed to really like her red lipstick. Hell, Michael wouldn't do her. He didn't like those semi-hippy chicks, no matter how much lipstick they slapped on to show they had a retail side. Sleep with them and forever wear their patchouli stink.

Besides, he just didn't like the bitch. He still thought of that one summer party, potluck which had him salivating uncomfortably like Pavlov's dog. Stupid Amber made jalapeño poppers, which he was sure she had told him were those new mild green bell peppers. They weren't. He almost went into anaphylactic shock. And she didn't seem too upset when he almost stopped breathing. Thank goodness he had his EpiPen with him. Didn't the bitch know that he was highly allergic to capsicum? She could have killed him. He'd never quite trusted her after that, but he thought she was just stupid. Now, he wondered if she was just cunning instead.

This morning, Amber found her voice, and now she couldn't shut up. How disgraceful! How common! Well, he doubted she'd talk that way in front of her husband, but really, how dare she speak to him in the way that she had? It was mind-blowing, but he considered the possibility. Jack had probably encouraged her independence because he was weak and didn't know how to keep his woman in line. This was the path of least resistance. No doubt Amber wore the pants in that family. He probably obeyed her like a dog to his master. Maybe they were into that S&M stuff. Maybe she made him wear a dog collar. How the hell would he know? If only he had a better relationship with Jack, he could help him with his wife. Offer suggestions. Make Jack's life better. But not now.

No, he had his own wife to consider. Amber would have to wait for another time.

He'd already been to Margaret's parents, who refused to answer their door as well. So he parked down the street, undercover, and waited. Eventually, a limo arrived, and the driver opened the trunk. No one never saw him, but he saw them leave with a lot of luggage. Her parents even paused by the front door to set the alarm, and then they left. It occurred to him at that moment that they had never shared the alarm code with him.

He wondered if they were joining Margaret somewhere or just taking their annual trip to Palm Springs was it? Or was it Mexico? He couldn't remember. He wished he'd paid more attention to their patterns. It would have helped if they hadn't made it sound so boring. My god, what was it with old people and the over-explaining? Jeez.

Margaret, or more likely Jack, must have found the trackers he'd used on her phone. Within a day of her escape, she was no longer emitting a signal. Lucky for Michael, the Apple tag he'd hidden in her car was still sending a signal. That's how he knew she was staying with Amber and Jack in the beginning. Then, about a week later, the signal showed that the car was at a dealership in town. A BMW dealership. The little bitch traded the perfectly good Honda in for something else. If it was a BMW, there would be punishment. They had conversations several times. She would not be getting a BMW. He forbade it. His word should be enough for her. He didn't care that her success in her little real estate business would pay for it! It was yet another thing for her to lord over his head!

She needed the attention-inducing German Sleigh like she needed a hole in the head. If she bought that car after he forbid it…

Air in, air out…he needed to relax.

The AirTag reappeared on his tracking, but it made no sense. It was aligning with a Mini Cooper. Mini Coopers were beneath his wife. She was a brand whore, but he couldn't discount this information. After he'd surveilled the Mini for an hour, it didn't take long for him to figure out that she or Jack placed it in one of the dealerships rentals. Well, little Margaret thought she had outsmarted him. He could do her one better.

So, he had done the smart thing about the car. He hadn't gotten mad. He'd gotten smarter. He'd tried to find a weak link at the dealership. It should have worked. But no amount of bribery would give him access to records that would show what she purchased. He couldn't believe that they denied him!

So much for this being a capitalist society. He was willing to pay cash for information. But no one would supply it. To add insult to injury, some steroidal security man escorted him off the property and threatened that they would call the police if Michael continued to harass the employees. Since when was a husband denied information about his wife?

Even her real estate company had gone all black ops on him.

THE VOICE OF REASON

They were suddenly tight-lipped. All they would tell him was that he could leave a message for her but that her license was on referral-only status, whatever the hell that meant. Even his contact inside her office didn't know anything. Had she gotten in trouble? He liked that idea but didn't like how that kind of reputation could hurt his business.

The hairdresser, his mother's as well, hadn't seen her in five weeks. Then he found out she canceled her appointment with Barbara for her six-week trim without an explanation. It was not only rude, but it also embarrassed and disrespected his mother. Mother would be upset if the dementia hadn't taken over. The disrespect, however, was another thing he needed to catalog. How she would make up for all the disobedience to him was one thing, but he wondered what on earth Margaret could do to make it up to Mother? His mother might not understand, but it was the thought that counted. Margaret better be prepared to pay homage to his mother. Why had she upended their lives so completely, so thoroughly?

My god, what kind of sick game was Margaret playing?

Chapter Sixteen
(Maggie)

Maybe Maggie was being oversensitive, but she could feel the eyes of her coworkers land on her and check her out as she sat in the impressive conference room with large windows that looked out to Stanley Harbour. Well, she knew she was dressed in a great suit and had the right look. But she was picking up on the tension. They probably resented her for her very presence because if the looks she was getting were any indication, they did not share Henry Hudson's thinking out-of-the-box idea about her for *GreatChef*. Their looks affected her. If she could, she would turn and run. Instead, she just tried to smile and look demure. It wasn't hard. There was a part of her that felt like a beaten animal. Memories of Michael's words were never far from her mind, making her feel downtrodden.

When I married you, I thought you were smart...

You've really turned out to be a total disappointment...

It is a good thing you know how to schlep houses because no one would hire you...

You should look in the mirror, but I bet you can't stand to look at yourself...

She did not want to make direct eye contact for fear they would see her inadequacy. Henry Hudson's blazing blue eyes fell on her once or twice. He was a good-looking man, tall, with a strong build. When she met him with her brother years ago, she thought he was handsome but still young. His potential hadn't been fully realized. Well, he had grown into his looks, morphing into a man that was very easy on the eyes. He had a kind, sincere smile, unlike Michael's. What must he think of her?

She could almost hear him.

How could she be powerhouse Jack's sister? She looks about as smart as the carpet... Maybe I've made a huge mistake...

It had been a while since she'd felt this uncomfortable in a public setting.

When the meeting broke up after an hour, Rick whisked her away to show her to her office. She had a sense that Henry Hudson wanted to talk to her, but he was surrounded by other people, and she was able to slip away. She wasn't sure she wanted to hear what Henry might say. This could be the shortest internship in history.

"Wow," she said when she first saw her office. It was a light and airy space with a view of Vancouver. Maybe it wasn't as nice as Rick's view, but it wasn't like she knew Vancouver well enough to know if it was good or bad. She knew she liked it and that it was kind of fabulous. She knew she didn't deserve it, but until they figured it out, which was only a matter of time, she would enjoy it. She had the same windows that the conference room featured, but her space was about one-third the size. But it was the nicest office she'd ever had.

She was considered one of the heavy hitters at her real estate company. They encouraged her to upgrade her office as she became more successful, but what that really meant was that she had to pay more money in monthly expenses to enjoy a good office. Michael decided it wasn't worth it, so she had always shared an office with another real estate "team." Still, her numbers increased each year.

Rick picked up the phone on her desk. He dialed a number then said, "Hey Issac, I'm in Maggie's new office. Yeah, bring in the stuff. Okay, thank you."

"We are going to fill your office with *GreatChef* products," he continued to Maggie. "Full immersion. So, feel free to research the competition online and in person. Take an afternoon. Take a day. Anyhow, take a look at a few stores and get a feel for their designs, point-of purchase displays, and the quality of the products. Take them home and play with them. Heck, if you can attend cooking demos, do it. You get the idea."

"Sure...Okay, is there a product you want me to focus on?"

"We have six core products we will want you to think about. We will start with their largest seller—"

A knock on the door drew their attention.

"Issac, just in time. Bring the stuff in and put it anywhere you can."

Issac said something that sounded like a greeting, but Maggie barely heard it. She sat in her chair and fought the urge to pull her legs up, wrap her arms around them, and curl into a ball. Issac was followed by a half a dozen associates carrying butcher blocks with knives.

Knives.

Knives were everywhere. In butcher blocks, laid out before her as if they were ready to cut something or someone. They caught the sunlight and glinted. So many knives. Such potential violence.

"Get familiar with the products, look at the ads online, check out their competition...you get it. That's why we got you some other brands as well for you to check out, not just *GreatChef*. Start making notes and build a file. I've got a meeting, then I'll check on you."

Why did it have to be knives?

Rick said, "Okay, can I leave you for a bit?"

"Um...sure," Maggie managed. "Thank you, Rick. Thank you, Issac."

When Rick left her alone, her body began to shake. Seriously, why did it have to be knives?

Sitting at her desk, she pushed the chair back and slowly pulled up her skirt to expose her thigh. The scar was still there.

Three inches long and jagged despite the sharpness of the blade that caused it. It felt a little bumpy as her finger gently rubbed the scar tissue and counted the thirteen bumps that equated to thirteen stitches. She hadn't told anyone about it. It was her and Michael's little secret.

She should have left then. But she stayed. It was the only time Michael apologized, and like an idiot, she'd believed him.

CHAPTER SEVENTEEN
(Maggie)

Maggie reverently touched the cool handle of the Henckel butcher knife in the block as if it might bite her. The way she was able to pull it smoothly and soundlessly out of the block was a testament to its fine design. She reminded herself; it was just a thing. It wasn't attached to an arm and body that wanted to hurt her. She was the one holding the blade, controlling it.

But she knew what it could do. She knew what she could do with it. It could kill someone. In a matter of seconds, it could render a wound so massive, so brutal, that someone could bleed out and die in a matter of moments before help could arrive. It could wound so severely that there could be no saving.

How did that feel? Did it feel like cutting a steak to cut the body with a knife? She wondered what Michael felt when he cut her leg. It had been quick, so quick. At first, there was no pain, but then there was lots of pain. And fear. If Michael hadn't stopped, if he slashed her again...if he'd hit her femoral artery...

Okay, okay...That was then, and this was now. For all she knew, these knives had never been used for anything other than display. Heck, the one in her hand probably hadn't even cut an orange or lemon for a cocktail. You did need a knife to do that.

Other items had the potential to injure and kill, but they looked happy or had an obvious purpose for something else, something benevolent. A bookend. A heavy object. A vase. A fireplace poker. A bottle of wine...The list went on and on. What really mattered was intent. What was the intent behind holding an object? If it was a vase, was it to arrange flowers? Or was it to break over someone's head?

People got hit by buses, but that didn't make the buses bad. It made the idiot who stepped in front of the bus guilty of not showing good judgment. Maybe the bus driver couldn't see the person, and the person had a clear pedestrian signal to cross in front of the bus. Who was at fault then?

"Hey Mag, see anything you like?"

The voice was male, strong, and direct. It came from the general direction of the doorway.

She couldn't have jumped higher if he'd tossed her in the air. Dropping the knife to the desktop where it made a clanking sound and then spun, stopping when it encountered her new coffee mug that bore the company's logo.

Putting a hand to her heart, she released air from her lungs and said, "You scared me."

"I'm sorry, I should have knocked. I was disappointed I couldn't talk to you this morning. So, I wanted to see if you were free for lunch," he said, softening his tone as he held up his hands as if to say, I'm a good guy. Maybe he was worried she would pick up the knife and use it on him. It was a valid fear.

He was a friend of her brother's. She could trust him. He was, from all she heard and for all intents and purposes, a good guy. She had met him before, okay, ten years earlier, but still, she knew him. People were probably jumping at the chance to spend time with him, but she wasn't. She wanted to be left alone and do her job well. But she had to fake it and be nice to this man. He was her key to getting out of town. Now, he was her boss, and she was on his radar.

Fake it and smile.

Glancing at her new Coach watch, a little gift to rid herself of the fake Cartier Michael had given her, she noticed it was a few minutes before noon. To her surprise, the morning had flown by.

"I don't have any lunch plans. That would be very nice of you if you don't mind entertaining the new employee," she said, adding some enthusiasm to her voice.

"I'm looking forward to it," he said. "I'd like to catch up and hear what Jack is up to now that he is a father. And I'll show you one of my favorite local haunts that has fantastic food."

"That sounds great. I'd like to try some of the local places." She wanted to get away from the knives, these people, this office, the whole bit. She needed a moment of quiet and calm to reset. That meeting and then the knives. It was a lot. Probably not a lot for an average intern, but she wasn't an average intern.

"Great. If you're ready, we can go now," he said as she grabbed her purse from one of the desk drawers. It was one of the only things from her past life that she kept, a Burberry satchel bag. After the Cartier debacle, she had it checked out and was delighted to discover it was real. She still couldn't believe Michael had given it to her for Christmas a couple of years earlier. It had to be the nicest gift he'd ever given her.

They rode silently in the elevator to the lobby and then left the building. As the awkward silence encircled them, she wondered if she should be asking him questions because he seemed more than comfortable with the silence. Really, she should show interest in him, the company, the upcoming pitch for *GreatChef*. What was wrong with her? Talk, damn it, talk!

She opened her mouth to say something as they paused for the light to change when he chuckled and said, "I remember how Jack used to talk about you when we were roommates in our frat house at Northwestern."

She looked up at him and put her hand up to block the sun so she could see him. He had a nice profile and looked good in his tailored navy suit with his coordinating tie. She realized he was very tall as she said, "Really? He used to terrorize me as a little sister. It is amazing I'm still alive."

"He said he could talk you into about anything," Henry said with a laugh.

Maybe that is why Michael got such a good hold of her. She was easy to persuade. That behavior had to end. This was a good reminder that it had to end today.

"When I was small, like five, he made paper wings out of construction paper which he attached to me and thought it would be fine for me to jump out of the second-story window to test them. To prove I could fly."

"Did you do it?" Henry asked, stopping her in the middle of the sidewalk.

"I would have because I worshiped him and had no doubts about my ability to survive. But, no, my mother stopped it right as Jack was helping me to step on the windowsill. She screamed; I fell backward, and we both ended up on the floor. It was a whole thing. I think she almost killed him that day. I think he was ten. From then on, she referred to him as the demon child she spawned from the bowels of Hell."

Henry shook his head and laughed.

She could see how Henry and Jack were friends. She felt comfortable with him even though he was her boss. She wondered how much Jack had told him. Although Jack said he hadn't told him anything, she wasn't sure if she quite believed it.

They ended up at a pub called *The Spread Eagle*. In a dark booth toward the back, her new boss shocked her by ordering a pint of Guinness when a waiter arrived to check on them. Seeing her expression, he smiled and said, "It is okay. It is your first day, so have a beer with your new boss. It will make the afternoon fly by."

But then he took in her expression.

"I'm sorry. I should ask. Do you drink alcohol?" he asked.

She nodded.

"Do you like Guinness?"

"I do," she said.

He turned to the waiter, "Make it two Guinness's, please."

Then they gave their orders for halibut fish and chips, and the waiter walked away.

Maggie was at a loss. She shook her head and said, "I...I...um, I've never drank on my lunch hour. I just want you to know that."

"Point taken. I do drink on my lunch hour sometimes, obviously," he said with a half-smile.

She hoped he wasn't an alcoholic like Michael. She wouldn't wish that addiction on anyone.

"I wanted to say that I thought the team was a little cold to you this morning. And I fear I set them up to see you as a rival, not a resource," he confessed. "It is my mistake, and I need to fix it."

"Well—" She did not want to stand out for any reason.

"So, I must apologize. I'm going to have a word and get them to understand that you are there to give them a little different perspective. I know you haven't worked in advertising despite your degree. That is why you are so valuable to me. You've been out in the world. Most of my employees resemble puppies in the whelping pen. They are right out of school and full of self-assured Gen Z sensitivity, fluid pronouns, and sexuality. I try to be respectful, but it is like trying to hit a moving target. I'm just too old to be hip."

"Do they say hip anymore?" she asked with a smile.

"See? I don't know," he said, lifting his hands in surrender.

"First, you are maybe thirty-two, so relax."

"I feel so much older," he said, shaking his head.

"I can relate. You know, they might come to respect me when they see that I'm no threat by the work I do," she said. She did not want the staff to know she was, in any way, special to the boss. If he talked to them, more attention would be paid to her.

"Don't worry, they will start treating you better immediately.

And they don't know about our Jack connection. I was vague and said I found you."

"Okay."

"Okay," he said with a smile as he looked at her closely. He wanted something from her. She could see it in his expression.

Stepping out on a limb, she said, "I bet you want to know why I wanted to run to Canada for a few months."

"I do, but I don't know if I should ask. I mean, the timing was really good, so Jack's call helped me when I needed it. I'm extremely happy to have you. But I know you are a successful Realtor in Minneapolis. I visited your website." A website that always featured her maiden name because Michael didn't want people to show her any favoritism by cashing in on his last name. Now, looking back at it, it struck her as all kind of messed up.

Before she could respond, the waiter placed Maggie's beer before her. She drank deeply, needing the liquid courage. It was cold and creamy, almost chocolatey, with a slightly bitter note at the end. She had not been honest in her past, and life hadn't rewarded her for being a martyr. If she had died, no one would have known what she had been through. The man across from her was watching her intently. He had kind eyes, and a good sense of humor. She doubted he would ever be abusive, but she certainly had learned her lesson. What if she told him, and he sided with Michael? She would make this vague. She wondered if he had any interesting perspectives about marriage.

She met his intense blue eyes and said, "I'm going to be honest with you. I'm going through a very contentious divorce, and my soon-to-be ex-husband is a very angry person. He liked to punish me. I left because I was pretty sure he was going to kill me. That isn't quite right. He told me he was thinking about it. I believed him."

He pulled back a little. His eyes gave away his shock. "Holy shit. I'm…I'm so sorry, Maggie. Did Jack know?"

"Thank you, I got out. I came clean with Jack, which wasn't easy. Now, I have a different car. A different phone. I fled with only the bags I could carry. I escaped, and I didn't look back. That was about two weeks ago."

"Only two weeks?" he asked incredulously, his eyes growing wide.

"It feels like two years. I'm so relieved and happy to be gone. He isn't as he appears, which is why I needed to get away from him and someplace he couldn't find me because he is very believable, and I don't think everyone will believe me when it all comes out."

She didn't tell him Michael's name. His podcasts were very popular in Canada as well as the United States. Heck, if it was an English-speaking country, he did well. For all she knew, Henry Hudson could be one of his fans. He could be a part of *The T Society*. She had to be so careful. She could not risk that the man before her would pop onto social media and mention her location.

"That is why you came to Canada," he said, his easy smile no longer present, worry lines appearing between his eyes.

"Yes. I can't get my life back if someone decides to kill me, but maybe time and distance will help."

"I'm glad you got out in time," he said, his hand starting to move across the table. He thought better of it and pulled back which was good. If he touched her, she would have flinched. He must be one of those tactile people. Maggie used to be like that, but she wasn't anymore.

"Well," she said. "I have a couple of scars from times when I didn't move fast enough—" She hesitated, felt embarrassed. "Look, I'm sorry. I shouldn't tell you all the gruesome details."

"I don't mind. I'll help you get through this however I can. Not all men are like your ex. That is what you need to know. I wish Jack and I had been in better touch throughout the years. Maybe I could have helped more. I think he'd told me you got married, but I don't remember any of the details. He said you were happy."

"I was happy in the beginning, but that didn't last long. It has been horrible, but I'm very thankful. I lost a lot, but I could have lost it all."

"I'm so sorry. Your real estate career? Tell me about that. Have you thought about what you will do?"

"I might pick up the real estate again, but I was getting burned out. Maybe it was the stress of my bad marriage combined with the real estate. And I can't trust him not to hurt me when I'm hosting an open house for the public. Anyone can walk in, and they do. I've had people creep me out or even steal things at opens. This job is a good change for me. And I will do everything to make you proud that you took a chance on me."

"I know you are going to do well. I have that sense about people. But tell me, is there anything I can do?"

"Thank you, but I'm fine. I'm very excited to be here. I need to pour myself into something as Jack is taking care of the divorce back in Minneapolis. So, I'm going to work hard for you on *GreatChef* and give it my all."

"I'm looking forward to hearing your ideas. And I'm serious. I'm here for you if you ever need me."

"I just don't want him to know I'm here...my ex-husband. So, I want to keep a low profile and put my nose to the grindstone. Thank you. If he should somehow find me and show up, I'll probably want to hide behind you because you're tall." She added the last part with a tongue-in-cheek smile, which he understood and smiled back.

Henry held up his glass and said, "Deal. Do you think our building security should be made aware?"

"I think they should know to alert me if anyone ever asks for me. No one should, and that would be the first step."

"What name would he use?"

"Probably my married name, and I'm not using that, so I think that's safe."

"Good idea."

She didn't elaborate. Michael's photo was instantly recognizable. He had reached celebrity status. No one would believe it if she showed them Michael's photo. He was a famous marriage counselor whom everyone adored. There was no way that he could have a bad marriage. Heck, Henry might not even believe it.

They clinked their glasses together, and Maggie hoped with all her heart she would never have to hide behind this kind man. He had no idea who he would be dealing with when it came to *The Voice of Reason*.

CHAPTER EIGHTEEN
(Jack)

When Jack arrived home the evening after Michael had shown up at their front door, he found Amber in their family room with a child in each arm, Pumpkin, and Wicca snuggling next to her like bookends.

"Daddy's home," she called out as the babies looked at Jack and smiled.

"That Daddy guy is the luckiest man in the world," he said as he bent, greeted them with sweet baby talk and kissed each baby on the forehead, and then kissed Amber with a kiss that lingered and used to be a prelude to sex, probably still was, but there were a few other factors to consider.

The dog chuffed, and Jack gave her a little attention, as well as the cat.

"Well, hello," Amber said.

"Hello, family," he said, shucking out of his suit coat and pulling at his tie as he smiled at them. Then he looked at Amber and asked, "And how was your day?"

Moving Wicca out of the way, he joined her and the children on the couch. Putting an arm around her, he cradled his little family to him as Pumpkin stretched to lick the hand that touched Amber's shoulder.

"Well, the bad man never made a reappearance, but a few reporters did invade the front yard. It must be a slow news day," she said in a tone that the babies wouldn't notice was anything but sweet. "I almost turned on the sprinklers. I wanted to be memorable."

"I'm glad he didn't come back, but I've been fielding a few reporter's calls and emails, too," he said, using the same tone. "They are on the scent, but that is okay by me. They need to stay interested."

"You have a point. It is going to get so much worse before it gets better. At least, I hope a lot of people find out about it," she said with a smile.

"It is definitely starting," Jack said.

"Locally, I think we need to increase our preparedness and maybe start tracking him a bit better to protect Maggie and ourselves from any surprises. Just in general, it would be nice to be able to track his whereabouts."

"I'm a step ahead of you, darling," he said, taking Clay onto his lap, who smiled up at his father. "I hired a private investigator today to follow him and put a tracker on his car. He hasn't done it yet, but he will. We just need to wait for him to take the car out of his garage and park it in a public lot."

"I like the way you are thinking," she said as her smile curved, and she added, "I like this protective side of you."

"Always. And we have hired a less-than-scrupulous PR company to control information that will somehow be shared to the press anonymously."

"What an interesting coincidence. But then we tend to think alike. I had a little dialogue with Neil today. He said to say 'hey' to you. So hey," she said with a wink.

Neil was her personal computer hacker who now lived on the East Coast. Amber had gotten close to him when she was still Dr. Kelan Smith. He was so close to her now that she referred to him as her honorary nephew. Jack was also fond of Neil and enjoyed the times they would bump into him while on vacation in some faraway land where they didn't know anyone.

THE VOICE OF REASON

He also had connections with various friends who were able to produce very good passports and driver's licenses.

"'Hey' back to Neil. That was a wonderful idea, to talk to him. What did he suggest?"

"You know it is so funny…he has access to a bunch of reporter's emails at large online and print media. He's going to reach out under a different name, of course. He loves this kind of thing. And he is not a fan of Dr. Michael Allan Drake."

"I knew I liked him, the little pot stirrer," Jack said with a smile.

"Yeah, a bit. I wonder who he learned that from?"

They both laughed.

"By the way, that little box you asked for is in the garage on a high shelf. I figured you could move it to the safe at your leisure."

"Good. Thank you. I need to think on it a bit, but I have an idea already forming as to how I want to use all the little goodies it has inside of it."

"I can't wait," Jack said.

"It isn't my usual kind of thing."

"Variety is the spice of life."

"Well, in this case, the spice definitely plays a role in life."

CHAPTER NINETEEN
(Dr. Michael Allan Drake)

The last few weeks had been unspeakable. Michael blew off several phone calls—his agent, his editor, the producer of his special blogs, and the book tour director. It might be undignified to say, but they could all suck it for all he cared. The last phone call he had with his publisher on Friday had not gone well. The officious little bitch threatened to cancel his contract after this first book. She was completely overwrought, but truthfully, Margaret was to blame. His wayward wife was the iceberg to his Titanic. He didn't have a chance once she ran her mouth and told all those lies about him.

Where in the hell was she? He was starting to sound like some common laborer. He was so angry at her that she was bringing out his baser male.

He sat at his desk and stared into the empty space of his office. It was getting dusty. Margaret wasn't there to dust it. The house felt empty. He didn't like his own cooking, and he was tired of DoorDash, but in a pinch, it worked. He needed to hire a housekeeper or two. It was highly unlikely one person could be relied on to get his house to the level of perfection he demanded. Well, score one for Margaret. She kept the house to about 80% of the way he wanted it. She could always do better, but at least she had done that almost satisfactorily.

He shook his head. On the other hand... What good was a wife? Maybe he should hire a cook and two maids and accept that Margaret might not be up to the task, which she realized and then left. Maybe she was doing him a favor. And, not having her around, well, that lead to a lot of freedom he could not explore with her in residence.

No, he had a standard to uphold. She could be everything he needed if only she was trained properly. If only she had the right initiative. Maybe it was just a lack of motivation. As the last six years passed, she had gotten lazy with him. He felt that.

He'd been spending too much time with the damn book. It diluted his concentration. Her education had slacked off. He felt some responsibility. He let her get lazy. Well, he'd just have to double down when she came back. Okay, he'd send her to the facility, and once they got a handle on her mental issues, then she'd be a clean slate. He'd be able to *reprogram* her, for lack of a better word.

Even horses needed to be broken. Dogs and children require boundaries and structure. Of course! She just needed to have her boundaries restructured.

He let out a large sigh. Where was Margaret? How could she have just left? Hadn't he thought of this? Hadn't he planned for this contingency? He failed and had only himself to blame. She was like some kind of small animal, a mouse. You didn't let a mouse run free. You let it live in a controlled environment. Well, Margaret had broken out of her cage.

Clearly his plan for a tracker on her phone and the Apple AirTag in her car didn't work. Overlapping safety measures had failed! A few years earlier, he'd even put a Tile in her purse, hidden so well, it was probably still there. Then he changed from Android to iPhone, and the AirTag was more compatible—

He sat up straighter in his chair.

Wait.

Wait a fucking minute...

She had a new phone. She had a new car. What happened to the old Tile he had painstakingly hidden in the lining of her damn designer handbag that she couldn't stop talking about?

He'd given her the designer handbag for Christmas a few years ago. It was expensive, and she didn't deserve it, but he had an ulterior motive. And the day before he gave it to her, he opened the side pocket and carefully broke an inch of a seam in the lining inserted the Tile and then repaired it so that no one could tell the difference.

But then he'd upgraded them both to iPhone and gotten a handful of AirTags. He put one in her purse that she knew about. But she never knew about the Tile. He turned to the computer on his desk and started doing some research.

To him, the Tile was inferior. It was a smaller network, so exact locations could be a problem, but Tile batteries could live up to three years. The Tile hidden in the lining of her bag was close to the end of its battery life, but it wasn't like he used it much lately.

He needed to get an Android phone.

"Jackals," Michael uttered as he pulled back the curtain from his living room window and saw all the reporters who gathered with their television vans and cameras. They barely parted when he turned into the garage after his little errand to Best Buy.

The only bright spot in this whole thing was to finally understand and allow himself to understand how popular he was to the general masses. What did his mother always say? "There is no such thing as bad publicity."

Yet again, Mother was right. He had to make sure they weren't on her doorstep, bothering her. Not that she even would know they were there, but his poor mother didn't need this grief and bother. He'd called Changing Waves, the memory care, but he didn't trust the twat who answered to actually take him seriously.

He told Mother about Margret's departure even though he wasn't sure if she understood him. She might be suffering from a terrible disease, but on some level, he was sure she knew. For the pain his words caused, he was even angrier at Margaret. His mother didn't deserve this.

As he fiddled with his new purchase on the now fingerprint-smeared glass top of his desk, his memories swirled around him.

After he shared his disappointment with Margaret last week with his mother, he remembered all too clearly what Mother told him when he announced he was marrying Margaret. Mother never liked Margaret, not from the first tense meeting. She didn't hold back. Margaret had never been the right life mate for him. It was something he now believed too. However, he still held hope that if he could get her back, he could train her to be the perfect mate for him. It was simply a matter of discipline.

He applauded himself for being such an optimist. Many people would simply walk away. He didn't like to turn his back on a challenge.

He heard the tapping noise and shook his head.

The reporters started knocking on the stained-glass front door. His phone was ringing constantly, and he had at least thirty emails. *Jackals.*

Was Margaret talking? He wouldn't put it past her to air their dirty laundry to the masses. Their marriage was their business, and for her to involve others made him very angry. How many times had he told her that? If only she would listen to him, *The Voice of Reason*, they could be happy together again. Instead, she liked to spread her lies like a virus among sticky-handed first graders.

He shut his eyes. He needed to be calm. He was leaving soon on a grueling book tour. He should be excited. It was his first, but he was not excited. Why? Well, Margaret ruined it for him, of course. *Breathe in, breathe out.*

He hit his fist on his desk, rattling everything on top of it.

Oh shit! He hoped he hadn't damaged the Android phone open in front of him.

Something happened. When trying to locate the Tile in Margaret's handbag earlier in the day, the system hadn't worked. But now, when he accidentally hit the command to play a specific chime to find the object as if it were lost. It was not only playing a chime in her purse, but it was also showing him where she was.

When he looked at the screen on the phone, he got the shocker of his life. Margaret was in Vancouver, BC. The Tile was moving along Robson Street. Then the Tile disappeared.

CHAPTER TWENTY
(Maggie)

Maggie discussed her thoughts on the knives with the team at their normal Monday morning meeting, only her third team meeting, signaling her second-week anniversary at *Graystone, Hudson, and Fields*.

"In conclusion, of all the knives I looked at, the *GreatChef* was the lowest quality in regard to hand feel and advanced ability when compared to their competition. Basically, they weren't great cutters. I think they bruised some tomatoes when they should have just sliced them. However, the knives were stylish and looked good in their block on the kitchen counter. They are available in seven fun shades, from magenta pink to poison green. I think you should target the young cook right out of school who can't afford much but really wants to have all the bells and whistles. However, if they are serious cooks, they will get frustrated."

"So what you are saying is that you wouldn't buy them?" Henry asked from where he stood, leaning against a credenza in the back of the room.

"No, but my reasons have nothing to do with price and everything to do with ability. Maybe if I had a second house, like a beach house, or was house poor with my first house, or they were my novelty knives, I might buy them, but not for my primary home. Not if I really liked to cook."

"You don't like them," Henry said.

"I do, and I don't. Here's the thing. I can buy a really good knife for $150. But when it comes to *GreatChef*, I can buy three, almost four sets at $39.99 a set, and end up with thirty knives vs. one. As a cook, I know which one I'm leaning toward. But the poor college student who eats a lot of ramen and takeout likes the look of the butcher block because it will impress his girlfriend. And if it isn't used much, it might do okay the one or two times a year he pulls it out and uses it."

"I hear what you are saying. They make nice accessories, but they aren't for the serious chef," Henry summarized.

"Yes."

"Okay, team, you heard what she said. I like the direction of someone who is buying knives for the first time and goes for quantity over quality—"

"Henry, if I may," said the woman who told Maggie to stay out of her way yet a week earlier.

"Yes, Amanda?" he asked.

"With all due respect, I'm sure Maggie is very good at being a homemaker. I just don't know if she understands the product and what we are trying to do here."

Henry, who was now sitting at the end of the conference table, rocked in his chair once, twice, and three times when he stopped and sat up abruptly.

"Maggie," he said. "What did you have for dinner last night?"

Maggie dropped the pencil she was holding. "Um…beef stroganoff."

"Amanda, what did you have last night?"

Giving a coquettish glare in Maggie's direction, she said, "I had a wrap from The Mediterranean Village cart outside my condo."

"Maggie, where did you get your beef stroganoff?"

"I made it," she answered quietly.

"So you cut up the mushrooms, onions, and beef?" he asked.

"Yes," she answered, not understanding.

"Show of hands, how many of you made your own dinner last night?"

Out of fifteen, three raised their hands.

"Congratulations, you will meet with Maggie this afternoon and brainstorm ideas."

"Wait—" Amanda protested.

"No, Amanda, I want this to play out," Henry said, ending the conversation.

Later, as Maggie walked during her lunch hour to clear her head after that surprising morning meeting, she occasionally glanced at the windows on Robson Street as she made her way to one of her new favorite delis. One thing was for sure, she'd made an enemy of Amanda, not like she really cared. She had much bigger fish to fry. At the very thought of Michael, she gave an involuntary shiver. Even though he was in another country, she was still hyper-aware of her surroundings.

In their phone call last night, Jack said Michael was refusing to agree to sign divorce papers. It wasn't unexpected, but it would mean that everything would take longer. Thankfully, Jack was already proceeding.

Maggie heard a soft ringing. Was that her cell? It sounded off to her. Considering she had new international service, anything was possible.

The noise was coming from her purse. Sitting on a nearby bench, she searched through her bag, finding nothing. She was perplexed but she could still hear the sound. Then she realized it was coming from a hidden place. She felt a lump in the lining of her handbag. What the heck was going on? Since Michael gave it to her, she didn't hesitate to rip at a seam in the lining. She had always been a bit suspicious of the gift. The lining gave easily, as if it were hand stitched.

A moment later, she was looking at the locator Tile that was flashing and ringing in her hand. She didn't think. Surprise turned to panic. She regarded the Tile as a bug that crawled out of some dark corner. And in some regards, she wasn't too far off.

She dropped the Tile to the sidewalk and then smashed it with her shoe. It had taken some effort, but she was fueled with adrenaline, the flight-or-fight awakening every cell of her body and kicking in hard. When the ringing stopped, and the small device looked mangled and damaged, she knew she was successful. She only hoped it hadn't signaled back to Michael where she was, but in her gut, she had a feeling it had. Something made it ring.

She looked around uncomfortably, noticing everything in her surroundings. Was he looking at her right now? She couldn't detect anything, which meant nothing.

With shaking hands, she took a photo of it with her phone and then tossed the mangled parts into the nearest garbage can.

CHAPTER TWENTY-ONE

(Amber)

Amber never questioned ideas when they came to her. Maybe it was some form of random divine intervention that kept her safe. She didn't want to mess with that. She just let any ideas that sparked in her brain grow into a plan, and then she executed them. She was a painter on a blank velvet canvas of morbidity; instead of paint, her medium was poison.

Today, she was in her monofilament gown, booties, goggles, and surgical gloves, out in her little greenhouse. She also wore a painter's breathing apparatus to make sure she didn't ingest any of the pepper mist. It would be like getting hit with pepper spray.

She loved her little greenhouse. It served her very well over the last few years. The twins had gone down for their naps and were peacefully unaware. Occasionally, she glanced at the baby monitor and confirmed they were still asleep. She would never do this kind of thing in front of them. She didn't want them to have troubling memories or wonder what she was up to when their brains developed into having that kind of contemplation. No, she would keep their world all rainbows and unicorns as long as she could.

She was soaking a bunch of dried peppers in ethanol to extract the capsicum. A dried-up Hawaiian lei of crown flowers lay in a little box to the side of her capsicum process. She was essentially making her own pepper spray. Only hers would be a little stronger than the pepper spray you could buy to use against muggers, rapists, and bears. The crown flowers would essentially be a little catalyst to help the capsicum do what it was meant to do. She thought of buying pepper spray or gel, but it would leave records, no matter how careful she was. This was just better. And she liked the challenge.

Jack knocked on the door of the greenhouse, waved, and then stepped back a good ten paces. He knew to always be careful when his wife was getting her recipes together. He was a smart man.

Amber glanced at the clock hanging on the wall. It was 12:30, and Jack was home, but it was unplanned. Sure, they occasionally engaged in nooners when they could, but she always liked a little warning so she could get into her finest lingerie. This could not be good news. She quickly opened the door, stepped out, and shut it behind her.

"Hey. Whatcha doing?" he asked playfully. She chuckled. He knew exactly what she was up to. He also knew how to fight his baser instincts and not run in for a hug and a kiss, something she was fighting as well. She knew she was the hottest pepper within a thousand miles of Minneapolis.

She nodded and smiled. Just because she was currently a bit hot didn't mean that she didn't miss physical contact with her husband. Heck, they'd been married for over four years, and she still craved him. It bordered on obsession, or she was just very horny for him and him alone.

"Tinkering," she said, and knowing him as she did, she asked, "What's up? You're home early, not that I'm complaining. I love it when you come home in the middle of the day." If he was there for carnal purposes, she could take a quick shower. He might even join her.

"Maggie just called. She found a tracking Tile in her handbag. You know the fancy purse that Michael gave her for Christmas a year or two ago?"

"No, not the cool Burberry satchel?"

"I don't know, it was kind of plaid. You have a couple."

"I think it shocked everyone when Michael bought it for her. I know it shocked me. It is the only thing from her old life that she kept when she drove to Vancouver. Damn, she should have left it behind. How did she find out it was there?"

"It was buzzing or chiming."

"He was trying to find her location," Amber surmised.

"Exactly," he said.

"Further, we need to assume that he succeeded," she said with a defeated tone.

"Thankfully, she was out walking in downtown Vancouver and not at her office or condo."

"But now he knows she is in Vancouver," Amber said.

"Yes," Jack said. "Unfortunately."

"Are you going to tell Henry? Get her a little added protection from the evil ex-husband?"

"Yeah, I know she didn't want me to tell him, but without me there, he will protect her, and that is more important. I just left him a message because Maggie won't want to bother him. But I want him to know. We will have to see if he can keep a secret. She would be pissed at me for telling him."

"Yes, she would, but I understand why you need to do it. What a mess," Amber said.

"How are you doing?" Jack asked, shrugging toward the greenhouse.

"Well," she said. "Everything is coming along nicely. I'm almost ready for the chocolate."

"Do you need me to visit a couple of See's Chocolates, pick up some truffles, wear glasses and leather gloves, pay in cash?"

"No, too close. Neil is going to pick up a few boxes with extra wrap, etcetera, in New York and send them to my post office box in Des Moines. I'll do a little road trip next week."

"Renting a car?"

"Already have," she said. It went without saying she rented it under one of her aliases.

"Then what?" he said, lowering his voice and looking around their vast backyard.

"Miss Violet is going to do a little shopping in Portland at the same time Michael is staying there for his book tour. She's a huge fan. Well, at least that is what she will tell him at the signing. Imagine that."

"Is she already onboard?" he asked.

"Yes, she agreed this morning. I think she is bored because she is kind of excited to do it."

"I think she is just bloodthirsty."

"For the role I've played to make her that way, I'm proud. She has learned patience and cunning. She is like my favorite aunt that I didn't know I had."

"Well, she's a character, that is for sure."

Amber recalled her earlier call to Miss Violet, the woman who guessed her secrets a few seasons ago and now ran a little shop in Yachats that Amber had started called *Madam Emma's Love Emporium*.

Miss Violet was in rare form today.

"Thank the Jerry Garcia holy ghost that you called," she had said. "I was about to seduce this stupid new piano player at the Salty Dawg in Newport. I'm bored as hell, and he looks like he has a big dick and needs to get laid, which, as you know, is exactly my type. How is life with mister tall, dark, and sexy, Little Mama? How are my precious honorary grandbabies?"

Amber smiled as she walked into her large backyard and talked on the burner phone always reserved for Miss Violet.

"We're all good. I climb Jack often, and the kids are sleeping through the night."

"Yabba dabba do. You get some for me," she said and laughed her Miss Violet laugh.

"I will, I do, and he would blush if I told him what we were talking about. Actually, I'm calling to ask—would you be up for a little adventure?"

"Only if it is delicious," Miss Violet replied.

"Oh," Amber said, "It is quite spicy."

CHAPTER TWENTY-TWO
(Maggie)

Was it a panic attack or a heart attack? Maggie sat at her desk and tried to get air into her lungs. She couldn't remember the walk back to her office. But now she was sitting in her chair, trying to come to terms with what happened during lunch. Her lungs were tight and seemed to be getting tighter with each breath she took, like her organs were flattening or imploding. What if she passed out? Would she start breathing then? What if she didn't? Would anyone find her? Was her office door shut? How long would it take for anyone to find her? There was a clean-up crew that came to the office every night, so maybe they would find her. She'd probably be dead by then, but oh well. At least she would be found before she started to smell up the place.

And at least she had a new will. Jack saw to that before she went to Vancouver so she could die without concern. If anything happened to her, Michael got nothing.

It hurt. She couldn't breathe.

Finally, she bent over, and stuck her head between her knees, and told herself to relax, but her ears were ringing. The same way they rang when she gave blood that one and only time and had fainted. She hoped she wasn't going to faint. Well, maybe it was better than suffocation. Maybe if she fainted, she wouldn't know when she died.

She glanced toward the hallway. Crap, her door was shut! Who would hear her or find her? Would they find her in time?

Maybe she should move toward the hallway. Maybe someone would see her. She might have to crawl. She wasn't proud. She could crawl.

She was so focused on her own misery that she didn't hear a soft knock. Then her office door opened, and footsteps crossed the plush carpet. A big, gentle hand rubbed her back in comfort as a warm voice spoke to her.

"Maggie, it is okay. It's going to be okay. Just relax, keep breathing," the soft voice that sounded like butter said.

The realization was swift. She wasn't alone. Someone was touching her. And it was definitely male. What if it was Michael? How could she have let her guard down? She was getting sloppy.

She sat up quickly, knocking the hand off her back, standing, and ready to fight, looking around for a weapon.

"Easy," Henry said. "It is okay." He held out his hands as if she was a wild animal he was trying to tame. Maybe she wasn't completely sane.

She couldn't speak, just wheezed, as she half fell, half sat unceremoniously in her chair.

"Just relax, listen to my voice. You're safe. I'm here. Nothing is going to happen to you."

He carefully grabbed her hand and started massaging it. She heard her own wheezing as she looked down at her hand encompassed in his much larger ones. His fingers were warm and strong. She tried to think of only how good it felt to have her hand rubbed. She tried not to think that it was her boss doing it.

"That's it. Just focus on your hand and my voice. It is all going to be okay," he said as she looked up and saw him smiling at her and felt her breathing hitch for very different reasons. Why did her boss, Henry Hudson, have to be so good-looking?

"But if I should be calling an ambulance, I can do that too."

A moment later, she blinked, took a large breath, and felt her lungs expand.

"No, please, no ambulance. I'm fine. I'm sorry, I didn't hear you come in. You scared me," Maggie managed, trying to find her composure. She relaxed in her chair and waited for the reprimand she was sure would come. Henry gave her hand a final squeeze and let go of it.

"I'm sorry. I didn't mean to scare you. That was not my intention. Are you okay?" he asked, sitting on the edge of her desk a safe distance away from her. His voice was soft, gentle, and also a little questioning.

He probably thought she was about to go postal or was just plain crazy. Some crazy American. Security was but a phone call away. Maybe he'd have her physically removed from the building. He had to be questioning if she was up for this job. It was too bad because she was starting to kind of enjoy herself. This little adventure in Vancouver had been an oasis.

"Yes, I'm fine," she added a fake smile, "I'm so sorry. Something stupid scared me earlier when I was out at lunch, walking, and it is just, well, stupid. I'm fine. I just had a moment when I replayed it in my mind. I was feeling a little vulnerable. Ridiculous, really..."

"I know what happened. He wouldn't want you to know, but I just got off the phone with Jack," Henry said with a nod. He wasn't buying her crap. "It sounds like you have a reason to be scared."

The fake smile fell from Maggie's face.

"Whoa, wait, what did Jack tell you?" she demanded as the realization took hold.

Maggie no longer felt panicked. She was pissed. Damn, Jack! Maggie didn't want her past to be a part of this future. They had talked about this. Jack wasn't supposed to say a word about her divorce. What she told him must have concerned him. A lot.

Knowing this made her a little scared. Once a little sister, always a little sister.

Henry surprised her by smiling, not a small smile, but a big one. And unlike hers, his was real. He really did have a nice smile. She wondered what his wife had been like. Jack was at Henry's wedding almost ten years ago, but Jack mentioned Henry was divorced.

Why couldn't she stop thinking about how attractive he was? Because she hadn't been around attractive men in years? Maybe. She wasn't even divorced yet. Maybe it was because she'd been in a loveless marriage for so long. She envied people like Amber and Jack and other couples she witnessed. They didn't fight. One person wasn't in control. They were a team. They had open dialogue. They had easy affection. No one was scared. That was all she ever wanted. But that certainly wasn't what she got.

"I'm not supposed to tell you what we discussed, but I find my loyalties pulled in a couple of different directions," he said, the smile never leaving his face. "Jack is one of my oldest friends. He is expecting a certain level of discretion. We were frat brothers. We took the secret oath and stuff. Yet you are here and one of my people."

One of his people. How did she feel about that? Well, she liked it because it didn't sound threatening. It sounded protective.

"What...what the fuck did he say?" she asked, shocking them both by her use of profanity. Her soft mouse voice found some teeth, and she sounded more like a roaring lion. She even sounded louder, enough so that she clamped a hand over her mouth in horror.

Henry laughed hard as he shook his head and said, "You are so Jack's sister. I think that is the realist thing you've said to me since you started here."

"No, I'm just a little mad at my big brother. He has a way of pissing me off! What the hell did Jack tell you?" She asked, then

THE VOICE OF REASON

clamped her hand over her mouth again. She was starting to feel like her old self, the Maggie of *before Michael*. How long had it been since she had cursed so freely? Years. It had been years, and somewhere, the old Maggie Daniels was cheering. She'd always been the most colorful, the most animated in the family. When did she stop? Maybe when she had started dating Michael. She had gone all demure and shit. He had conditioned her. He had groomed her. And she let him do it.

"I'm sorry, my brother brings out my gangster self."

"Sure," Henry said, shaking his head and smiling.

Finally, Henry got serious and said, "He said your ex put a tracking Tile in your handbag possibly years ago, and you found it when its little tracker alarm went off. Since you didn't know it was there, this is of concern. The whole idea of coming to Canada was to get away from him. You wanted to have him be clueless as to where you'd gone. Now, he might know you are here. I'm sorry."

Was he mansplaining to her? She decided not to hold it against him. He was in a weird position.

"Yes, the asshole stitched a tracker in my handbag probably before he gave it to me. You know, when he bought me that bag, I was more than a little surprised. I was so downtrodden that I almost felt unworthy of it. How messed up is that? And why didn't I buy one for myself? That is all kinds of messed up. Now...*now* I know why he did it. It had nothing to do with buying me something nice. Something nice for the woman he supposedly loved. No, the bastard wouldn't do that. He wanted to track me and knew he had to give me something I'd always wanted to have with me. I should have known, the asshole. He'd always bought himself the top-of-the-line item but forgot it when it came to me. Heck, the engagement ring I've lived with is a joke. *'It is only until our tenth anniversary, then you'll get an upgrade.'* Yeah, sure. You should have seen my mother trying to be supportive. All the jewelry she and Dad ever gave me was nicer than the diamond chip he gave me. What the hell was I thinking?"

He shook his head and said, "My mother always told me that engagement rings should hurt a little. If they were easy and affordable, you weren't spending enough."

Maggie pointed at him and said, "Exactly. I like your mother."

"You would. She is very likable. Dad's good, too."

"I can tell. They raised you right."

He smiled and shook his head.

She knew she should shut up, but now that the swearing flood gates were open, she didn't know if she should close them again. She couldn't stop talking. It was like he was her best friend. What was wrong with her?

"What did you do with it, the Tile?" he asked, redirecting her.

"The tracker Tile? I smashed it to hell with my heel and tossed it in a trashcan on Robson Street. Here, I have a photo." She showed him the broken Tile on her cell phone.

"That's impressive," he said. "They are pretty indestructible."

"If you are angry enough, they go down fairly easily."

"I don't doubt you had a moment of pure adrenaline. Remind me to never make you mad," he said with his smile...again.

"I'm sorry that you are getting bothered with this," she said. "I can't tell you how embarrassed I am. I never wanted anyone in Canada to know. I'm trying to forget." The little voice inside her head couldn't figure out why she couldn't stop talking, disclosing things she had no business telling him.

"I don't consider it getting bothered. And you should not feel embarrassed. It kind of livens things up for me," Henry said.

"I highly doubt that your life is that boring," she retorted.

"Well, I like to keep it interesting," he said. "And this is the most interesting thing that has happened today...for sure."

"I'm embarrassed by all of it. You saw me looking weak. This is too much drama for an intern. I look like a mess, and I sound like a mess, but you have to believe me, I'm really not a mess. I was once a strong, competent woman. I'm trying to find her again. I think she is coming back. I missed her."

He looked at her and folded his arms, then held up his hand to stop her from saying any more.

"Okay, here is what I see. One, you are at least five years older than my typical intern, so let's call you a consultant from here on out. I mean, damn, we are almost peers. Two, this isn't drama. It is life, which is filled with good, bad, and so-so. This is a more challenging moment. Three, you are not a mess. You've propelled us in a whole new direction with the campaign. You've only been here a few weeks, and you are doing great work. At the end of this time period, when the consulting is done, I might ask you to consider staying. I need more people like you and less like the young idiots that I've got who are always kissing up to me. They are so fake I wouldn't trust them as far as I could throw them. Heck, I wouldn't trust them to feed my pet fish."

"Fish? You have pet fish?"

"I have a very nice tropical aquarium in my office. You should drop by and check it out sometime. And four, you are kind of family, kind of like a sister by proxy, so relax."

"So you're treating me differently?" she asked.

"Yeah, I guess I am, but you're impressing me. I'm proud."

She shook her head and looked away. This day was just getting odder and odder.

He picked up her cell phone again, shook his head, and set the phone on her desk.

"That little Tile didn't have a chance. Okay, back to the menagerie," he said. "I have to ask because I know you won't bullshit me. Have you noticed the attitude they have? They act like they are doing me a favor by being here, by trying to actually work. They are incredibly sensitive. Makes me wonder what I was like at twenty-two."

She ignored his concerns and asked, "We were all idiots at twenty-two. So I'm doing okay?"

He smiled that smile again that lit up his whole face and gave him dimples.

"Yeah," he said with a nod of his head. "I came here to ask you something, but I don't want to add more stress to you. It isn't anything you have to do. I just saw it and thought it might be good for you. Now, I hate to bother you with all you have going on."

"What is it?" she asked, relaxing by degree. The big scary ad man was much more approachable and human than he appeared on her first day, even after that lunch they'd had.

He looked away, possibly struggling with whether he should tell her or not.

"Um...well, the client George McKenzie with *GreatChef*, he told me about this. You see, occasionally, the *GreatChef* supplies cooking classes with all of their tools with the hope people will then buy their tools once they've been given a demo and had a bite to eat."

"Like co-op dollars."

"Exactly," he replied.

"Is *GreatChef* sponsoring a cooking class near Vancouver?"

"Yes, there is one in Maple Ridge, at some little cooking store, about forty-five minutes away. I thought I'd go, and I wondered if you'd like to go with me. It would give us some good marketing feedback as we watch how people interact with the tools."

"Yes! I'd love to go. I like cooking classes in general."

Being married to *The Voice of Reason*, Maggie had to become proficient at cooking all kinds of dishes. When Michael had a hankering for something, it wasn't like she could experiment until she got it right. It had to be right to begin with, or he had a problem with her motivation. Still, she could perfect something like Chicken Mole, and he would still tell her the seasonings were off. Because of his allergy to capsaicin, she had to be very careful. She had to be exact. She had to be perfect. That started a chain reaction of teaching. She'd have to make her normal dinner each night, and once she was finished, she'd have to practice the other dish she hadn't quite gotten right. In the case of Chicken Mole, she had gotten it right on the twenty-third try. And after all of that, he never asked her to make it again because he was tired of it. Privately, she used to think she could make one heck of a cookbook. Maybe she's even title it *Pressure Cooking: An Abused Wife's Guide to Trying to Make Her Abuser Happy.*

"The menu is some chicken dish with a radicchio side and some kind of chocolate orange dessert. Does that sound at all appealing?"

"Yes, sure. When is it?" she asked, feeling excited to be going out to do something different without any expectations. Something new. A new adventure. And she had never been to Maple Ridge. Despite the hours she was putting in at the office, she was a bit lonely. But she had to admit that not having rules made her want to park herself in front of the television, order DoorDash, which she discovered was available in Canada, and do nothing.

"Friday night. I'm sorry, it is the beginning of the weekend."

"No problem. But I have no idea where Maple Ridge is. Are you driving?" she asked.

"Yes, if that is okay with you."

"That would be great!" She smiled. It was the first genuine smile she could remember ever delivering to Henry Hudson.

Maggie frowned as she connected to her brother's cell phone.

"Hey, how are you?" he asked.

"I'm stressed out, and my stupid brother told my boss all my secrets, so now I'm embarrassed, too."

"Henry doesn't know who Michael is. He just knows that you had a shock today, and if you ever need him, he is there for you. Truly, Henry is a good guy. He is your older brother in my absence. He wrestled in college, if I remember correctly. But he isn't good at keeping secrets, obviously. He couldn't keep this from you like I asked, but he won't tell anyone else."

"He is loyal to his employees. I just wish your friend at the agency was anyone but Henry Hudson. *My boss*. I don't need my boss to think I'm some hothouse flower."

"He's a nice guy," Jack said. "I've known him for a long time. I'd do the same for him. Seriously, I wish you'd met him before he met his ex-wife. He'd have been a better husband for you. Too bad the timing is bad again."

Maggie let that thought roll over her for a few moments. Henry Hudson did make her heart beat faster. Talk about a strange complication with all she had on her mind.

"Gee, thanks for that. Now, I can think of him in a whole new way."

"Besides, he went through a divorce a year or so ago. Not like yours, but he gets it."

"Please stop speaking. It just gets more embarrassing with each word you say."

"Okay, enough about Henry. Are you being careful? You weren't followed or anything?" Jack said lightly, but they both knew he wasn't kidding.

"I walk everywhere with my pepper spray out and armed."

"Good," he said. "Just please be careful. And don't hesitate to use it on Michael. We have a restraining order in place."

"I was feeling peaceful until that little Tile started chiming in my purse. Now, I'm looking around at every dark corner, wondering if he is there…waiting."

"You should be practicing situational awareness all the time."

"Of course, I am. I couldn't have lived this long with Michael and not been aware of my surroundings."

"Do you want to come home?"

"No, I'm starting to remember who I was before Michael. I like the work here. I didn't like the knives in the beginning, but now I'm on to their tools, like can openers and small choppers. It's fun."

"If you see anything or hear anything, do not hesitate to dial 9-1-1. It works the same way ours does."

"Gee, I hadn't thought to check that out, being a completely helpless female."

"I'm sorry, I know you're being careful and know what to do," Jack said.

"No, I'm sorry. I didn't mean to snap at you. I'm just freaked out at the moment. Thank you for worrying about me."

"Always."

CHAPTER TWENTY-THREE
(Dr. Michael Allan Drake)

Thanks to the same-day delivery from Amazon, a newly purchased map of Vancouver, BC, was stretched on one wall of Dr. Michael Allan Drake's home office. Due to his keen, heightened intelligence, Michael had all the streets downtown memorized. And it wasn't because he and Margaret traveled to Vancouver, BC, for their first anniversary, but he did feel the irony. Fine. That was a trip from hell anyway. Margaret had shown a lot of weaknesses. It disappointed him greatly.

Something was going on, but he was a man who liked a challenge. This is why others should never be encouraged to compete with Dr. Drake at anything where a superior brain would win. Because Dr. Michael Allan Drake always won.

He had a red push pin in the position Maggie had been in earlier in the day when he accidentally tried to locate the Tile in her purse, only to discover she was on Robson Street. Was she there on vacation? Shopping? They spent some time on Robson Street when they were vacationing there. Margaret liked the shops and the people. He concluded that Canadians, on the whole, annoyed him. They were very nice. Too nice. No one could be that nice.

What if Margaret was hiding out in another country…just to annoy him? He looked at the clues at his disposal. It had been close to noon, so even a simple-minded idiot could deduce that she was headed somewhere for lunch. Seriously, did she have a job in Vancouver? How had she gotten a job in Canada? It wasn't an easy thing. What was she qualified to do? Real estate? That was a laugh. She wasn't smart enough to do anything else. If that premise were true, she had to be living in Canada. She was too timid to ever do anything like that. She couldn't handle the complexities of living in another country.

It wasn't like her real estate license could transfer. He was missing something. He had to be sharp for his book tour and be ready for the adoring fans, the women for whom he was their ultimate fantasy. But this little thing, the "where in the world is Margaret," was going to eat at him nonstop until he found her. Damn her for ruining this for him.

Vancouver wasn't on the list of destinations for the tour. Heck, the closest he got was Seattle in two weeks' time. Well, at that point, he was only a couple of hours away from his intended. He was intelligent enough to multi-task. So, he'd asked for a two-day break between Seattle and Portland to visit "friends" that did not exist.

What if she wasn't there? A nice little walk through downtown Vancouver never hurt anyone. If she wasn't there, it would be a nice break from the book tour. Heck, he might even set up an event at one of the local bookstores. Maybe he should talk to someone about a Canadian book tour. A few days in Canada wouldn't be too bad. Heck, he might even convince his publisher to promote it. PR companies were a dime a dozen. They could toss some money at one and have them arrange for radio and media interviews. Hell, it could be profitable. He'd make a call to Stoner Benjamin.

Planning. It was all about planning. It took time and a lot of strategy, but it was worth it.

Michael compartmentalized his feelings about Margaret. She was on the agenda, so he would just leave her there as if she were an item, like picking up dry cleaning. A box to be unwrapped at another time. On his list, it read: *Reunion with Margaret*.

He had a red pen in his hand and had printed out the itinerary his publisher put together for him. After discussing it, they liked the idea of him extending the tour to the west coast of Canada. They stretched his two-day vacation to a generous three days, but because they were assholes and he was their show pony, they had booked him for some events around Vancouver, BC. He circled the three days and wrote next to them, *Margaret*.

He still hadn't figured out why she was in Vancouver, BC, but he would. It was just a matter of time until one of his sources came through. Okay, he'd had to make it worth a little something for them, but it would be worth it to find his wayward wife. A receptionist here, a gardener there, someone would hear. And thankfully, he had some connected friends. Someone would tell. And when they did, he would be there to listen.

A nagging little thought entered his mind. What if Margaret gave the purse to someone else and she wasn't in Vancouver at all? No, she loved that purse. It was the nicest thing he'd ever given her. Her engagement ring was sparkly, but he'd purchased that at a pawn shop for about $1,000, although he told her it was his grandmother's. The purse set him back at least double what the ring cost. But it fit into his plan, so he justified the expense. No, she was there. She was in Vancouver. She had destroyed the Tile, and he didn't think she would have done that if the handbag was owned by someone else. He knew, just as he had known that she was planning something, that she was in Vancouver. He could feel it.

Back to his list, he needed to pack perfectly. It was something he prided himself on. But today, perfecting his list of exactly what he'd needed was proving problematic. His cleaning supplies for the dirty hotel were contained in one little black back that fit nicely in his luggage. He'd start with the handheld black light, which was sure to disgust him. Lysol spray for the bathroom and doorknobs. Disinfecting wet wipes for everything else he found. He also packed his own top sheets and pillowcases to wrap himself in, like a cocoon.

He was taking two suits, two sports coats, and several shirts, including several pairs of coordinating trousers and seven ties for this little tour. He packed three paperbacks from authors like Lee Child and Harlan Coben, his contemporaries if there ever were any. The thought of watching television in a hotel room, or anywhere for that matter, was abhorrent to him. It was a way to lose your intelligence. Margaret liked watching television. But this time, this time when she returned, television wouldn't be part of her life. Not anymore, anyway.

So he had his wardrobe and room security against germs thought out. The problem came when he thought of what he would need to reunite with Margaret. Those things, those supplies, he wouldn't be able to take on the airplane. He'd come up with a workaround. He convinced his publisher to let him rent a car and drive from Seattle to Vancouver. Stoner Benjamin hadn't conveyed the message well. Although they liked the idea, it looked like he might have to pay for it himself. His publisher was one cheap bastard. He'd acquire what he needed when he had a little privacy. He added a baseball cap and sunglasses to blend in. He wouldn't want to be easily identified if he was shopping for things like rope, knives, and enough chemicals like bleach, alcohol, and acetate to make his own chloroform. Because although he considered rehabilitating her, if he couldn't get her to agree to his demands, well, he didn't have a lot of alternatives. She was willful and stubborn. He couldn't let that behavior live freely. He'd better add a shovel and a tarp to his shopping list. Who knew how dark this might get?

Margaret had taken the good luggage because, in her little mind, she thought she deserved it. He had to go out and buy several new pieces. He took the receipt for the luggage and tucked it away in an envelope in his desk. It was just another expense he incurred because of her.

He decided to think on the bright side. Not *if*, but *when* she was finally back home, rehabilitated, and subservient, she would pay for this outlandish expense. But it wouldn't be just cash, no. He had some other ideas in mind. Maybe he'd pay her a dollar for every day that she pleased him. And that way, he could fine her twenty or fifty dollars every time she did something that displeased him. He liked this idea. He'd have to think more about it. Heck, if he reflected back to the week before she left, he had years of fines for her to make up. Hadn't she had five pairs of shoes in the closet the day she left? Yeah, that was worth at least twenty dollars. By his math, that would take almost a month of perfection to clear the fine. He liked this idea a lot. He bet his friends at *The T Society* would like it too. He'd have to write one of his suggestion memos. They would be used to it by now, as he'd already sent them twenty-three of these memos as his thoughts evolved magnificently.

He went back to the packing with a smile on his face. His special list for Margaret was added to the pile of other detritus he was taking with him. Everything was TSA-approved and able to fit in a carry-on bag as long as others didn't try to take the space above his seat with their property. People were so rude.

He added several prescription lung steroids for varying degrees of his lung issues, Afrin, eyedrops, and saline sinus wash to the list. Flying was hell on his asthma and by default, the sinuses. He added an EpiPen. Who knew how the air would be on the West Coast. All those alternative lifestyle folks. The air was probably thick with the secretions of marijuana. And the weather...it rained so much that the air was probably thick with mold.

CHAPTER TWENTY-FOUR
(Jack)

"What are you thinking?" Jack asked Amber, who was looking up from the book she'd been reading in bed. "And if it involves freeing yourself of that restrictive nightie, let me know."

"You are a bad boy, and I like it," Amber said, giving him a little coy smile.

He leaned over and gave her breast a playful squeeze through the red silk nightgown.

She smiled and leaned against him. "I *really* like it when you are bad."

"Wait a minute. Tell me what you were thinking, then we can play."

"Spoilsport."

"I'm sorry, baby. I just could almost sense your stress. Share with me, then take it out on me."

She leaned with him back into the pillows and said, "I like how connected we are. It is so rare and so wonderful. I was alone for such a long time."

"So was I. But we don't have to worry about that anymore. I love you," he said and kissed her.

"I love you too," she said when they broke apart.

"Now, tell me what's on your mind."

"I'm still thinking about the Tile from a few days ago. It kind of changes everything."

"I know, I don't like the Tile. Now, he knows she is in Vancouver."

"Yes, and tomorrow, we look to see if he has added any stops in Vancouver to his stupid book tour. If he has, things will change."

"Should we get Maggie out of there?"

"Maybe temporarily until we find out that Michael isn't there any longer. It sounds like she really likes Vancouver. Just how handsome is your friend Henry?"

"I don't want to think about it, but they would make a good team. I'm betting that you've already got a contingency plan," he said as he freed her shoulder of one of the red silk spaghetti straps.

"I do," she said and leaned closer to him. "Enough shop talk. Time for you to perform some husbandly duties on your wife. Take away my stress."

He kissed her and asked, "How would you like to be serviced this evening? Sweet and slow or hard and fast?"

She smiled and pulled him close. Then she whispered in his ear, "I need my husband to treat me like a cheap hooker he met on shore leave, who offers him a good price to do anything he wants."

He leaned close to her, his lips barely touching hers as he said, "Aye, aye."

CHAPTER TWENTY-FIVE
(Maggie)

"We are just Henry and Maggie, a young career couple. *GreatChef*? Never heard of it," Henry said as they drove in his car toward Maple Ridge.

"Okay, I get it. We are incognito. We don't work at the agency on *GreatChef*," Maggie said.

"You bring up a good point. What do we do?"

"Okay, you could be a lawyer or accountant," Maggie said. "I'm a teacher."

"Couldn't I be something more interesting?"

"Special Forces?"

Henry laughed. "Maybe I'm writing a novel."

"Okay," she said, "You're an author of an unpublished book. What is it about?"

"Early Canadian settlers."

Maggie smiled. "Let me guess. You really are writing a book on early Canadian settlers."

"I've been playing with the idea," he admitted.

And despite all that Maggie had been through, ignoring that she was in the process of divorce from a published author, and the thought of a man touching her was slightly repulsive, she felt like she was on a date as they drove in Henry's big black BMW to some far-off location called Maple Ridge that was popular with American filmmakers.

It had been over a week since she found the tracker Tile in her handbag. A week of hellish fear. Since then, she was scared of her own shadow, always carrying her pepper spray, anticipating that Michael was lurking in every dark corner. At 5 p.m. sharp, someone appeared at her office doorway to escort her to her car. It was either Henry or the security guard. She felt a little exposed when it came to the extra attention, but she knew it was a necessity, and despite her slight embarrassment at the special treatment, she appreciated it.

They left early Friday evening in anticipation of traffic and Friday afternoon exodus from Vancouver. Now, they were sitting in Henry's car with an hour's drive ahead of them in heavy traffic.

"Let me know if you ever want me to read what you've written." She had read Michael's book several times, although she hadn't offered any criticism. He didn't like that kind of correction, especially from her. She knew how to read something and not say anything negative.

"I'd be embarrassed," he said.

"Don't be. Wow, there is a serious amount of traffic."

"I'm glad we left early," he said.

"I'm lucky. I had no idea how much traffic there actually is leaving Vancouver. My commute is less than ten minutes because I live near the waterfront."

He turned toward her, looking surprised as he said, "I live by the waterfront too."

"Did I know that?"

"I don't think so," he said and then mentioned his address, which was only a block or two from hers.

"We are practically neighbors," she said and gave him her address. "It is a great neighborhood. My little rental condo is pretty nice. I have views of downtown out one side and of the harbor in the other direction."

"I know that little stretch of condos right by the water. You picked a lovely spot. I have always liked having a view. Before I got divorced, my house was ten miles from downtown, but it took an hour to commute each way. It didn't matter what time I left. In the winter, I only saw it in daylight on the weekends. And the view was that of trees, which is peaceful, but the waterfront always has something happening."

"Do you miss it? Having a house with grass and space?" Maybe what she really wanted to know was if he missed his ex-wife. She started picturing what the woman looked like. She remembered after her brother graduated, there was a flurry of weddings, Henry's being one of them.

"I miss grass and trees, but I don't miss the unhappiness that house represented. I had huge hopes and dreams when I bought that house with my ex-wife. I had one of the unhappiest marriages in the history of marriages. All my dreams weren't meant to be. We were too young, too opinionated, and had way too many ideal notions. Neither one of us realized that marriage took work. We didn't share dreams and goals with each other. We fought to see who would win. Then, it no longer mattered. The trees and grass that I loved, she hated, although she picked the house. She was too young to settle down, and I was too boring to live with."

"Boring can be good," she said.

She had a little movie in her head of him and some beautiful faceless woman picking the perfect house and assuming it would be where they would be happy for the rest of their lives. Add children and pets. It was an all too familiar scenario for her. Well, not the pets. Michael killed that dream.

"It is rather insensitive of me to say all that in light of what you've been through," he said. "We were never scared of each other, just disappointed."

"No, it is not. Pain is pain. Mine was different than yours, but you still had it."

"How are you holding up since the Tile stuff?" he asked, looking straight ahead and not at her.

"Well, it changed how I thought of Vancouver. I thought this was a safe place, but I'm remembering the fear I felt living in Minneapolis. It is like riding a bicycle. It just comes back."

"I'm sorry. Vancouver is such a wonderful place. I'm sad that now you're feeling that way about our little city."

"Well, until he shows up here, it is still my safe place, right?" she asked.

"Can you think of any way that he would find you? I mean you were on Robson when the Tile sent your locale. Thankfully, not at home or the office."

"No, those are just my nerves talking," she said, but she knew, just knew, Michael would not be able to deal with the curiosity that was probably eating him up over her whereabouts. She just hoped she'd see him before he saw her.

"I'm sorry. I have a question, but it is rather personal."

"Go ahead," she replied.

"Were you ever worried that he would be physically violent? Jack alluded to that but didn't elaborate. When we had lunch that first day, it sounded like your ex was unhinged."

"Yes, he was physically violent," she said quietly. "He was a very large man. He'd punish me if I broke one of the rules he had in the house. The violence was escalating. It started with something small that he apologized for and said it would never happen again. Within two weeks, it happened again. More stuff happened after that. I thought if I didn't leave, he'd kill me. No, that isn't right. He would have killed me either way."

"I didn't know. I'm so sorry. Holy shit. I don't even know what to say."

"I appreciate that you believe me. It isn't something that people would actually believe. They would have thought I was exaggerating. You see, my soon-to-be ex-husband was a bit of a pillar of the community. People don't like it when you start knocking down one of their idols. Even if I showed bruises. I'm just glad that when I went to Jack and Amber, they didn't question it."

"Something I once heard was that women don't make up that kind of thing."

"No," she said, "They don't. In fact, it is embarrassing. We can't believe we are in this situation. We can't believe that someone who promised to love us would do something so violent to us. It shatters our dreams, makes Swiss cheese of our confidence."

"What a horrible outcome. I'm very glad you got out."

"It took me long enough," she said.

"But you did it. And I'm proud of you. That could not have been easy," he said, still not looking at her and staring straight ahead.

"It was the hardest thing I've ever done," she murmured. "But I'm remembering who I once was. That girl was no shrinking violet."

"I remember hearing Jack speak about you at school. He didn't say anything specific, but I thought Jack seemed…well…a bit frightened of you, like you were a force. My divorce was easy. No one could understand how wrong it went so quickly. Despite all the evidence, they couldn't believe that Gina would do that to me. You see, she strayed…people kept asking if reconciliation was an option. Heck, even my parents asked that. They wanted to know if she was just going through a phase. So what? Did they really want me to take her back, knowing another phase could kick in at any time? Like after we had children. Even if she wanted to come back, the trust was broken. With your situation, going back should never be a question."

"I would never go back. I don't care if he is rehabilitated. I'd rather be alone for the rest of my life than deal with him again," she said.

"Good, I'm glad to hear that. Sometimes, everything around you gives you signs you ignore. Then, when you get hurt enough, you decide, no, I don't want to hang around and wait for another round of the pain."

"Exactly, you're right," she said.

They were at a red light, so he turned to her and said, "I need to say this. Don't let him take all the good work you've done and sully it. You've really brought us some wonderful insights. Things we never would have considered. I think that if we get this account, we have you to thank. I won't let you forget how valuable you've been to me. It doesn't matter how you got here, I just glad you came."

"Thank you, but anyone could have supplied you with the *GreatChef* info if they had taken the time to research the products," she said and smoothed the skirt she changed into before they left.

"That is just it. They wouldn't have taken the time. You were the right fit. Only you. Please don't discount what you've done."

"You give me too much credit."

"Thank you, Henry," he said formally. Then he responded in kind, "Oh, you are welcome, Maggie."

She chuckled and said, "Thank you, Henry."

"You are welcome, Maggie," he replied.

Second-guessing her gray silk blouse and the gray herringbone skirt with the scallop edge, she said, "Despite what led me to being here, this has been a wonderful adventure. Coming to Canada, meeting everyone."

Henry wore chinos and a white button-down shirt. They looked the part of two professionals on an evening out after a long day at work.

"Why do I think that you're still doubting yourself?" he asked.

"I think it is a hangover from my bad marriage."

"It might be. But if you asked The Menagerie, they would tell you that I don't give out compliments easily."

She was quiet for a time and then volunteered, "I was never good enough for my ex-husband. He held me to a standard that he didn't hold anyone else to. So, I was never happy enough. I never smiled the way I should. If I smiled too much, it looked fake, yet if it was a small smile, it was smug or just not enough. If I laughed too long, I was loud and obnoxious. If I didn't laugh, maybe I wasn't smart enough to comprehend the joke. My lipstick was too red. My blouses showed too much cleavage. I had too many pairs of shoes in the closet at one time. I wore too much makeup. My hair was dyed like a whore. The corrections, and my failure, well, the constant scrutiny, it never ended. Now, I think it makes me second guess myself with everything that I do."

"I cannot believe he said those things to you. He sounds like a controlling asshole. How long were you together?"

"Too long. Life is precious, and I gave him six years of mine. Time I'm not getting back."

"Quality, not quantity, so please don't focus on it. Be glad for every day you aren't with him."

"That is a good way to think of it. I'll never go back. I was lucky to have escaped," she said and checked her makeup again in the mirror.

There was no humor in his voice when he said, "I'm serious, Maggie. Never, no matter how much he begs, never, ever go back. Because if you did, Jack and I would show up and remove you."

"Does it sound weird for me to say thank you?"

"No," he said.

She was too curious for her own good. "How long were you married?"

"Just long enough for my wife to get bored with me and start having an affair with my client from London. He flew in for a few days, and I suggested dinner so that he could meet Gina. We went out to dinner, but Gina added a few other lunches in the suite of his hotel that I didn't know about. I found out when she cried at the thought of his leaving. I was a little dense, but I could see the fire through the smoke, as it were. I guess they had a lot more chemistry at that dinner than I noticed."

"Unbelievable," Maggie said. And it was. Who would cheat on him? She couldn't believe it. He was a catch.

"I'm dense. It took me a couple of days to fully realize that my marriage was over. Then there was the awkward way she told me I was boring when compared to him. After I agreed to the suggested and surprise divorce, she said it was his sexy accent. She couldn't resist it. I lost my wife and future in about four days to some shady businessman with an accent. That is how fast my life changed. Four days. They are married now, living in London, and expecting their first child. The house I mentioned earlier was sold because I couldn't stand living there after everything went down. The end of a dream."

Henry was a handsome man. Charming, and a bit like a Ryan Gosling. Boring wouldn't be in the first hundred words she would use to describe him if asked.

"Tell me you didn't send them a wedding gift or are still in contact," she said.

He looked at her then and gave a small, sly smile.

"She is allergic to sulfites in wine, and he doesn't drink due to his religion, so I sent them a very expensive case of Pinot from Napa Valley. He is the only client I have ever fired. Because I guess I hold a grudge, according to her."

"You're a monster," she said and laughed.

They both laughed then, and he said, "I can admit, I wasn't a real gentleman when it came to the man who swept my wife away."

"No judgment from me. I think they got everything they deserved."

They talked about Vancouver and restaurants and places she'd been and places she needed to go.

"Tell me about Jack's wife," he said.

"Amber? She is wonderful. They are what you would call

soulmates. He came alive after they got together. I guess she reminded him of someone else he had a fling with during a vacation to Saint Barts. Anyway, he nursed a broken heart for months and decided to visit our cousin in Oregon to get his mind off that other woman. Our cousin's fiancée had a dinner party for him, and neighbor Amber was there. They hit it off in a big way. It was like love at first sight. Within a few weeks, they were living together in Minneapolis. Within a year, they were married. Now they've got the twins, a boy and a girl, Clay and Libby. I guess she looked a little like the woman from Saint Barts."

"I guess he knew when it was right. He seems very happy. I'm happy for him."

"They are very happy. In fact, they have the kind of marriage I was looking for but didn't have. They really respect one another. He worships her, and she kind of does the same to him, which, as his sister, is hard to watch. Serious ick factor, but I'm happy he's happy. They are just in sync with each other. I don't know how to explain it, but they fit like two puzzle pieces. You almost feel like you are in the way when in their company. They move as one almost. Point and counterpoint. It is like they are the same person, anticipating each other's movements before they make them. They don't mean for you to feel this way. You just do."

A half-hour later, Henry parallel parked the BMW in front of a cute little bistro in a town square of Maple Ridge that Maggie remembered seeing a dozen times in movies.

"Hang on, I'll come around. I have a huge umbrella."

Maggie waited and then huddled with Henry as they shared an umbrella and walked to the front door of the bistro and cooking store.

Had Michael ever held an umbrella for her? She didn't think so. It was caring and kind of intimate. She liked it, possibly more than she should.

People turned and smiled as they entered the warm space.

An older woman intercepted them and greeted them, "Hello! Are you here for the cooking class?"

"Yes," they both answered at the same time as Henry stood in the doorway and shook the rain off the umbrella back onto the sidewalk.

"Wonderful! I'm Helene, and we just need to wait for a couple more people to arrive. How would you like a glass of wine? Since we are making chicken, we are serving a lovely Chardonnay from Forget-Me-Not winery from Yamhill, Oregon, outside of Portland. May I get you a glass?"

Henry looked at Maggie, and they both nodded. Eventually, they were shown to side-by-side chairs at a big wooden table that looked like it had come from an old farmhouse. The entire space had a rustic, almost European feel to it. It was the kind of place maybe you'd stop in on a Saturday afternoon for a bit of shopping and a little lunch with a glass of wine. It was homey and kind of romantic. Maggie liked it and especially liked the displays of kitchen equipment, including *GreatChef*. Discretely, she took photos, Henry nodding his approval.

They met other people who were there for the class, but most of all, they talked with each other and drank the smooth wine.

"You know what I really like about this setup?" she whispered.

"No, what?" he asked, angling his head toward hers.

"They have mixed *GreatChef* with Le Creuset, so low- and high-end cookware and equipment. Anyone who could afford Le Creuset is not going to purchase *GreatChef*. Yet there is still something for every price point."

"Well," he said quietly, "They wouldn't be buying *GreatChef* if they knew better."

"Yes, whoever put on this class packaged these two brands together, or maybe they will say, well, if you cannot afford Le

Creuset, here is another alternative that looks good. Just don't try to use it."

Helene, who greeted them, took up her position on the other side of the table. She was big on eye contact and looked at each one of them as she spoke.

"Welcome, everyone. I'm Helene, and today, we will be making Swiss chicken with mushrooms and wine in a clay pot. On the side, we will have sautéed radicchio and, for dessert, chocolate almond Grand Marnier brownies. Any questions so far? Now, is everyone set with wine?"

They got refills on the wine and settled in.

"First, you shake the chicken in the herb and flour mixture and then sauté it in olive oil to get a quick sear." She demonstrated while Henry and Maggie continued to drink their wine.

"Now we layer it in the clay pot with the chicken, mushrooms, and onions that I sliced with my *GreatChef* knife. Let's deglaze the Le Creuset pan with our featured wine of the evening from Forget-Me-Not Winery. As it simmers, add the sour cream and the herbs." She also gave instructions on how to clean mushrooms, which was the same way Maggie cleaned them with a damp cloth.

During a quiet moment, Henry leaned close to Maggie.

"Already smells good," Henry whispered. "She has a good handle on branding."

"My stomach is growling. My apologies."

"Next time, we leave with enough time to grab a burger before the cooking class," Henry whispered, but he caught Helene's attention, and she decided to punish him.

"Excellent," Helene said, "Thank you for volunteering, Henry, isn't it?"

"Oh...I..."

"Thank you for volunteering! Right here next to me, we will get you to roll some radicchio in bacon and stick it with toothpicks to secure it before you place it in the deep Le Creuset pot that I have waiting over medium heat with two tablespoons of olive oil," Helene said with a smile as Henry reluctantly stood and joined the instructor.

Maggie watched as Henry washed his hands and was tied into a pink floral apron and then tried to cut the radicchio. She bit her lip to keep from laughing as he fought with the bacon. The *GreatChef* knife wasn't good for the one thing it was supposed to do: cut. At one point, their eyes met. They shared the thought about the knife without saying a word, and he winked at her.

A silent assistant refilled her wine, and she found that her mouth hurt. When she figured out why, she was surprised. She was smiling. How long had it been that she smiled so naturally and for so long that her mouth hurt? She couldn't remember, which told her it had been too long.

Once Henry had the radicchio in the Le Creuset pot and squeezed in a lemon, he was excused to wash bacon grease off his hands and return to his seat next to Maggie.

He sat next to her and whispered, "You enjoyed that too much."

"You did well," she said with a chuckle.

He smiled, and they clinked their glasses together. They watched Helene slide the chicken into the oven and then did the demo making the Grand Marnier brownies using a *GreatChef* zester that seemed to not know what its job was. Poor Helene was incredibly flustered as she switched to a Good Grips microplane.

Maggie looked at Henry, who nodded. They had both seen it. The tools were only nice eye candy kitchen décor. If you had to use them, it wasn't easy. In fact, it was downright frustrating.

While they waited for the chicken to finish, Helene gave them a rundown of all the tools she had used, including the clay pot, which was from Romertopf. The woman managed to get four sponsorship endorsements in one class. That was rather impressive.

At the end of the demo, Maggie said to Henry, "I think I could use a clay pot like that."

"I have one. It is really useful."

Surprised, she asked, "You have one?"

"Yes, and I cook with it," he said proudly. "And sometimes what I make is pretty good. I'm very good at roasting vegetables. But heck, you toss root vegetables, wine, and butter into a pot to hang out together, you are going to do okay."

"What's your specialty?" she asked.

"Well, my specialty is pasta, and I do it in a pan on the stovetop. The good thing about that dish is if it isn't perfect, you just add cream or cheese, and it makes it good. I think the original recipe is called Chicken Davide, but I use that term kind of loosely."

"You are right about the cream and cheese," she said with a laugh. "And you seem to have a handle on the use of butter and wine."

"What about your specialty?" he asked.

"Name something. My soon-to-be ex-husband liked me to perfect very popular and complex recipes, like coq au vin or chicken mole. Seafood risotto is easy. That way, work colleagues would always be impressed by his little wife and what a good little homemaker she was. Of course, he had me make it and perfect it until I was an expert. The stress was incredible. I made the mole over twenty times before he was satisfied."

"I'm so sorry. I mean, that is horrible. It sounds like a kind of torture."

"I survived. I got out. And now, if you ever have a craving for coq au vin, you know who to call."

"I don't think I'd ever ask you to make something that you'd had to perfect. That would bring back bad memories. I think I should have you over for my pasta instead. It is kind of rustic, but it's edible. I have by no means perfected it. The garlic bread is always good. I mean, you split a baguette, melt a stick of butter, add some crushed garlic, top it with parmesan, and broil it. It always comes out."

"I'd like that. I could bring dessert," Maggie said.

And it wasn't until later that she realized she had accepted a dinner date with her boss. They hadn't picked time, but the invite was out there.

The chicken was sublime. They enjoyed it along with the radicchio.

"I've never liked this purple stuff, but I like it like this."

"The fat from the bacon and the lemon juiced hides the bitterness of the radicchio. It is all about the balance of acid and fat with the salty bacon," she said.

Henry looked surprised. "How do you know all that?"

"Because, believe it or not, I actually like to cook. I like to put ingredients together and make things for people and myself. I just don't like to be forced to cook."

"I'm glad your ex-husband didn't ruin the joy of cooking for you."

"He didn't. I actually like to entertain, just on my own terms. What is your favorite dish?"

"I love Italian, French, or Mexican," he said. "But I don't know how to make my favorite, which is beef bourguignon."

"Would you like to know how to make it?" she asked.

He wrinkled his brow. "You know how?"

"Of course," she said with the hint of a smile. Michael had her perfect it. It had only taken eight tries and became one of her early specialties.

"If I got all the stuff, could you show me how to make it?"

"Sure," she said with a smile. See? It wasn't a date. It was a cooking class.

"I've already taken up a bunch of your weekend, maybe some night next week?"

"I'm free tomorrow or Sunday, so if you'd like to do it sooner, I could." That way, if he had a hot date to cook for, he'd know how.

"I'm free tomorrow, but is that too soon?"

Maggie shook her head, "No, we could do it tomorrow night."

"I'll get the stuff. I just need a recipe."

"Look, since I've made it before, let me get everything. You can bring the wine. Bring a nice red, like a Bordeaux."

"Are you sure?"

"Yes, come by about six, and we'll make it. And bring something to take notes."

They finished dinner, and then he surprised her by buying her an expensive Romertopf clay pot and a matching cookbook.

"You didn't need to do that," she said.

"I want to. Besides, you might want to make dinner with it, and I don't want to buy any *GreatChef* stuff. I know you probably don't need the cookbook, but they look nice together."

"Thank you, that is very nice of you. I'll make the beef bourguignon in this pot tomorrow night. It is ironic," she said, shaking her head. "I used to have this cookbook. I used it a lot. It wasn't something I took when I left so quickly that day last month. That book is probably gone forever. But now I have this, and there is a good memory with it. Thank you. I'm glad to have it back."

"Good," he said. "You're welcome."

They drove back to Vancouver in peaceful silence. Occasionally, one of them would talk about the class or the food, but mainly, they just enjoyed the company and the drive.

Henry took her to the parking garage across from their building, where she left her car.

"Let me just have a look around before you get out. I want to make sure it is safe."

"Thank you," she said.

"By the way, could I get your address for tomorrow night? Otherwise, I'll be knocking on a lot of doors."

When she gave him her address, he said, "I can walk to where you are. You're a block away from me. Maybe I should start driving you to work."

"I don't want to be a bother," she said.

"Maybe it would make me feel better," he said. "Until we know the extent of the Tile's meaning, I need to keep you close. I'm going to follow you home tonight, just to be on the safe side."

Her automatic response would be to tell him it wasn't necessary, but she really appreciated it.

She nodded and said, "Thank you."

But he didn't stop there. After they drove to her condo, he parked behind her and escorted her to her door.

"This was above and beyond, but I really appreciate it," she said as she paused at her front door. It felt like the end of a date. Should she hug him? Kiss him on the cheek? He had crossed the line from boss to friend.

"Do me a favor," he said.

"Sure," she replied.

"Let me have a look around inside. It might be paranoid, but it would make me feel better."

She let him in and followed him around as they opened all her closets, looked under her bed, pulled back her shower curtain, and finally proclaimed her condo was "safe" and very neat.

Maggie wanted to say something witty that would make him smile. Oddly, she wanted to offer to have him stay, have a drink, and keep talking to her. But she remembered the old gambling motto, "quit winners." And she would be seeing him tomorrow, which had little butterflies fluttering in her stomach.

And so, what had been a lonely weekend ahead was suddenly filled with possibilities.

CHAPTER TWENTY-SIX
(Dr. Michael Allan Drake)

Michael despised the book tour so far. The idiot who planned out his stops should be fired. Probably some officious woman. It had to be a woman with no sense of direction. Today, he had three signings in Chicago with barely any breaks. He didn't even have time for a civilized lunch. He had rushed from place to place like a bicycle delivery person and act as if he should be grateful for the people assembled waiting for his autograph. Whoever planned this trip failed to recognize that he was the star, not his fans. The trip should have revolved around him, not the other way around. It was like his publisher thought he should be pandering to his fans. That was so messed up.

Almost all of the audience members were women. He felt himself scowling. These weren't the kind of women he should attract. No, they were sad, pathetic, fat, middle-aged housewives who lost all hope in their lives. And oh, how they looked at him, like he was sex on a plate, and they were all hungry...Make that starved. They wanted their photo with him, probably to fantasize about later while they were with their fat, sweaty husbands, grunting like pigs in mud.

They wanted to touch him. Heck, if he wanted meaningless sex with someone's mother, it wouldn't be hard. They would line up willingly to be serviced by him.

Occasionally—and let it be known, it was the exception, not the rule—there would be a hot MILF (A hot mother he'd like to fuck.) But it didn't happen too often. He was tense in a way that only men got. He might have to pick someone out at the next event to service his needs since Margaret wasn't around to see to them. He could use a quick little blow in the men's room. And wouldn't he be doing the woman a favor? She could get up and personal with the famous Dr. Drake. Well, part of Dr. Drake. He chuckled at his own joke.

A sedan, not a limo, whisked him away to the airport, and now he was on a short flight to Detroit, which seemed to have more turbulence than it should. Could he talk about the seats for a moment? They hadn't even upgraded him to first class. He flew in the main cabin like a piece of meat...like cattle. This could not continue. He had a call into his agent at the moment with a threat to stop this treatment, which wasn't what he deserved. And as for these low-budget hotel rooms, that had to end, too. He required a suite, nothing less. And there needed to be room service at the hotel. Really, really good room service. He had to have all the amenities available to him 24/7. Nothing less would be tolerated. Who did they think he was?

He had 24 hours before his next jaunt to San Diego. There had better be some damn changes, or he would take matters into his own hands.

After San Diego, there was Los Angeles, then San Francisco. Eventually, he'd go to Seattle, then Vancouver, for his personal getaway, and finally Portland, which made no sense. He should be in Portland before Seattle. Did the planner of this trip have a mental deficiency? First, he'd gone east. Now he was going south, only to head north and then to head south again. What the hell was she thinking?

It gave him a headache. All he knew was that in a few days, he'd be in Vancouver, British Columbia, where his wayward wife was currently living. Well, he'd show her a thing or two about trying to hide from him. He couldn't wait to see the look on her face when he showed up and surprised her.

He sighed as the plane lurched from side to side. If it wasn't one thing, it was the other. His publishing and PR team had him on a tight leash. Heck, they'd even asked him not to answer any personal questions, as if he would. They asked him not to discuss the pending Margaret divorce or restraining order, which was complete bullshit. He explained to them more than once that Margaret was confused and had mental issues. As soon as she calmed down, possibly with the help of others that he had already arranged, she would be fine. It was almost like they didn't believe him. Well, they weren't the smartest of humans.

He pulled his iPad from his briefcase, which barely fit under the seat in front of him. Once he'd secured Wi-Fi with his credit card, he checked his private email, the one only one other person had.

Jerome Osborn, his private detective, sent him a message. Michael tried not to get excited at what might live inside the email when he clicked on it. There already been disappointment. The man was slow. Michael only hoped this wasn't another dead end. Hadn't he told him to only make contact if he had something to share? Michael didn't like getting his hopes up, and his little stop in Vancouver was but a few days away.

He tapped the screen and opened the email. Jerome knew not to waste time with small talk. It simply read: *She is going under her maiden name, Maggie Daniels*. The detective then gave her place of business and current home with the address. Bingo and Check Mate all rolled into one glorious moment.

Jerome wrote that Maggie worked at an advertising agency. What did she know about marketing? So what? She had a degree, but that meant nothing. For a moment, he wondered if the other man had found the right Margaret. The last line in the email put all his doubts to rest: *Her brother, Jack Daniels, and the managing partner of the advertising agency, Henry Hudson, went to college together.*

Oh really...

That did it. Jack had interfered. He'd deal with him and his little hippy-dippy wife too.

Just six days until he was in Vancouver.

CHAPTER TWENTY-SEVEN
(Amber)

On Saturday afternoon, Amber played in her little greenhouse in the backyard while Jack entertained the twins. She didn't require much alone time away from her husband and the children, but Jack always insisted she have a little time to herself. Maybe he knew her better than she knew herself because she thoroughly enjoyed these stolen moments.

Today, she decided to catch up in the greenhouse. She was trying to get a chunk of plumeria bark shard that she'd gotten in Hawaii to germinate with her special ministrations. Plumeria was one of her favorite flowers, and she hoped to make a tree from the little start she had. She thought there was a possibility she could get the tree to blossom in the middle of winter in Minneapolis. And wouldn't that be fun? She would make it happen. She loved a challenge, after all...

A chime noise, not unlike breaking glass, cut through her contemplative thoughts on the plumeria. It was her special burner phone that was in a drawer nearby, and she knew immediately who was calling. Only one person had this number, *Miss Violet*. Amber had been expecting the call.

Gently placing the plumeria back in its tray, she went to the drawer, opened it, and picked up the phone next to a lucky silver coin, the only part of her old life she still kept with her. She answered warmly, "How are you?"

"Well, I've been having some fun in the Windy City. I just visited a special friend who is staying downtown."

"Did you learn anything new after touring the special friend's temporary habitat?"

"Well, he wouldn't be my cup of tea. Too neat, too tidy for my liking. Very repressed and disciplined. Looks like a boring partner in the sack if his possessions give any clue."

"Big ew," Amber replied. "I never asked her directly, but I surmised as much."

"My thoughts exactly. What he needs is a big doobie and a cabin in the woods to find himself. Maybe dance naked around a big fire with the blood of innocent animals smeared on his face."

"Yes, leaving him in the woods is an excellent idea," Amber said. "Maybe he'd choose to stay there forever."

"Yeah, but shovels are so heavy."

"And they wreak havoc on the manicure."

They both laughed at the idea of burying Michael in the woods.

Miss Violet was a wild thing. Amber couldn't picture Michael or Miss Violet in the same room at the same time. She doubted Michael ever smoked a doobie in his life. She knew that Miss Violet loved her doobies. Thankfully, Miss Violet retained some mental capacity so that she never was in jeopardy of discussing secrets. And Amber and Miss Violet had a lot of secrets.

"My only complaint is that my seasonal allergies are really bothering me. I'm going to have to get some of that sinus wash. I can't remember the name, but you know the brand. It starts with an S and ends with an X. You know, the ones that have little blue and purple packets of oily saline salt that you mix with distilled water, and then you use a little bottle to squirt it up your snout?"

"Yes, I've seen it. You can buy it at almost any drugstore. It's become very popular. And very helpful if you have asthma."

"Our friend downtown appears to enjoy the product, so he must be a devout user. Or shall I say, a daily user?"

"How very interesting," Amber said, already considering the possibilities.

"I've heard warnings about not using the right water or salt solution. Bad things can happen just from tap water. I'd worry that if you didn't have the real stuff and put some variation up your nose, how would you make sure to get it back out again?"

"That's why you have to be very careful of what you use with it. And seriously, use only distilled water. Because if you don't, little parasites that live in the tap water can get up into your sinuses and your brain," Amber cautioned.

"That sounds awful."

"It can be fatal. In fact, people put a little vinegar in the water to kill anything, but it burns going in, which is unpleasant."

"Yikes. I'll have to remember that. Well, it's been fun catching up with you, but I have to catch my plane back home," Miss Violet said.

"Thank you. We'll be in touch. Safe travels."

"Hugs to man, children, and dog."

"Don't forget the cat."

"Of course not. She gets a special hug because she's a special girl. I think I love her the most."

"Oh please, I've seen the way you look at the man."

"He is rather delicious."

Amber pulled off her gloves as she thought of the new information that Miss Violet had given her. The plan had always been to do something with chocolates because she knew that Michael had a sweet tooth. They would leave them for him with a faux note of welcome, so they looked like they came from the hotel management, but she wasn't sure it was enough. He'd know after one bite and could spit it out. But sinus spray, well, it was kind of foolproof.

Michael was extremely allergic to capsaicin. Amber had seen it with her own eyes. That was the day that Amber almost killed

Michael with a jalapeño popper. She hadn't been trying. If she had been, he'd be dead. He still acted like a kindergartener who just lost his achievement sticker on the playground. Finally, Maggie supplied the EpiPen and give Michael a life-saving injection. Amber and Michael hadn't liked each other since. Maggie didn't hold a grudge. She acted as if it hadn't happened. It looked like an accident. If it happened again, Amber wondered if Maggie would have been as fast with the pen. Somehow, she didn't think so.

In fact, Amber was testing to see if he was allergic to capsaicin. Well, the degree of his allergic reaction. He hadn't disappointed. After a lot of swearing, coughing, and choking, and an EpiPen later, she learned that yes, he was allergic. She had a feeling that he didn't like her reaction, which was nothing much of a reaction. She had met men like Michael before. Men who were controlling and abusive. She knew this day would come. She just wasn't sure how it would come, but now she knew.

This new information that Miss Violet offered Amber flooded her mind with a plethora of new ideas. Possibly, she could take the capsaicin and crystallize it or mix it with salt and replace his normal salt packets with doctored salt packets.

After all, if you weren't looking for it, you wouldn't know it was there. She wondered what the consequences would be for an asthmatic who used this special salt wash on their sinuses. This would get the capsaicin right into their mucus membranes and next to their brain.

With every interesting solution that Amber came up with, she always asked the same question. Would it work? Time was wasting. She needed to commit to a solution.

Amber smiled in the empty greenhouse. She'd bet on the future blossoming plumeria tree that she had found the perfect way to deal with Dr. Michael Allan Drake.

CHAPTER TWENTY-EIGHT
(Maggie)

It was a cooking lesson, nothing more, nothing less, Maggie thought as she got ready for her day, taking a little more time with her lotion and hair prep. Then why was Maggie so nervous at the thought of having her boss in her home? Maybe she was a mix of nervous and excited. That was bad. She only used to get that way when she had a hot date many years ago. It kind of felt like that. Damn. Okay, she could admit that she had fun with Henry the night before. Did she wish her brother introduced her to Henry before Henry had a serious girlfriend? Yes. That realization tingled her to the bone. What did she think? She and Henry would have ridden off into the sunset together? That was crazy...okay, maybe...

So she liked Henry. So what? Men and women usually liked each other for reasons other than attraction. They might have the same perspective in business. They might share the same values and goals. The other person might be a good role model for what she might look for in a man one day. Right?

Only she was attracted to him. Why? She questioned herself about it constantly, thinking about what other people would say. How could she even look at another man after what she'd been through? Rebound much? Didn't she need a break? Didn't she need to recover? Was she just interested because he was the first decent man she'd met?

Possibly, but that wasn't it alone. A little voice told her the perfect time never existed. Stupid little voice.

Okay, and this wasn't her home. She had to remember that. It was a rental. Heck, it was like she was on a vacation from her life. But it felt more like home to her than her home with Michael felt in the entire time she lived there. When she looked back on that time, it felt like a nightmare. It made her shake in fear. Had she really lived that?

Now, she felt free despite the old ghosts making their appearance.

This life, this experience, this everything was temporary. She'd be leaving in a few weeks. But she hoped the joy would follow her wherever she ended up. Heck, she'd miss this time. She'd miss Henry. What did that mean? And what should she do? Tell him she had feelings for him and ask to stay? Pathetic much? She could not think about that.

Back to the rental. What did it have that she liked and would integrate into her next home? She wasn't responsible for the décor of her rental, but she liked it. She even liked the colors blue, green, and sand, which she'd never use with Michael. In her past house with him, the colors were in his vernacular "rich," but she found them dark and depressing. These colors were soothing. They reminded her of the ocean, always flowing.

Maybe she'd decorate in warm red, soft greens, and butter yellow. Inspired by Italian warmth. The colors of Tuscany. Not like she had been there, but now there was hope that she would visit one day. She was so tired of dark, oppressive colors. She could change the surroundings where she lived, much like she had changed her hair. Still her hair, but different. The way she wanted it. The way that gave her pleasure.

Maggie had always been messy growing up. Her way of organizing her shoes was more of a theory than a reality. Then Michael punished her for not adopting his sense of organization. She learned quickly. Almost overnight, she became a neat nick.

After almost six years with *The Voice of Reason*, she'd turned into a Pavlovian dog, and nothing was out of place, or she shook with anxiety. She took great pains to make sure everything was tidy. This wasn't a good thing. Maybe that anxiety would lessen in time, but as she looked around her space, it felt perfect, almost too perfect. It looked like it did the day she moved in. Aside from the luggage she'd unpacked and arranged in the closets and bathroom, nothing had changed. Okay, she bought several new plants, and the curtains were open to their fullest to bring in all the light.

Earlier in the day, she had gone to the Granville Market and got everything she would need to make the beef bourguignon and a couple of appetizers. It was like going to Disneyland if Disneyland were all about food. She couldn't stop smiling at all the happy people and colorful interiors. She felt free, carefree. And the food she sampled was amazing. She bought flowers, chocolate and a couple more plants to liven up her little rental: a fern, and a little topiary ivy that was variegated in light and dark green with sage undertones, which enhanced the color of the living room.

She kept looking at the space and felt a little thrill when she saw the plants. Michael didn't like indoor plants. He would not approve. It made her smile. She kept the smile from the grocery store all the way through prepping everything. She cut the carrots on the diagonal in perfect little shapes. Then she peeled the pearl onions and sorted them for their uniformity.

When it came to beef, she didn't use chuck. She used several filet mignons, which she cut into little pieces and placed in a Ziplock bag in fridge next to her bag of carrots and onions. She added a few mushrooms because she had seen it done, although it was a little controversial in the recipe. In fact, it wasn't included in the basic recipe, but she liked to add them to round out the flavor of the vegetables.

Henry said he'd bring the wine. She had a couple of bottles of exactly what she needed for the recipe, just in case. She wasn't sure if he liked the recipe over noodles, mashed potatoes, or with buttered garlic French bread. She could do any of them, and had the ingredients for them, depending on his preference.

She made a dill dip with vegetables that she had always served when Michael wanted to impress guests. She tried to use the pink-handled *GreatChef* knives she had, but they didn't cut well, so she moved on to a butcher knife that came with the condo.

She had a small, triple-cream-Brie cheese from France that she topped with marionberry compote and then wrapped in puff pastry she had purchased. When Henry arrived, it would be almost ready to come out of the oven. And it would be delicious.

The table was set, and she had even picked up some tapers to light, but if the mood was wrong, she would conveniently forget to light them.

Her outfit choice almost put her over the edge. Yet again, it felt like a date. He always saw her in a suit, but she couldn't wear something like that on the weekend. She had a cherry red silk ribbon sweater that was expensive and looked shabby casual when paired with a pair of jeans. At a little over six hundred dollars, the sweater was anything but shabby. Along with jeans and a pair of Italian red patent flats that matched exactly, she thought, ironically, that her Saturday outfit cost more than any of her suits.

Twenty minutes before he was set to arrive, the Brie went into the oven. She took off the oven mitts and held out her hand. It shook a little.

"Get a grip," she said aloud. "It's just dinner, for shitssake." She would be as nervous if it was one of her friends or relatives, right? Well, maybe not.

Why did she have to find him attractive? Why did she have to feel like this? It was so damn fabulous and confusing at the same time. She was married, like yesterday. Heck, she was still technically married. How she could even speak to another man she didn't know, but Henry was kind, and she liked the way he smiled at her. It was real, sincere. He didn't appear to want to change her at all. He liked her the way she was. Maybe it was a façade, but she didn't think so.

When there was a knock at her door at six sharp, her first reaction was fear tempered with logic. Still, she approached the door carefully and looked through the peephole. Henry waited on the other side. He even gave a little wave and a smile.

Her heart beat so fast, she wondered if it was visible through the sweater.

He was in jeans, too, but she had a feeling there was nothing inexpensive about his outfit either. He wore a camel-colored cashmere sweater over a white t-shirt and loafers that were Gucci, if she wasn't mistaken. The logo was discreet, but she recognized it.

"Hey, good evening," he said, holding up a couple of bottles of wine. Next to him on the ground was a grocery bag that held a bakery box.

"Hello, oh my goodness, you really didn't need to bring anything."

"Well, I don't know if these wines are any good. And it was a good excuse to get my favorite dessert from *Scrumptilicious Cakes*."

"What kind of cake is it?"

"Black Forest. Is that okay?"

"It's one of my favorites," she said, smiling. "It was completely unnecessary, but thank you. I love cake." In her marriage, she hadn't been allowed to eat cake for years. Michael watched her weight carefully. A few months ago, he'd determined that she had gained five pounds, so he had forbidden her to eat any sort of sweets at all. That first night after she left Michael and stayed at Jack and Amber's was the first time in years she'd had something sweet. Amber's famous cake. Nothing had tasted sweeter. She hadn't splurged since. Life was too short not to enjoy cake every now and then. She was due for a splurge.

He stepped inside. She took his coat and then asked, "How has your day been?"

"It is hard for me to savor the weekend. I'm still thinking about the office," he admitted.

"Well, hopefully, you could at least sleep in?" she asked.

"No, I usually remember it is Saturday right after I shower and am wondering which suit to wear. You?" he asked.

"Nope," she said with a laugh. "I'm conditioned. I can't sleep past six."

"Me neither," he said.

"Maybe tomorrow morning I'll sleep in, after this dinner and the wine," she said.

"We'll have to drink this whole bottle. I'm a lightweight, so it'll knock me out," he said. "At least I can walk to my place."

"You really are that close?"

"Yes, I walked tonight. It took less than five minutes."

"Then we can share the bottle with no guilt." With Michael drinking enough for three people, she always watched what she drank. Because he wasn't a nice drunk, and she never knew when she might have to run for her life.

"I should have said something last night, but I think this is a very nice place," he said.

"Thank you, I know. I kind of lucked out. Come on into the kitchen. I've got everything ready to go. And I've got a Brie in the oven, and it's about ready to come out."

"I love Brie that has been in the oven," he said.

She smiled and let out the breath she didn't know she'd been holding in. He was gracious and enjoyed everything. It was a far cry from entertaining with Michael watching over everything and judging. She had held back a lot of tears over the years.

They stood in the kitchen, drank the wine, and ate the Brie

as they talked. She started assembling what they would need. It was fun. It was easy.

Cooking with Henry was a joy the likes of which she hadn't ever experienced. She let him fiddle with the condo stereo system, using an iPod piped music into the whole space. He put on Latin dance music, and before she knew it, they were both dancing and laughing in the kitchen.

"I feel like we've already had a few glasses," she said. "Not just the one."

"It's good for us to let loose," he said as he grabbed her hand, and they danced in harmony.

"I haven't had this much fun in a long time."

How long had it been since a man grabbed her hand in joy and not to punish or harm? This was the first time she could remember since her brother held her in his office. Before then, well, she couldn't remember.

Finally, she said, "I've got to stir the stuff."

"Stir that stuff," he sang as she stepped toward the stove.

She moved the beef around in the pan on the stove as they stood next to each other and continued to move to the music.

"We be searing!" she said with a laugh.

"Searrrriiiiinnnngggg," he sang out in a deep baritone.

Then she added the veggies and tomato paste and deglazed the pan with wine.

She smiled as she took a deep inhale.

He joined her, his face close as he seriously asked, "Does it always smell this good?"

"Hell yes. I'm making it," she said, realized what she'd said, and started giggling. He joined her.

They laughed at the sizzle of the wine hitting the hot pan, and at last, she reached for the clay pot that was soaking in cold water in the sink.

"Thanks to this pot, we can cut the cooking time down considerably."

"Fantastic," he said as he toasted her with his wine glass.

Before long, her new Romertopf clay pot was in the oven, and Henry watched her with a strange expression on his face.

She took a self-conscious sip of wine and waited, swaying to the music.

Something in his expression changed.

"What is it?" she asked softly. Had she done anything wrong? She didn't think so, but she worried she had been forgetful.

"Watching you cook, I mean, it's like watching art. You're so graceful. I'm kind of blown away. And you've got some smooth moves."

She nodded self-consciously, a deep blush on her cheeks. She felt shy and vulnerable but not scared. No, not like she had been conditioned to feel so many times with Michael. This feeling was a quiet excitement. It started in her tummy and spread warmth through her body like tingling electricity. Not quite meeting his eyes, she said, "Right back at you. Let's go sit in the living room. Please bring the Brie. I have some other munchies in the fridge."

She was aware of him in the way you were spatially aware of certain people. It seemed so wrong, so inappropriate, that she didn't know what to do. Yet they had just danced in her kitchen. If she met him six months from now, after the divorce was final, different story. What was wrong with her? A month ago, she had been someone's wife. She had shared a bed with another man. Well, she hadn't enjoyed sharing a bed with Michael. She didn't know if she'd had a good night's sleep for the last few years. Yet, here she was, dancing with her boss, wondering what it would be like to be in his arms. How could she even look at another man after what she had been through?

Her problem was that she couldn't stop thinking about Henry. Everything about him called to her. She liked the fact that they held hands as they'd danced. She liked the feel of her hand in his. She felt strength in those hands, the warmth of his skin, and it didn't cause her to be scared of what that strength could do. No, it made her feel reassured. What was wrong with her?

She wanted to run her fingers through his thick hair. They had danced at a distance. She wanted him to wrap his arms around her. She wanted those hands. The man had gorgeous hands, and she wanted them on her. She wouldn't fear his touch. How could she?

And he was looking at her. Really seeing her. And if she wasn't mistaken, he felt this odd, cloying tension, too. She could read it in his expression. Or maybe she could sense that she had a little...what? Crush on him? What if he felt the need to discuss it and how inappropriate it was? Oh, man...

The room, the space between them, was filled with tension that made it hard to breathe. It was thick like smoke, the most beautiful smoke she'd ever seen. And he was her boss. Had she forgotten that little fact? Heck, he probably thought she was pathetic. Sad. Pathetic.

The music changed. Now, it was a ballad. Something she recognized as sexy and sultry. Sade... Uh-oh.

"Maggie?" he whispered as she sat on the opposite end of the couch that he occupied.

"Yes?"

"I...I'm so, I don't want to...I haven't enjoyed myself like this in so long..."

Oh, damn. He'd read her mind, and he wasn't interested. Well, he was her boss. This was so complicated. Embarrassing.

His fingers closed over hers as she held her wine glass. Then, he took it from her hand and placed it on the table.

"I don't want to mess this up, but I need to tell you something," he said.

She nodded but said nothing. The next words he spoke would have the power to decimate her. She was so damn fragile.

"I'm out of my element here. I worry I'm going to do something like kiss you. I'm just...well...I'm sorry. I didn't mean to make you feel uncomfortable. I just can't stop thinking about you. I'm sorry, I didn't mean to do this..."

He liked her, too. She couldn't believe it. He. Liked. Her.

Her hand reached up and touched his lips.

"Please kiss me," she said. "If you don't, I might implode or explode. Damn it, just kiss me."

She didn't need to tell him again. He pulled her close, his arms wrapping around her, and then he kissed her. She was in the Sahara, and he was a much-needed oasis. Sinking into the kiss, she gave it as good as she got it. She stretched and moved against him, his arms tightening as she tried her best to get under his skin. His hands were warm as they sought to pull her tighter to him.

They rolled around on her couch, taking pleasure from each other until the oven timer loudly interrupted them.

Maggie sat up too quickly and had no sense of balance. Henry caught her as she fell against his chest.

"I'm sorry," she said.

"I'm not. Easy, we'll go together," he whispered in her ear, his arms guiding her to the kitchen where the timer on the oven interrupted their peace.

Keeping one hand on Henry, she used the other to silence the buzzer. Then she turned the dial and cracked the oven door. Glancing at Henry, she smiled and let herself be pulled into his arms, where he kissed her again.

She whispered against his lips, "What would you like, rice, pasta, or garlic bread?"

He smiled, kissed her, and whispered, "I would like you."

"Really?"

"Yes."

"Well, we should let the beef cool." She turned off the oven.

"I agree," he said, smiling as he pulled her away from the oven.

They weren't teenagers. She was an adult, which gave her a certain amount of freedom. She hadn't enjoyed the pleasant company of a good-looking man in longer than she could remember. Reckless freedom egged on by two or three glasses of wine that her mostly tea-totaler self drank with reckless abandon. Why stop making bad decisions now?

"Would you like to see the rest of the condo?" she asked with a sly smile.

"I thought you'd never ask," he said as she led him to her bedroom. The dinner long forgotten as other appetites took over.

Maggie slowly opened her eyes. There was light in her bedroom, moody light skewed by rain, which meant she'd slept in for the first time in possibly years. Thankfully, she knew it was Sunday. She had no place to be except in the warmth of her bed. And at the moment, it was a very appealing place to be.

A hand gently spooned her, wrapping around her middle and fitting comfortably between her breasts as she lay on her side. She was aware that a warm, furry chest nestled against her back, and the owner of both was gently sleeping behind her. She could hear the soft inhale and exhale of his breathing.

Usually, she didn't like to be touched when she slept, but this was different because the man spooning her was Henry, not Michael. It was unlikely he'd hurt her in her sleep.

In the years she had been married to her husband, she had never been free with her body. Maybe in the beginning, before she realized that being naked wasn't freeing, it was vulnerability.

Michael deduced that there was obviously a problem with her. She was cold. Her body didn't want to experience pleasure. She should talk to someone. Maybe get some therapy because she wasn't sexy to him. *If things didn't improve, he'd have to look outside their marriage because he had needs... He'd done all he could do... This was her problem...*

She never thought of herself as cold, but she was. How had she gotten into this position with Henry? It had been stupid and slightly humiliating to let it get this far. She'd have to leave, find another place to hide from Michael. She didn't know how she would face Henry this morning. And if Jack asked what happened? It was mortifying.

Slowly, carefully, she placed her hand lightly on the one that rested between her breasts. This might never happen again. A man might never be in her bed again. A tear slid down her cheek. She had so much pain. She was so sad. How could she ever find herself again?

Behind her, Henry snuggled against her neck, the point of his nose tickling her as his hand moved from between her breasts to tightening his hold, his hand gently cupping the soft mound. She had gone from feeling a little trapped to being trapped.

"Good morning," Henry murmured.

"I...um...good morning," she said. "I'm sorry about last night."

"What? Why?" he asked, his tone changed, now slightly alarmed. "I don't understand."

"I know...I'm a disappointment. I know I'm cold. I'm sorry I didn't mean to ruin things...You've been so kind to me—"

"What are you talking about?"

"I know I have intimacy issues. I hope...well...it isn't you. You're fabulous. It is me. I'm the one who has issues, and I'm sorry—"

He pulled away so that her body lay back in the bed. He looked down at her, confused, as he shook his head and said,

"You are the most passionate woman I've ever known. You have more passion in your little finger than most people have in their whole bodies."

"It was okay?" she asked, embarrassed.

"It was fabulous. Seriously. This isn't about us, is it?"

She looked away, unable to meet his eyes.

"I don't know what this ex-husband of yours did to you, but he was wrong. You aren't cold. Hell, if you are cold, I think you'd kill me if you were hot. It's like asking someone who has only driven a dump truck to drive a Ferrari. And you, darling, are a Ferrari. Totally, *totally* out of his league."

"But I'm kind of frigid."

He started laughing. "I'll take you being frigid anytime."

"So you didn't think it was bad?" she asked.

"Um...no. Did you?" he asked, wrinkling his forehead.

"No...I felt good. Really, really good."

"I thought you had a good time. I thought we both did. I care about you, Maggie. I like bringing you pleasure. I like seeing you lose control because of what I'm doing to you. The way you respond... It is just...so...wow."

She started to speak but then just nodded and bit her lip as he slowly lowered himself to her.

Later, after Maggie found Henry a requested toothbrush and they'd taken a long shower together, they made breakfast, their bodies leaning against each other in pleasant silence. Every now and then, Henry would stop working on their omelets to kiss her. She couldn't believe this was happening and blushed, finding it hard to meet his gaze.

"I can't do this," he said as he turned off the burners. "I think you broke me."

Had she ruined it? What had she done now?

He pulled her close and smiled, "I've forgotten how to make basic scrambled eggs."

"I thought you were making an omelet," she said.

"Oh, yeah. That's what that was supposed to be," he said with a smile. "I'll order us a pizza later."

And before she could comprehend it, he'd picked her up and carried her back to the bedroom, where he kicked the door shut behind them.

CHAPTER TWENTY-NINE
(Amber)

On Sunday morning, Amber snuggled her face down in her pillow as Jack, who lay beneath her, ran his hands along her back and down to cup her butt, which he squeezed playfully. They were both in the mood for a good morning round of sex. Then, the baby monitor came to life and let them know that their mornings of debauchery were in their past.

"Ugh, them again?" Jack asked.

"Yeah, you just had to knock me up, didn't you?"

"I can't seem to keep my hands off you."

"Such is my burden to bear. You know, they can be a lot of work. It's just too bad they are so damn adorable," Amber replied.

"Yeah, and damn it, kind of smart."

Amber nodded, "Well, with the DNA we gave them..."

"How could they be anything but?"

"Exactly," she said.

They heard a chuffing at the door.

"Good morning, Pumpkin," Amber called and received a whine in reply.

"Breakfast or babies?" Jack asked.

"If you toilet and breakfast the animals, I'll handle the teacup humans," Amber said.

"Sounds like a plan," he said, reaching up and giving her breast a squeeze.

"You know something? I'm in love with you," she said with a smile.

"I'm in love with you, too. Maybe during their morning nap, we could also...take a nap, pick up where we left off?" he suggested.

"Yummy," she said as she cupped his groin and slipped off him.

When Libby and Clay were in their highchairs, eating little pieces of egg and cereal, Jack looked longingly at his wife. She smiled, reading his mind. "Two hours and counting."

"Good," he said. "Hey, did I hear you talking to Neil late last night? How is he?"

"He's good. I just have a little errand for him to run for me."

"Really? Something besides the chocolates?"

"Yep," she said with a smile as she sipped her coffee. "Something a little more personal. Still forming in my mind, but when it comes together, I think you will like it."

"Will it be ready in time?" he asked.

"Neil is making it a priority, and he is going to be on the West Coast in a couple of days."

"Do you want to visit him?" he asked.

"I don't want to be anywhere near this. However, he might have a layover that would allow a visit."

"Sounds like it is showtime."

"Let's just say the audience is entering the theater."

CHAPTER THIRTY
(Dr. Michael Allan Drake)

Finally, he was ready.

Michael wore a baseball hat and clothes that made him feel less-than as he carefully, methodically walked around the different aisles of the Bellingham, Washington Home Depot. Uber had given "Lyle" a ride to the nearby Biscuits Diner. The ride was booked and paid for using a burner phone and a prepaid Visa card. In a matter of moments, Michael watched the Uber leave and then quietly walked the two blocks to the nearby Home Depot.

He pulled uncomfortably at his plaid flannel shirt. How did men wear these damn things? Seriously, could plaid be any uglier?

He got an orange plastic cart—which was disgusting, filled with the detritus of a thousand shoppers—and ran a hand sanitizing wipe over the handle. It wasn't perfect, but it would help. Then he went about the business at hand.

A little duct tape here, a little rope there...ah yes, don't forget the zip ties! He really liked zip ties. Margaret hated them because he'd had to restrain her a couple of times, and they had cut her skin. Oh well, a little skin irritation paled in comparison to what she had done. He smiled a little when he placed the ties in his cart.

He pondered the items assembled. What he needed looked like what he'd once read was a murder kit. Add some bleach and a tarp, and he was set! Ah, modern paranoia and the group think of the masses...if one fan who recognized him and took a photo...well, it wouldn't be good.

What was a fella to do? Well, he knew. He added caulking and plastic pipes. Screwdriver, hammer, X-Acto knife, and even a couple of basil plants.

This wasn't a murder kit. It was just another day of a stressed-out helicopter dad trying to help his kids with a last-minute school science project. He added some balsa wood and some wood glue. Heck, he had to smile. Those darn kids! Always waiting until the last minute to get their homework done...Well, by god, they had better get an A on this project. He was missing a baseball game for this! And he wasn't going to do it for them. He'd done that in the past. What good had it done? Had it taught them anything? No. They would have to do it all on their own. He might have given them some advice, but that was it.

He paid for the whole bundle in cash.

Once outside, he used his burner phone to make a call.

In a matter of moments, two late-model Black Escalades pulled into the lot.

The men, dressed in plaid shirts and hats, both stepped out of the driver's seats and tried to hide their excitement at meeting the famous Dr. Michael Allan Drake.

Members of *The T Society* couldn't quite believe that not only were they called upon to help their unofficial leader, but he was also standing before them in the flesh.

Michael did again what he liked to call "putting on the dog." It was a bit ostentatious, but they expected it from him, and he certainly didn't want to disappoint them. He could smile and glad hand with the best of them.

Ten minutes later, they handed him the keys to one of the Escalades and bid him good luck. Now, he had a car that could not be tied to him. His rental was back at the hotel, where he was taking a bit of a break from the tour. He stopped back at the hotel, parking the Escalade a few blocks away. Then, he grabbed one of his bags, specifically packed for his journey, and made his way north on I-5.

Yes, border patrol would record him going across the border to Canada, but so what? He was going to visit his wife. Thanks to the Escalade with the special modifications made by his loyal *T Society* men, he'd be able to travel back to the United States with Margaret happily, discretely restrained in a way border patrol would not be suspicious as long as he was cool and they didn't search the vehicle. Well, that was easy. He liked being downright cold.

CHAPTER THIRTY-ONE
(Amber)

Amber and Jack parked their car three blocks away from the mall on a side street and walked to a nearby Macy's, one of the anchor stores in the large structure. From there, they went inside and came out, having purchased something small that was in the Macy's bag Amber now held. No one seemed to take notice of them, which pleased Amber. She liked to be noticed when she wanted to be noticed, but this wasn't one of those times. It is why they didn't exactly look like themselves. She was dressed more like her previous persona as Madam Emma from two seasons earlier. She drew the line at the candy apple red hair she had worn then. The color was murder to remove. Jack wore a beat-up jean jacket, a ball cap, a bunch of bead necklaces, and trucker boots.

They sat on a bench in front of the store, and Jack used his burner phone to call an Uber.

The Uber took *Everett and Paula* to the airport. They walked inside for a few minutes, went to baggage claim, and quickly went out the doors with a crowd of people. They hailed a taxi that took them to one of the chain hotels that was around the airport.

Inside the hotel, they encountered no one as they made their way to the elevators and took them to the fifth floor. At the door of 509, Amber knocked and then stood back.

Her honorary nephew, Neil, answered with a big smile and

then a quiet laugh. "Awesome," he said as he stood back to let them enter and checked out their outfits.

After hugs, they settled in around a small table.

"How did you get here today?" he asked.

"You know, cautiously, to make sure we weren't followed. We started at a parking lot, then we went to the mall, an Uber, the airport terminal, and finally we took a cab here," Amber said.

"I always learn from you, Auntie," he said.

They ordered room service lunch and caught up.

Amber reached into her handbag and pulled on a pair of gloves, then pulled out a Ziplock

bag that had a box inside it.

"Nice," Neil said.

She handed him a pair of gloves. "Check out the seams of the little packets."

Neil put on the gloves and looked at the packets. He nodded and smiled, then asked, "They are perfect. How many, if you'll excuse the pun, are hot?"

"All of them. I didn't want to take any chances."

"How did you get them so perfect?"

"A little hot spoon to reseal, the edge of a metal file for the pattern," she said and mimicked the action with her hands. "Steam to open."

"Wow, that should take care of business."

"She never messes around," Jack said, looking admiringly at his wife.

"Thank you for doing this," Amber said.

"It is my pleasure. I'm going to meet your friend along the riverfront tomorrow afternoon."

He meant Miss Violet.

"I'm a bit jealous. She's fun," Amber said.

Room service arrived, and they had a good lunch of club

sandwiches, fries, and brownies for dessert. They caught up and discussed plans for the annual trip they always make.

"Harder with the children, of course," Amber said.

"I have an idea. It is a little out there," Neil said.

"We tend not to like run-of-the-mill nowadays," Jack said.

"I was thinking about the kids. Making it easier for them. What do you think of us renting a cabin at one of the lakes? It would be mellow, and we wouldn't have to fly."

"I like it a lot. Only if you wouldn't miss something tropical," Amber said. "I mean, Minnesota in the summer isn't the Caribbean."

"I think it would be great, just not in the Uber heat of the summer," Neil admitted.

"July and August are the worst," Jack said.

"How about the first week of September?" Neil asked.

"A week with babies? Are you serious?" Amber asked. "I don't want to put you off ever having children."

"You are my family, so yes."

Amber smiled, placed her hand on her chest, and looked like she might cry. "Well, in that case, I love it."

CHAPTER THIRTY-TWO
(Dr. Michael Allan Drake)

Michael took the elevator to the lobby of the pretentiously named *Graystone, Hudson, and Fields Advertising Agency* in Vancouver. He'd arrived late the night before and was staying at some substandard flea trap on the edge of town. It lived up to his expectations of a hotel. He really couldn't handle a hotel that would be considered "slumming it." Perhaps he should consider moving to the Fairmont. It was something to consider.

Today was full of possibilities. He had legitimate business to discuss, but if he happened to see someone he knew...well, wasn't that all for the better?

He would be discussing the promotion of a Canadian book tour to start as soon as his current one ended. Well, that was his story, his justification for this early morning visit. Besides, he knew this man, this Richard Fields, who appeared to be very excited at the prospect of working with him. He was a disciple of Michael's behind-the-scenes teachings. Michael had an eleven o'clock appointment this Tuesday morning with the man. Michael started seeing the man's name on *The T Society* sites on the dark web several months ago. Richard was not just an employee of the advertising agency. He was a disciple.

What were the odds that life would gift him with all this shared coincidence? Margaret in the exact location that a loyal follower also favored?

Well, Richard would be in for a surprise when he told the man about Margaret.

He wondered if Richard knew Margaret. Michael's associations with *The T Society* were starting to really pay off. He hadn't asked the other man yet, but if things went well, he would.

Sure, there was the book tour that made all the little chubby mommies swoon, but this message, the message he was spreading with *The T Society* about traditional roles and old-fashioned family values with the male at the head of the family... well...it was taking hold. He was starting to get quite the following. Soon, they would pull back the curtain and let the general populous in on their movement. Michael smiled. He was slated to be at the head of it. There was talk that he should run for political office. Now, wouldn't that be fun?

Crawl... Walk... Run... He had a wife to get in line first.

Margaret was working as an intern, and Richard was the advisor of the interns, according to the company website. How ironic! That was about right, Margaret being an intern. More than menial labor could not be expected of her. With any luck, he'd see her today.

Could it be this easy?

Would she come with him willingly? No, he didn't think that would be the case, but at least by seeing her, he'd crush her independent streak, which was totally out of control. And then, when she thought that maybe he'd given up, maybe the game was over, he'd reacquire her.

As the elevator doors slid open, another idea came to mind. Instead of asking for Richard, he knew he could just ask for Margaret and see what would happen when she appeared and realized it was him. But, come on, that was too easy. He worked for his success. He hunted for his food. If it came too easy, he didn't trust it. Besides, when it came to cat and mouse, he enjoyed every part of it. The hunt, the chase, and the capture.

"Good morning," the overly made-up whore-twat behind the ostentatious tall desk greeted him.

Someone should tell her that magenta hair and lash extensions made her look cheap. And her outfit, well, he'd ponder that later as the thoughts and images of fabric and skin flooded his mind.

"Dr. Drake to see Mr. Fields," he replied, as if she should just snap into line because of his tone. It would be a good test of her obedience. She didn't grasp the importance. No surprise there.

"Sure. If you just have a seat, I'll let Rick know you're here. Would you like a coffee or Red Bull while you wait?"

"No, thank you," he said, wondering just what kind of place would offer him a Red Bull. It seemed so relaxed. A. Red. Bull. What was he, some student cramming for finals? His opinion of Richard Fields was plummeting. Well, this *advertising agency* hired Margaret, so they appeared to be flawed from the start.

He sat on plush leather sofas, his eyes traveling to the table before him. It was a glass top triangle balancing on metal funnels and bowling balls. How odd. Well, the creatives weren't wired correctly. He actually was having a hard time relating to the creative types now that he had written a book. He wasn't, and would never be, one of them.

Richard Fields kept him waiting seven minutes, and since he was five minutes early, the man was technically two minutes late.

Michael used his time wisely, continually checking out his surroundings. Heck, at any moment, Margaret could appear, and then it would be a checkmate. He actually hoped this was but a tease. He wanted the pursuit to last longer. It excited him. Heck, if this space were a little more private, he might want to hump the twat behind the desk. That would be so satisfying! She needed to be broken, and he felt like breaking someone. It wasn't like she wouldn't enjoy it. Heck, she was a walking invitation to sex. He just wanted to give her what she was asking for...

"Dr. Drake, I'm Rick Fields," the man before him said with a cosmetic dentist-enhanced smile. The man was short and a little pudgy. He had rolled over on his back when middle age came a knockin'. Middle age was winning. And he had a gold pinky ring. Like he was supposed to be gangster-tough? Michael could break him in half.

"Richard," Michael said, standing to his full height.

"Why don't you come on back to my office so we can chat," Rick said and extended his hand, a "right this way" gesture, which seemed unnecessary.

Michael silently followed behind him, taking in each door he passed. People were working, chatting on the phone, and having small meetings, but no Margaret.

They ended up in a corner office where they sat on the couch and chairs that were near a wall of windows that looked toward the harbor. It was a million-dollar view, but Michael didn't think this man, this pudgy, short little man before him, had any need for such grandeur. Michael's book sat on the coffee table between them. It looked well-worn, as if it had been read several times.

"Let me just start out by saying that I'm a big fan," Richard said. "Our entire world has become so unrecognizable, and I'm all about returning to family values. I know of the work you do behind the scenes with *The T Society*. Aside from book promotion, I just want to know how I can help you."

Michael liked the humble honesty.

He leaned close as if he were listening intently, pushed his glasses with clear lenses up his nose with his middle finger and said, "Well, Richard, there is something I could use your help with. I'm in Vancouver to see my wife."

Chapter Thirty-Three
(Maggie)

Maggie took a deep breath on Tuesday morning as she looked at the appliances on her desk. Then she shook her head and smiled.

The butcher knives were still on the credenza next to her windows, as were the kitchen tools she had investigated. Today, it was all about the larger tools, the choppers. Well, Cuisinart wasn't going to have to worry. They were safe in the market, just for their sturdiness alone, not to mention the way they cut vegetables.

GreatChef's *Veggie Cut N Go* had mauled the vegetables in the office kitchen a few minutes earlier. It was a total loss. She had hoped a side benefit of these machines might be a crudité snack platter that she could make for her coworkers right before lunch. They started to accept her a bit more, and food tended to be a great equalizer. But those dreams of a little surprise snack were gone. She wondered what she would do with all the dill dip she made for the occasion.

She painstakingly cleaned everything, only to watch the *Veggie Cut N Go* mutilate carrots, cucumbers, celery, and squash in a matter of seconds. It was so bad that after she had taken photos of the carnage, she had tossed the bruised and battered vegetables in the garbage can. No one wanted to eat something that looked pre-digested. At least she saved the garnish, the cherry tomatoes.

She sat staring at the machine and wondered if it presented a risk to any of the women or men who chose to operate it. There were a lot of spinning blades. She was really worried the whole machine might break apart. She didn't, couldn't, think of the children. They might be maimed for life. For a moment, she worried that she might be maimed for life if she kept trying to use it.

Initially doubting herself, she read the directions again. Unfortunately, or perhaps fortunately, she had done everything correctly. Right as she was folding up the directions, Henry stuck his head in her partly open doorway, smiled, and asked, "Do you have any lunch plans?"

She was hoping he'd drop by and see her. They had rarely been apart since that Saturday night when he learned to make beef bourguignon. Aside from getting clothes from his condo, he basically never left. He spent last Sunday showing her around Vancouver. And last night, he'd taken her to his favorite restaurant in the Gaslight District.

She'd read about love bombing, which concerned her. It was what Michael had done to her in the beginning. It involved over-the-top affection and attention to influence her. It was very clear now that it had been Michael's goal, so she was very sensitive to it. But with Henry, the thing was, she could tell it was honest and real. She didn't feel crowded or like she didn't have any time to herself, far from it. They had silences where one of them read a book, called someone, or even paid bills. There were comfortable, normal silences. And they didn't agree on everything. But they agreed on the things that mattered. They had the same values, goals, and morals. That meant something.

"I hope we are going somewhere to eat," she said and smiled. "I'm starved."

He stepped into her office and shut the door. She stood, and he opened his arms to her. She went into them willingly. They didn't kiss; they just held each other. She sank into his arms and felt safe, as if all was right with the world.

"I need to say something," he said seriously. It gave Maggie a bit of a chill, but considering all that she had been through, she knew that whatever it was, she could deal with it.

She stepped back and met his eyes, which had become very serious. "Okay," she said.

"I know it has only been a few days, but I feel like we've known each other for a very long time."

"I do, too."

"I don't think we are moving too fast. I think it is more that I found you after a very long search."

She couldn't speak, so she nodded, feeling tears tickling the corners of her eyes. He kissed her then, softly, and pulled her close once again.

"I can't wait for the end of the day when I get to hold you," he said.

"I can think of nowhere else I'd like to be."

He leaned against her, and she sighed at the feel of him in her arms.

She couldn't look at him as she said her next words. "You know, we have leftover spaghetti from last night. It would be quite tasty for lunch should we be so inclined to leave downtown and stop by home."

He whispered playfully, "Are you suggesting we drive to your condo, maybe take a little nap, and then eat cold spaghetti for lunch? Then we could come back to the office as if nothing happened?"

"Well, I don't know...it was just a thought...but I should tell you, I'm not tired."

"That's fantastic. Because I'm not tired, but I still want the nap. If we can't sleep, we will have to think of something to do. Come on, let's go."

Maggie grabbed her purse and followed Henry into the hallway. Did her coworkers know about her evolving relationship with the managing partner? Had Henry told anyone? She didn't care.

They walked quickly down a long hall, through the lobby, and to the elevator.

Behind them, another door opened. Rick and Dr. Drake stepped into the hallway. Their current business was finished with plans ready to be executed in the future. He hadn't mentioned that Margaret worked in Richards's office, but he was about to. Right on cue, something happened.

A fleeing couple that was ahead of them and didn't see them practically ran down the hallway. It answered all of Michael's questions. He tried not to look interested, but how could he not be? That was his wife!

He stared at her back as she and some tall man hurriedly made their way through the lobby and disappeared.

"That's our managing partner, Henry Hudson. I would introduce you, but it looks like he is in a rush to get somewhere with our intern," Richard said.

"He looks weak. I hate weak men," Michael said contemplatively.

He'd found Margaret.

It appeared that she hadn't taken her vows seriously enough and was two-timing him with another man. Well, he'd put a stop to that. "And by the way, I know that intern. She's my wife. Her name is Margaret."

CHAPTER THIRTY-FOUR
(Amber)

Amber was so conscientious about her well-thought-out plan that she worried with the angst of a teenager hoping to get a little action on Prom night. When whatever she planned was showing signs of actual execution, or there was a tangible end result, Amber remained calm. Her blood pressure would drop, and her heart rate would stabilize. But leading up to that moment, she was a ball of nerves. She just hoped she wasn't sensing something. After her stint as Madam Emma the psychic and Tarot card reader when she owned *Madam Emma's Love Emporium*, she never quite discounted her intuition as she once had.

When she handed off the tainted sinus wash to Neil, who was then going to give it to Miss Violet, Amber was nervous. There were so many ways this could go wrong, from Neil making it to Portland and meeting Miss Violet to Miss Violet needing to break into Michael's hotel room unseen and switching out his sinus wash for the tainted wash. What if she had the wrong brand? What if someone got caught? What if the wash wasn't powerful enough? During her last season in Yachats a couple of years earlier, when she'd first met Miss Violet, she was plagued with overly potent mixtures. Hadn't Amber, then named Emma, killed someone she only meant to make sick? That was on her. Sure, she was going to eventually kill him, but not the way she wanted to, not in her living room where the man had dropped off his chair and slid to the floor.

She shuddered at the memory. She'd had to get rid of the

body. That was not her thing. It was too close for comfort. That time, she could have gotten caught. She still had nightmares with the police pulling up to the abandoned cliff right as she rolled the body into The Pacific.

And now here she was... Amber didn't like endangering other people or asking for help. She usually did her own work, but this was a special circumstance, and she needed to be far away when Dr. Drake took his last breath of air. Michael was her brother-in-law. When the police figured out what caused his death, there would be an investigation. She, Jack, and Maggie had to be untouchable.

Amber stood at the window in the twin's upstairs bedroom and watched as the garbage man slowly lumbered around their cul-de-sac.

Finally, the truck stopped in front of their house, raised their can, and dumped the contents into the back of the garbage truck. The automatic arms slowly lowered the can back to the ground.

Amber gently bounced a happy Libby, who was still wiping the sleep away. She smiled at her beautiful, perfect baby. The evidence of what she'd used to make her capsicum oil was now swimming around with other neighborhood detritus. Heck, she'd even bagged it in the neighbors' preferred garbage bags to further push suspicion away from their house. Although, let's be real. How many people would question the remains of pepper? Well, she had used several dozen Scotch Bonnets for their slight fruitiness and ghost peppers to push the heat from unbearable to fatal. She was most proud of her utensils. She'd bought most of the things she needed, the knives, the cutting boards, etc., at Goodwill. She'd worn a disguise, of course, but oh my, the trace DNA it might have added...delicious. And when she finished with the tools she needed, they all went into a twenty-four-hour donation bin.

Her gloves and protective clothing had found their way into a

THE VOICE OF REASON

garbage can just outside a very popular Walmart. She thought of how she had once thought Cayenne pepper was hot. Cayenne next to Scotch Bonnets was the equivalent of crayons next to spray paint.

Jack came up behind her and wrapped his arms around her and baby Libby. He was dressed for the office, but he always made sure to kiss everyone before he left for work, including the dog, which Amber loved.

"A penny for your thoughts, Mrs. Daniels."

She turned to him with a worried look on her face.

"I have a bad feeling about this, but I'm trying to shake it," she admitted.

The sweetness between them vanished. Jack's brow furrowed as the conversation turned serious.

"Normal anxiety or something else?" He had seen her in this situation before. But this time, she shook her head and looked at Libby.

"It is going to be okay," he said, trying to reassure her.

"Too many moving parts. Maybe we should just have invited him for dinner and slipped him some capsicum and made sure he didn't have his EpiPen."

He pulled her tightly to him, then gently stroked the baby's head.

"Maybe you are too close to this one because it's Maggie. I could never have been civil to him. I don't think you could have been either. Or maybe all the angst is because others are taking care of business for you. You are relying on friends. You like to do it yourself, and I respect that. It doesn't make you any less of who you are because other people are doing the dirty work."

"I feel like I'm letting everyone down."

"Darling, none of this would be in motion if you hadn't planned it."

"I just need to believe that."

"What can I do?" he asked.

"That's just it. I don't know if there is anything you can do."

"Last night, you mentioned the house needed a little look over."

"Since you mentioned it, we have some work to do around here," she murmured as he nodded. "We need to make sure that none of my special supplies are visible. We've looked to secure the space because of the babies. We just need to do that again."

"That we can do," he said.

She would need to go through the house and make sure it told the story she wanted the police to know.

"May I ask you a question? It's kinda creepy," he said.

"By all means, that sounds kind of delicious."

"Do you get a natural high when you know it has worked?"

"You know I do."

He nodded, "I'm sorry. What I should have asked was, once Michael is dead, will you get a bit of a high from it?"

"I'm not sure. I won't be there to see it."

"I understand," he said and kissed her on the cheek.

Getting a bit of a high…did that make her a monster? Maybe. But when it was done, she didn't feel bad.

Did she really think the police would come for a visit? Maggie was going through a divorce. Jack was representing her, and Michael was high profile, even if he was a jerk. The happy couple wasn't all that happy behind closed doors. Yes, the police would come. She and Jack needed to be ready for them when they did show up.

The red padlocked box, the safe, everything needed to be put in order. Tax returns and jewelry needed to be placed in the safe as decoys. All the tools of her trade needed to go, which included her special tea made of hemlock and foxgloves. She was out of the mad honey the bees made several years earlier. Miss Violet liked it when there was a problem to take care of.

"Miss Violet is calling at two, noon her time, so we can finalize everything."

"Good, you'll feel better after talking to her," Jack said.

"I hope so," she said and held Libby tighter.

At precisely two that afternoon, Amber was in the greenhouse repotting several orchids, having rinsed their roots to rid them of mineral salts that naturally build up and hurt the plant. It was a monthly labor of love that she had down to a science. Each week, she had fifteen pots to flush on rotation that eventually got to all sixty of her plants of cattleya, phalaenopsis, and lady slipper orchids. Yes, she'd chosen the easy orchids, but she had her eyes on some cymbidiums if only she could get them to blossom in Minnesota. She might take them skiing or just find a high elevation, leave them overnight, and pick them up the next day. It was an idea she hadn't completely abandoned.

Her Miss Violet burner phone rang from its special drawer inside her workstation in the greenhouse.

Amber answered before the second ring. "Hello."

"Hello, darling. Isn't that boy a cutie?"

She was obviously talking about Neil. This was good. The handoff had happened.

"I've always thought so," Amber answered happily.

"Listen, kid, we have a bit of a change."

The unease settled over Amber. Something was wrong. Damn it, she hated being right. Was the entire plan ruined?

"Our friend has changed his schedule."

"Is he coming to the city of roses?" Amber asked, trying to tamp down her panic.

"Yes, but I heard he is delaying for a few days to visit close friends up north."

"How up north?" Amber asked, heart in her chest.

"Exactly," Miss Violet replied. "Vancouver."

"He knows," Amber whispered.

"If he doesn't, he's in search mode."

"Shit," Amber whispered. Maggie didn't know.

"You took the fucking word right out of my mouth."

. . .

Jack pulled into the garage fifteen minutes later, and Amber met him.

"I'm sorry," she said.

"No problem, and you shouldn't be. I was going to work from home this afternoon anyway. I've been trying her, and there is no answer," he was nervous, his shaky voice giving him away.

Jack's hand trembled as he tried Maggie's cell and then her office. "Where the hell is she?" he asked Amber, who stood nervously by and waited.

"Call Henry," Amber said.

"I'm already dialing," he said. "Aw shit, voicemail...come on...come on.... Finally...Hey, Henry, it's Jack. We heard that Maggie's deranged asshole of a husband is in Vancouver looking for her. His name is Dr. Michael Allan Drake, and before you wonder, yes, he is the famous marriage counselor you've seen on TV. Listen, I don't know how to say this. He's dangerous, and he has hurt Maggie in the past. Please, please look out for my little sister."

After he hung up, he pulled Amber close and held her to him.

CHAPTER THIRTY-FIVE
(Henry)

Henry glanced down at his cell phone as he returned to his office. Crap, he had nine calls to return. He flipped over to his voicemail when Rick stepped into his office. Henry tossed the phone on his desk and looked up at the other man without seeing who called.

"Did you have a nice lunch?" Rick asked sarcastically with a knowing glance.

"I take it that you saw me leave with Maggie, and you don't approve for some reason that you are about to tell me."

Rick shook his head and looked at the wall before meeting Henry's gaze.

"She's a married woman. That I know," Rick said.

"Really? Did she tell you all about it?"

"No, but I heard rumors that she is here, deciding whether or not she should get a divorce. I don't know if you should muddy the water. There is also the fact that you are her boss and that this whole thing feels a bit rash."

"Her past is her business. And for the record, this isn't rash," Henry said. "I met her maybe ten years ago through her brother, and I've never quite forgotten it."

"More reasons for you to be careful. You have history with her family."

"I intend to talk to her brother about it at the earliest opportunity," Henry said.

"Well, let me know when I need to contact our attorneys to

keep from getting brought up on charges involving the Canada Labour Code or heck, maybe the lawyers need to look into what it takes to get a visa extension," Rick said sarcastically.

Henry smiled, looked down at his desk, and said, "Well, thank you for being so on top of it. I highly doubt she will consider suing for sexual harassment."

"You know that I always protect the company, first and foremost," Rick said. "She is a threat."

Henry held up his arms in a "who cares" gesture and said, "No, she's not. She is getting divorced."

"Well, you don't want to get in the middle of that. She isn't using you to live in our beautiful country, is she?"

"Rick, take it down a notch," Henry said, the smile falling from his face as he tried to keep his composure in check. "Change of subject. How was your new client meeting today?"

"Fabulous. He's a very nice guy. An author named—"

The noise of someone running down the hall had them both turning to the open door.

A very distraught, panicked-looking Maggie appeared at Henry's doorway, silencing Rick. Both men focused on her as Henry asked, "Maggie, what is wrong?"

"I left my phone on my desk. I never do things like that. It is so stupid..."

"It is okay. What happened?" Henry asked, keeping his voice low and slow.

"It is my crazy ex-husband. He is in Vancouver. I've got to leave. I've got to hide before he finds me—before he punishes me. Before he kills me..."

"Maggie, take a minute. Tell us what happened," Henry ordered.

"My brother called me. When I didn't pick up, he left a few voicemails. Jack said that he knew that my ex was supposed to be in Portland today, but he decided to drive north to find me. It is that damn Tile he had in my handbag. He figured out where I am. I'm not safe."

Rick asked skeptically, "Come on. Is he really that dangerous?"

"Yes, I don't have time to explain, but believe me, he's psychotic. I'm scared to death of him," Maggie said. "He's a monster."

Henry stood, crossed to her, and took her in his arms. "I'm here, Rick's here, nothing is going to happen to you."

"You don't understand. You'll think he is charming, but he isn't. He's a monster. What if he has a gun and comes in here? You can't defend me then."

"Good point. We need to let security know. Do you have a photo of him?"

"Yes, I put one on my burner just in case."

"We will lock the front door and call in Bethany from the front desk and make sure she has the photo," Henry said.

Still with an arm around Maggie, Henry picked up his desk phone and instructed the receptionist to lock the front door and come to his office. Rick just leaned against Henry's desk with his arms folded in front of him.

Before long, Bethany appeared, looking nervous.

"Don't worry, everything is fine. But we have a bit of a situation here. Maggie's soon-to-be ex-husband has found out she is in Vancouver and might come here to harass her."

"Harass?" Maggie asked. "He's dangerous. I don't know what he will do."

"I'm sorry. He put her through hell. We don't know what he might do next. I think we should all be concerned that he might show up here. Maggie has a picture to show you."

"Here," Maggie said, holding out her shaking hand with the burner phone in it.

Henry glanced at the photo as Maggie passed it to Bethany. He said, "He looks familiar, but I don't know why."

Bethany's eyes grew wide as she looked first at Maggie and then at Rick. Then she said words that cut the air like a knife.

"He was here this morning. He had an appointment with Rick. I think he said his name was Dr. Drake."

"The marriage counselor guy?" Henry asked as he looked pointedly at Rick.

All eyes immediately focused on Rick, who held out his arms and said, "There must be some mistake. The man I met this morning wasn't an abuser. He was a soft-spoken gentleman. We talked about Canadian promotion for his book tour."

"You were married to Dr. Drake. Wow," Bethany said.

"He's a monster," Maggie whispered.

"Maggie, if he is here for you, it says more about what you might have done to him than what he did to you. He is a very nice man. I really liked him," Rick said, drawing stares from the others in the room.

"Rick, you need to shut the fuck up," Henry censored.

Maggie rounded the desk and approached Rick. She had a height advantage, so she towered over him, met his gaze, and said, "You have no idea how cruel he can be. You have no idea how it felt to go to sleep and not know if he would kill me in the night because he threatened to. You have no idea what it is like to live under his roof, under his rules. I'll never forget the torture if I made a mistake and violated a rule. It is men like you who don't believe a woman when she comes to you. You totally discount what it takes for me to admit my husband, my famous, infamous husband, isn't the wonderful man you expect him to be. Maybe you'll tell me that you believe me, but we know that down deep, you just don't think it is true."

Rick said, "Margaret—"

Maggie gasped.

"Do not speak," Maggie said, holding up her hand to stop Rick. Then she pulled up her skirt, and both men saw the jagged scar on her thigh. Henry had seen it before. It was one of those times when she hadn't gotten away from Michael. She told Henry about it when they'd spent that first night together, but it hadn't prepared him for the reality. Each time he saw it, it still bothered him, making him grit his teeth for the pain she had suffered.

She fought with her husband; only in response to her words, Michael escalated the fight. He'd grabbed a knife from the butcher block in their kitchen. What had she said when she told him about it? Never bring your words to a knife fight unless you are holding a gun.

"Your *gentleman* did this to me," she said. Then she ordered, "Look at it. It represents his rage. I should have left him then. But when he started telling me that he wanted to kill me, I believed him."

She turned to face Henry again.

"I'm sorry, but I need to go," she said.

"You aren't going alone," Henry said, scooping up his phone with one hand and her hand with the other as they walked toward his office door.

Bethany, who was still standing there wide-eyed and a bit frightened, looked like a deer in the headlights waiting for instruction.

"Have building security come up here," Henry instructed her. We need them to walk us to my car across the street. Call them now. Go!"

Bethany nodded and left, running down the hall to her receptionist's desk.

Henry turned to Rick and said, "I reluctantly say this. You are in charge. We are leaving. But when I get back, we need to have a serious conversation about your loyalty and future at this company."

"Come on, Henry, you have to know my loyalty is to you and our company," Rick said unconvincingly, "I didn't know that he hurt her. It changes my opinion of him."

"I don't believe you," Maggie said.

Henry stepped close to Rick. "If I find out you have any further communication with him, it won't be good for you. Do we have an understanding?"

"We will go to your place first," Henry said after the security guards walked them to Henry's car without incident. "He won't think to look for you there for another couple of hours. I doubt he is lying in wait. Then we drive to my place so I can pack a bag."

"Then what?" she asked as they drove out of the parking garage.

"I was thinking that we could go to my cabin at Whistler."

"You have a cabin in Whistler?"

"I like to ski in the winter months. Kayak in the summer around the lakes."

"Are you sure you want to be with me? I really don't know what he is capable of. You could just drive me to the airport."

He turned his head, looked her in the eye, and said, "I don't trust him not to think of looking for you there as you buy a ticket to Minneapolis. Let's get out of town and think it through. We are in this together."

CHAPTER THIRTY-SIX
(Henry)

Henry called Jack as they drove to their condos and again from the road as they made their way to Henry's cabin at Whistler.

"Henry," Jack said when he answered the phone. "What is happening?"

"We packed a couple of bags and are now going to my cabin."

"Are you making sure you weren't followed? I wouldn't put anything past him. He's dangerous."

"Yes, I took some time in the city, making turns that no one could follow. And I have more to tell you. He was in the office this morning visiting one of the partners on the premise of promotional help for his book tour of Canada, which will commence after he finishes up in his tour in the States."

"Holy shit," Jack said.

"Exactly," Henry said. "He never saw Maggie, but it was close."

"So I'm not being paranoid. He's there."

"Most definitely," Henry confirmed.

"Should we come up? I don't think you have enough for the police, but I might be able to show them our legal issues, and maybe that would make a difference to them. They enforce Temporary Restraining Orders in Canada, but there is a process that takes time."

"I just want to get Maggie someplace safe and away from him. The office, her condo, well, none of it feels safe at the moment. I have a little cabin in the gated community of Pinecrest. It is a little south of Whistler, but very few people know about it. I figure we will stay there for a few days. From what Maggie found through internet searches, he has to get back on his book tour in two days. Once he is gone, then I think Maggie should consider going back to Minneapolis."

"Definitely if he chooses to resume the book tour," Jack said.

"If what you and Maggie said rings true, I don't think we can count on anything that is logical."

"You're correct," Jack said. "Listen, Amber wants to talk to Maggie. Are you on speaker?"

"We are both here, Jack," Maggie said.

"Okay, we've got you on speaker, too," Jack said.

"Maggie?" Amber asked.

"I'm here, Amber."

"You be careful. I don't trust him. If he comes for you and you need to defend yourself, try to kill him. I mean it, don't just try to injure him. Take him out. Go for mid-chest and stomach if you can get to a knife or anything sharp. Don't underestimate just hitting him over the head. Use anything you can get your hands on, anything can be used as a weapon if you have the confidence to use it. It is self-defense. He is frightening and violating multiple restraining orders."

"I hear what you're saying," Maggie said.

"I wish we were there. It would take us at least a four-hour flight and a two-hour drive to get to where you are, so I need to know you can defend yourself," Amber said.

"I wish I had a gun," Maggie said. "But, seriously, you don't need to come here. I don't think Henry will let me out of his sight."

"I won't," Henry murmured.

"If it would make you feel better, we will come," Amber said.

"Not necessary yet."

"Okay, Mags, don't forget we are here for you. I'll give you back to Jack."

"Thank you, Henry, this is above and beyond," Jack said.

"No, it isn't. I like your sister, Jack," Henry said as he glanced at Maggie. "I mean, I really care for your sister. My feeling are only going to get stronger."

"Interesting," Jack said.

"Mind-blowing and a surprise, but I thought you should know."

"I trust you, Henry. Don't give me a reason not to."

"I won't," Henry said.

After a few more back and fourths, they ended the call with promises to stay in touch.

Henry said tentatively to Maggie, "Um, your sister-in-law…"

"Is damn scary."

"Yeah."

Silence.

Then Maggie said, "You told them about us."

"They will find out eventually. This is important, Maggie. I'm not going anywhere."

"Good," she murmured and placed her hand on his thigh.

They drove mostly in silence for a few minutes. Henry felt the glances Maggie would make in his direction.

Finally, he said, "It is so strange. I've heard of Dr. Drake. I've heard him speak, but I've never liked him. I thought he was pompous and full of crap. I couldn't believe how popular he was for nothing."

"Good," she said. "I don't think I could be with you if you liked him."

"I always thought there was something off about him," Henry said.

"He's evil, and it was just getting worse."

"Why would he come here? Why would he want to be

anywhere near you? You could ruin him with everything you have on him. A smart person would be far, far away."

"He thinks I'll get over it. Maybe I've had a mental break with reality. He cannot believe that I would leave him for being an abusive asshole. He probably wants to plead his case—because I'm so horrible, he had to do what he did. He needs to save face."

"He's such a classic abuser. Whenever or whatever you want to tell me...I'm here. You won't scare me away. I just can't believe anyone would raise a hand or speak to you in the way that he did."

She turned and looked at him for a long minute before she answered. "He was big on punishment. I think he's probably got a lot of notes on how he'd like to punish me for what he thinks I've done. It was kind of his thing, making lists with a broken rule and the resulting punishment. Write it all down so he wouldn't forget any of it. One bad meal could result in a whole legal pad page of notes. It was only a matter of time until he killed me. He told me when he punished me that he was sorry I made him do it. He said it was hard not to do more to me because I deserved so much more."

"I can't believe someone would treat someone they supposedly loved like that."

"I still can't believe I got out. I escaped. And when I think of all the rule violations he has probably attributed to my escape, well...it will be a long list."

"I don't know what to say. You survived, and you are never going back," Henry said as he pulled her hand to his lips and gently kissed it.

"It wasn't easy," she murmured.

When they were only a few minutes away from the cabin, Henry stopped at a small grocer where they got provisions, and then Henry called in a to-go order to a little diner where they got burgers, fries and milkshakes, which were ready when they finished grocery shopping.

"I'm going to step out on a limb here. I bet you aren't hungry."

"Bingo," she said with a small smile.

"I'm not going to force you to eat the best cheeseburger and shake you'll ever have, but I hope you will try them," he said as he placed the order of food in the back seat and handed her a milkshake.

"I'll try it for you."

"Thank you. Now, don't get your hopes up. This little cabin isn't much, but I like it."

"I don't care, as long as it has running water. See, I don't even need electricity?"

"It has electricity and a very nice bathroom. Remind me to turn on the hot tub so it will be warm for us tonight."

"It has a hot tub?"

"Well, yes."

"Is it outside?"

"Yes. Oh, damn. I take it we won't be using it."

"No," she said.

"I'm sorry, I need to start thinking a bit more cautiously. There is a very nice fireplace inside. We can cuddle up in front of that."

"Despite the circumstances, this place sounds kind of romantic."

"A little side benefit. I was going to suggest that we go there for a weekend, but this opportunity came up faster. I hope it won't ruin your perception of it."

"Nice spin, you are really kind to me," she said. "I'm sorry to have drug you into this."

"There is no place I'd rather be."

CHAPTER THIRTY-SEVEN
(Dr. Michael Allan Drake)

Michael had a second double Canadian Club whiskey on the rocks in the dimly lit bar just two blocks from Margaret's 'office,' where she played dress up, the ungrateful little bitch. *I mean, let's be real,* he thought. *She wasn't smart enough to have any real job that required critical thinking. And she was sleeping with someone else?* It wasn't hard to come to that conclusion after what he'd witnessed. She always was a bit of a whore, loose and wanton. But for her to have sexual relations with another man while married to him? That was unforgivable. That part of her belonged to him and him alone. Her punishment for breaking that vow would have to be something unusual and fitting. He'd have to think on that for a bit.

He glanced at his watch, almost 3 pm. He had some time to kill. He wanted to be near Margaret's office parking garage to follow her back to her condo. When asked about Margaret, Richard was a fountain of information. He mentioned the condo neighborhood where he thought she lived, helpful little disciple that he was. It was a good connection, what he had with Richard, but seriously, the man was so narcissistic...jeez. Michael wanted to show him his place as a disciple, but he couldn't, not while he still needed the man to be congenial. Richard would know his place in time.

As for Margaret, it wouldn't be hard to spot her new car. She would have Minnesota plates on whatever car she drove. There was nothing wrong with the car she traded in except her delusions of grandeur, wanting something else. He'd have to punish her for that, too. She was making it so easy. It was like taking candy from a baby. He wondered if she had a BMW. She always wanted one, like a child hoping for a special gift at Christmas. It would be easy to pop over and check it out. Heck, he might even hide in the parking garage. His car was there too.

He paid his check and gave neither a good nor a bad tip, just a little something in the middle to not be memorable. And he paid with the funny Canadian money. He heard it smelled like maple. It couldn't be true, but he held the money up to his nose, yes it did. It was faint, but it was there. The money had a whiff of maple to it, curious...

It was when he was on the sidewalk in front of the bar that his phone buzzed. It was, of course, the burner. He didn't need anyone tracking his activity in Canada.

Looking down at it, he smiled. Well, well, well, wasn't Richard being obedient? Good, he was starting to know his place.

He took the call, standing taller, putting out his chest as he answered with a curt, "Dr. Drake, here."

"Hello, sir, it is Richard Fields. I have some news for you about your wife, Maggie...Margaret. I wanted to call you a few minutes earlier, but I had clients our stupid receptionist put in my office."

Michael did not care about Richard's lack of ability to get done what needed to be done. He was an incredibly weak person.

Enough of the damn small talk.

"Tell me," Michael ordered.

"Well, Margaret and Henry have been warned that you are in the area. Margaret appears to be very scared of you."

As she should be, Michael thought.

"Henry showed your photo to our stupid receptionist. It was obvious that she knew something. Then she admitted you'd been in the office to see me. When Henry turned his questions to me, I told him part of what we discussed. Your book tour in Canada. Nothing else was mentioned. Henry is a good guy, but he isn't the kind of man who would be good for the movement."

"I'm glad you recognize his flaws," Michael said. Maybe there was an inkling of hope for Richard yet. As for Margaret's Sidepiece, he was a dead man walking...

"But Margaret freaked out, went full-blown scared, weak female, and said she was leaving Vancouver. She totally wasn't thinking and wasn't in her right mind. She has Henry dick-whipped because he said he'd go with her. He blew off his years at the company and his loyalty to us in a matter of seconds. It was rather a disgusting display."

"Did they actually leave?" Michael asked. Why was he hearing this now? He had a feeling it happened earlier.

"Here is the thing, I didn't know where they were going, then I remembered something. It was something that all the partners agreed on. We can track each other's cell phones. Henry might have left an hour ago, but I just used the app on my phone, and I know where he is going. It will be easy for you to find them."

"I wish you'd told me the minute he'd gone," Michael stated.

"It really wasn't that long. I heard Henry mention that they would go to their mutual residences and then head out. Here's the thing, he's headed to a bit of an isolated location. I didn't want them to see you going all Cape Fear on them. Better you arrive when they think they are comfortable."

He had a point, but Michael did not want to give it to him. Still, there had been an opportunity to re-acquire Margaret, and he missed it. Well, he wouldn't be so clueless next time.

"Where is he going?"

CHAPTER THIRTY-EIGHT
(Amber)

Wicca meowed. Jack swore. Amber cried. They were all in the living room of their Minneapolis home, feeling helpless and worried.

Amber was not used to feeling like a weak female, waiting for other things to happen.

Amber dabbed at her eyes as she paced. "I should have predicted this. The moment Maggie heard the chime on her Tile, we should have told her to come home. I should be there for her. Hell, I feel worse since we talked to her. She and Henry don't know how to deal with this. Psychotics are my specialty. I should have prepared her for this. She's family. I'm worried they are way out of their league. What if she is in danger, and I do nothing to stop it?"

Jack immediately stopped swearing when one of the babies in his arms mimicked him and almost perfected the art of saying, "Motherfucker." His wife didn't need any additional stress.

The animals, Wicca and Pumpkin, watched Amber pace, as did Jack. At the sound of Clay's attempt at swearing, Amber stopped, and Jack cringed as she said, "Jack, for freakin' sake, if that kid starts calling me his mommyfreaker, you're not going to wake up one morning."

Knowing the woman she was, the threat had a certain ring of truth to it.

"I'm sorry, honey," Jack murmured, sitting a little taller on the couch and getting a look on his face that could be considered fearful. He was a powerful man in his own right, but he knew better than to cross his wife. Was he scared of her? Yeah, a little bit.

Amber noticed the fear on her husband's face, the love of her life. Her savior. She sighed. She hadn't meant to do that. She didn't want to make it worse, and she had done just that. Jeez, she couldn't even kid about murder. She should know better. He'd seen things. Things she wasn't proud of.

"I'm sorry, I didn't mean it. I'm just stressed. I'm too madly in love with you to ever harm a hair on your head, you know that. I was trying to sound like I was kidding. But it came out wrong."

"I know that," he said, nodding unconvincingly. "It is just that I respect who you are. I respect your talent because you are good at it. And I love you, too."

Amber sat next to him on the couch as Libby climbed from Jack to Amber's lap. Leaning close, she kissed Jack. Then she held her baby close and murmured words of love to her. Pumpkin, feeling left out, nuzzled at Amber's hand.

"I love you too, my pumpkin-spiced Weimaraner."

"Aw, Pumpkin. Don't listen to Mommy. She's upset, and you're a regal Vizsla."

Amber grimaced, "How could this have happened? Why didn't I take care of Michael when he was still in Minneapolis? Now the plan is screwed. Everything is screwed."

"You didn't because it would not have been safe. You taught me to be careful. Now, I'll tell you, you need to be careful. We have too much to lose. He will be dealt with. It just might not be the way you planned. I have faith in Miss Violet to see this through. The plan is solid."

She kissed him again, lingering a bit longer than before, and said, "You're right."

He gently ran a palm over her skin. "You still have your original plan, but how can we modify it for these unforeseen issues? Or can Miss Violet do it on her own?"

"I don't know, but if Michael ever comes back to the United States, specifically Portland, we will execute the original plan. But strangely, I wish we made the plan for Vancouver and not Portland. However, if Miss V goes up there, there is a record at the border. She can't go. Henry and Maggie are alone. And from the sound of them, there isn't a mean bone in either of their bodies."

"Henry is no shrinking violet, but he is a good guy."

"But Michael fights dirty."

"And Henry doesn't, but he might if the circumstances warrant it."

Amber turned and met her husband's eye. "That is bad."

"Should we go to Vancouver?" he asked.

"I don't know," she said and shook her head. In her short but dangerous life, she had never experienced anything like this before.

Chapter Thirty-Nine
(Maggie)

From the central console of his car, Henry pulled out a garage door opener as they drove through a gate that announced *Pinecrest*, and then he clipped it to his visor. They entered a heavily wooded neighborhood that was shadowy and had narrow streets filled with a mixture of cabins and nice, high-end houses set off the street among the edge of the forest.

Although she couldn't see inside, Maggie was able to see the cars parked in several of the driveways. Audis, Volvos, and Lexuses seemed to dominate the neighborhood. It confirmed what she suspected: this was a higher-end resort community. It reminded her a bit of Black Butte or Sunriver around Bend in Oregon where they used to spend a week each summer as kids. All the properties had a certain level of privacy, and the dwellings themselves were very expensive. People didn't have a lawn. They had trees and views.

It was still light, early spring making everything lush and green, but there was a decidedly cool feeling about the neighborhood as if the forest was enveloping them and spring had not quite reached this deeply quiet place.

"My cabin isn't fancy, but I think you will like it," Henry said. "It is cozy in that I wanted it to be comfortable, not necessarily a cabin that might be featured in Architectural Digest. It is one of the smaller properties on the street."

"It is far away from my soon-to-be ex. That is all that matters. I'm...well... a little in shock that he showed up today.

It is very brazen. I should have told you who he really is. I'm sorry. It is just that people won't believe he is capable of such things. There are women who write him love letters. You should read what they say and what they offer. It is absolutely ridiculous. They don't know how lucky they are not to be with him. He's dangerous, but I'm not sure if it is to everyone or just me."

"Either way, it doesn't matter. It is unacceptable. It is mind-boggling, but then I know there is a lot we don't see when it comes to celebrities."

"You believe me, don't you?"

"Yes, Maggie, of course," he said, glancing her way. "Never, ever worry about that. I could hear the fear in your brother's voice, and when you arrived in Vancouver, you were shell-shocked. You were scared of your own shadow. You've come a long way in a short amount of time. I just hope he never has such power over you again. But today, I saw your fear firsthand."

She shook her head. "I don't know if we did the right thing. We just fled a very populated area to a less populated area. Maybe I should have stayed and waited. Eventually, we have to have a face-off. I can't have him chasing me my whole life."

"Remember, something made you drive to another country to stay away from him. Don't forget that. It is one of those stupid comments. *See what I do, not necessarily what I say.* You were terrified today. Your first instinct was to run. You need to pay attention to that because I am. Our basic instincts are rarely wrong."

She listened and decided to change the subject. "You are right, thank you. Now, I need a distraction. Tell me more about the cabin. This is a really pretty area. How long have you had it?"

"I've been coming here since I was a little kid. It was one of my parents' favorite places, but we always camped in a tent and had an outdoor fireplace as in a firepit. It was fun. We roasted marshmallows and had flame-grilled burgers, you know the drill. We even went to the diner for dinner one of the nights we were here. It was a big treat when I was a kid. But a few years of that, you learn to appreciate the finer things like hot water, showers, and a real bed. Because despite what avid outdoor people always say, the ground is not soft. And I don't like bugs. Bugs crawl on the ground. You're on the ground, and bugs crawl on you."

"I don't like bugs, either," she said.

She sucked on her chocolate milkshake and thought about him as a small child. She would have to ask to see a picture. She bet he was very cute.

He was right. The milkshake was going down smoothly. It was thick and heavily laden with ice cream, chocolate, and cream, if she wasn't mistaken.

"I'd always get the same thing I ordered today," he said. "There is comfort in that."

"We need a little stability right about now," she said.

"I bought this place for myself right after my divorce. Most people buy sports cars, maybe get a much younger girlfriend, or dye their hair. I bought a cabin in a resort area. My ex-wife didn't like it up here."

"It's beautiful. You made the right choice. Just in case I didn't say it earlier, I mean this when I say it. Thank you for doing this for me. I don't know what I would have done. I guess I would have probably just finished packing up and driven to the border. Maybe I'd have gotten as far as Bellingham tonight, but I'd be leaving you...I don't know if I could have done it. I'm sorry, I don't want to scare you, but I'm feeling something I don't know if I've felt before."

He grabbed her hand with the hand that wasn't on the steering wheel and pulled it to his lips, where he kissed it and said, "I know, I feel it too. I see something here that has been missing from my life. Now, let's look at a few things. First, I feel a strong need to protect you. That isn't going to change. I know how fresh this relationship is. I know that lots of people would just say it is infatuation, but that isn't it, Maggie. This...I don't know if I've ever felt this way before. I can't be without you. I don't want to be without you. I don't think I could bear it."

"Good," she said, "I don't know how it happened. I mean, I'm going through a divorce, not that my relationship felt like a marriage. I'm terrified of him. How can I even look at another man? I don't know, but you are different. I care more about you...possibly than I ever cared for him. Does that make any sense? Or does that make me sound incredibly shallow?"

"No, that just makes me incredibly lucky."

"How did this happen so fast?" she asked.

"I don't know, but I'm happy it did."

"Me too."

He pulled into the driveway of a modest-looking house with a newer metal roof, looked around suspiciously, and as the garage door rose, he broke his concentration and kissed her quickly.

After they'd pulled into the garage, he shut the door behind them, and then they got out of the car.

Henry opened the door to the kitchen and disengaged the alarm.

Maggie stepped inside and shivered. It might be spring, and it was close to summer, but the heat wasn't on in the cabin. And she wasn't dressed for an evening at the base of the mountains.

Henry moved around quickly, turning on the breakers on the circuit breaker box for hot water and then stacking firewood next to the fireplace. It was a small cabin, just one bedroom. The stone fireplace dominated everything. She loved it.

They were hidden in the trees. She liked being hidden. She didn't like wondering what might be in the forest watching them. It didn't appear that the cabin had many curtains. A quick check of the bedroom assured her they wouldn't be seen in there. It was the only room with curtains. She needed to calm down her thoughts. They were safe. Michael didn't know where they were.

"Are those kayaks that I see?" She asked, pointing out the window.

"Yes, we are close to Alpha, Pinecrest, and Retta Lakes. Retta is about a seven-minute walk. If I really wanted to get out, Daisy Lake is about a five-minute drive. I used to like to row for exercise, so I've tried them all. At the time I first bought the cabin, I was just upset, and it was a way to get out a lot of aggression after my divorce. When winter comes, the skiing is amazing."

"If we weren't hiding from Michael, I'd suggest we see them all," Maggie said as the doubts crept in. "But I don't trust he won't find out about where we are."

"I think we are pretty safe," he said.

Maggie shook her head, "That is exactly why we aren't. We can't have a false sense of security here. Michael is angrier than he's ever been at me. One time, he threw a glass bottle of olive oil at my head because I left a wadded-up paper towel on the drainboard in the kitchen. Garbage wasn't supposed to be left in the kitchen. It was filth and was supposed to be removed immediately. I'd had a lapse that day, I guess. I remember I was trying to perfect a shrimp curry dish, and I was excited about it. It was one of the few times perfecting a recipe was exciting for me, not stressful. But the prep was messy. The bottle smashed against the wall behind me. I had to clean it up because I'd violated a rule. The olive oil was just punishment for what I'd done. He explained he'd had to do it. I'd made him do it. But all I could think was that if I hadn't ducked, it would have hit my face. My face would have stopped a glass bottle. I wonder if it would have broken. The least it would have done was hurt. It probably would have cut me."

"That is all kinds of fucked up. You know that, right?" Henry asked, surprising her by swearing, pausing as he sat with her on bar stools by the small kitchen area and unwrapped their cheeseburgers.

"Yes, of course, and that was just a soiled towel. I've left him, ruined his reputation as a marriage counselor. I'm with another man, and I'm divorcing him. You think he might be angrier this time?"

"Yes, when you put it like that. I hadn't thought about it, actually."

She shook her head and said, "Unfortunately, you have to. We need to think like him in order to be safe."

"I don't know if I can. People in my life have never been like that. I…I believe you, but to believe that someone would treat their wife that way… It doesn't come easy for me."

"I just don't want you to think of me differently," she said.

"I think you are brave. Braver than anyone else I know."

"I stayed with him for too long," she admitted.

"You did a lot of things right. You didn't have children. You didn't endanger them. You left when you could, not next year or twenty years from now. You left a few weeks ago. Be proud. That wasn't a marriage. That was a prison."

"Thank you," she said quietly. "The idea of what marriage would be like and what it was…the reality of life with Michael… that reality…it did not come easy for me. I was so stupid. I thought we'd have a marriage like my parents. I thought there would be mutual respect and caring. I was naïve."

She took a bite of her cheeseburger but didn't really taste it.

"How was he when you were dating?" He asked.

"Wonderful, happy, fun-loving. But the courtship was fast, six months. Too fast. But about day two of the honeymoon, I felt that first inkling of concern. All of a sudden, he was drinking much more. Everything I did was wrong. Even the way I walked, dressed, or spoke. I've heard such things described as a light switch being flipped. It was like that. I wondered if he was having second thoughts about marrying me. It was so much worse than that. The spider had caught the little ladybug in his web."

Henry shook his head.

"I figured we were probably the most unhappy honeymooners that ever existed."

"Honeymoons aren't supposed to be like that," Henry said. "They are supposed to be one of the best parts of your marriage. Husbands, they aren't supposed to be like that."

"I know. This time that you and I have spent together, although it has only been a few precious days, has meant more to me than any of the best moments that I spent with my ex-husband. And I think all of those happy times with Michael, well, they were before we were married."

As they sat beside each other, he asked, "Was he ever nice to you after you were married?"

"I think there were moments, but the trust was broken. I feared him, so I didn't trust him. One day he complimented me on something, and then he had an issue with my shoes in the closet. Then it became personal, about my personality and my behavior. Why was I always so loud and obnoxious? Why was I so stupid? He thought he married a smart woman. Why did I always want to see my family? Why did we always have to go there for the holidays?"

"He was trying to isolate you from your family," Henry observed.

"We would be out for dinner, and I'd ask them to leave cilantro off my Mexican food, and he'd make the same request. I'd ask him why, and he said if I had to be difficult, he could be too, although he loved cilantro. I'm allergic to it, but he didn't care. It was just a way to make me feel bad about ordering something the way I liked it. I should conform to his likes and dislikes. I shouldn't rock the boat. And then later he could complain about that because I had to have it a special way that it took from his pleasure. It started not to make sense. Then came the punishment."

Henry reached out, but she didn't meet him halfway. She didn't want to be touched, not while she was talking about this.

She nodded, not able to meet his eyes. "The physical stuff, it started with little things, a critical word, a shove, a punch to the wall by my head. Then, when it wasn't enough for him, he threw things at me. And if he hit me with a book or a shampoo bottle or anything nearby that he could get his hands on, he'd smile and tell me he wished I wouldn't make him mad. When I was no longer scared of objects, he moved on to things like knives."

"Like the scar on your leg?"

"Cloaked as an accident, but not really. As he said, it was my fault. He never would have done it if I hadn't moved into the blade. Funny thing, I don't think it bothered him at all to cut me with the knife. And how messed up is this little added piece: he wanted my sympathy after he saw the blood and got scared of it."

"And we asked you to work on the *GreatChef* knife campaign," he said, shaking his head.

"I think of it as de-sensitizing me. It did a good job of that," she said, then pulled her purse close and pulled out a *GreatChef* knife with a pink ceramic handle. There was a safety sleeve in matching pink on the blade, but it still looked lethal. "I keep it with me always."

Henry looked from the knife to her and back to the knife. "Actually, considering the story you just told me and that neither one of us has a gun, I'm glad you have that. Do you have another in that big handbag?"

She shook her head, dropped the knife back into her purse, and grabbed her burger. "No, but I noticed a few in the block on the counter. You know, this really is a good cheeseburger."

CHAPTER FORTY

(Dr. Michael Allan Drake)

Michael parked the SUV three blocks from the address he received from Richard. He hoped the SUV that he was borrowing would not stand out. It had Washington State license plates. The street seemed a little desolate except for the rube resident he followed through the open gate to the community, who just let him in. The ability to break through one layer of security seemed like a good omen.

It was twilight, and he hadn't decided what to do in regard to Margaret, although he thought about it the entire drive up because his mind kept wandering. Damn, the scenery and his troubled mind. He used to be quite impulsive, but space and time matured him into knowing it was best to have a clear head and a plan when dealing with something that really, really was upsetting.

He wasn't going to pull into the Sidepiece's driveway and demand that Margaret get in the car and disappear with him into the night. First, she wouldn't do it because somewhere along the line, she stopped obeying him, and secondly, she couldn't listen for shit. Besides, there was potentially a hostile witness involved. After all, he could not control the actions of others. He could only guide them to better solutions. What if the Sidepiece guy decided to get involved? What if he had some sort of delusion when it came to Margaret? Would Michael offer the man advice? He was a man, so Michael could be generous…

to start. But the Sidepiece was guilty of having carnal relations with Margaret, and that cut deep.

Michael was too angry to think about what she had done with the other man. It proved his point. She was but a common whore. There was a lot there to look at, to examine and dissect. But he could do that over time. He prioritized and put his pain over what she had done. He would simply move it to the back of his brain in the short term. Now, it was about getting her back. What she had done, well, they had a lifetime to go over every little detail of that. She had years to make it up to him.

He shook his head at how far they had fallen. It was unbelievable. He was so glad his mother would not be aware of this because of her dementia. Why was his mother, a once vibrant, smart woman, afflicted with such a curse? Margaret was a waste of space. Why couldn't it have been her?

His mother called it before they had even gotten married. He was humble enough of a son to admit when he'd gotten it wrong. He owed his mother her due. She never liked Margaret and didn't think Margaret had what it took to make a difference. She'd been right. He'd learned his best life lessons from Mother, who raised him as a single mother after his father died. Her guidance molded him into the man he was today.

Margaret always called his corrections, which led to better solutions, punishment. Well, she didn't have the mental depth to understand that there was a method that she chose to ignore, to be disrespectful of…

He sighed. She just didn't get it. Margaret just wasn't smart enough. She didn't respect him. He was the head of the household. Part of Margaret's job in life was to be his mate and make his life easier. When they got married, the minister hadn't said "Woman and Husband." Nope. He'd said, "Man and Wife." Duh! He had thought that was clear. What? Did she need it written down for her?

He had a feeling Margaret wasn't going to come back from

this disobedience easily. Well, why would she? She had a hard time grasping the good things in her life. He could admit that her little escape act surprised him. Such insolence after all he'd done for her! There were a thousand women who would trade places with her. Didn't she realize how lucky she was?

He sighed again. He wondered for the hundredth time if he really wanted her back. He'd put years into her education, and he wanted to prove to the world that it meant something. Obviously, he needed to amp up her discipline. He hadn't been hard enough, and this was the result.

Hell, he knew the press would crucify him if the divorce went through. Margaret always created drama like a petulant child. It was always something. How often had he said, "You should look in the mirror, but you can't stand to look at yourself, can you?" She always had the stupid indignation to look offended. That and the crying. Damn, was she emotional! He pulled the polaroids from a pocket on the duffle he'd brought. Photos of Margaret crying. How she could work it! She looked so overwrought. What a little actress!

The bottom line was this: they had been through a lot together. He just needed to tweak her education and her discipline. Then she would finally be the woman he deserved. He didn't want to start over with someone else. The very idea was exhausting.

Maybe it was time to think of the other sordid business because shoving it to the back of his brain wasn't working. She had cheated on him. She had sex with another man. Okay, he should have anticipated that she would degenerate into a whore, but what was the path back? Another man living on this planet who knew what it was like to be inside his wife?

"No, no, no!" he shouted, hitting the steering wheel with his fist.

He wasn't sure that he could live with that, knowing another man had carnal knowledge of his wife. Michael opened the glove box and got out a long butcher knife from the butcher block at home. The exact knife he'd used on Margaret when he ended up slashing her leg because she couldn't sit still. It was a simple direction, and she ignored it, causing the injury. He hadn't meant to do that. It was too visual. And it marred the perfection of her smooth skin. He'd wanted to cut her where the scar wouldn't show so easily, but she'd messed that up too, denying her punishment and his pleasure.

It was strange that you could get a knife through customs at the Canadian border but not a gun. To Michael, knives were much more interesting. He'd had more practice. That might be one way to take care of her wife's adulterous affair. Eliminate the competition, as it were...

CHAPTER FORTY-ONE
(Maggie)

A fire in the fireplace always scared Maggie a little bit. Maybe it was the way Michael built a fire. The way he used the poker. She just hoped he'd never have a reason to turn the red hot poker on her. On nights when she displeased him, and he built a fire, she stayed in an opposite room of the house. Did that mean he couldn't heat up a poker and chase her around the house? No. But she would hear him coming, and that gave her a chance to escape. To run. To hide. To avoid being branded.

"How about a fire in the fireplace?" Henry asked after they finished their dinner.

Maggie couldn't speak for a moment.

"Maggie? Are you okay?" He asked, concerned.

"I'm sorry, I'm fine. Sure, a fire would be nice, but when it gets too dark, I hope you won't mind, but I want to move into the bedroom where there are shades. I don't want someone looking in the windows from outside."

"I will never discourage you from suggesting going into the bedroom. At best, we might end up naked. At worst, I get to hold you as we sleep."

She smiled. She couldn't help it. He did that to her.

She watched him build the fire, putting in paper on the bottom to build the heat, then the kindling and logs. Then he sat with her on the couch and pulled her into his arms. It had been a long time since she enjoyed a fire without fear. And having the room only lit by the firelight almost made her forget why they were there.

"Does Rick know where this place is?" she asked.

"No, he knows I have a place up here, but we are business associates, not really friends. He has some different philosophies than I do, and he is very religious. We struggle to find common ground. I've never invited his family to join me here."

A trickle of unease crawled up her neck. "I sensed that, but could you expand a little? What kind of different philosophies?"

"He's very conservative. He is the head of the house. His wife stays at home. He's old school. Not that there is anything wrong with that, but I prefer partnerships. I've told him more than once that our office is not moral ground zero. The receptionist is good, and I don't care if she has pink hair. I don't care if the creative team smokes pot on the weekends as long as they don't smoke it in the office and do good work."

"No wonder he liked Michael. Michael is very well-liked by this group of whackos named *The T Society*—"

"The Traditionalists of Society?" Henry asked.

The chill became much worse, all her nerve endings jerking alive.

"You've heard of it? *The T Society?*" she asked, her voice a little ominous in the fluttering light.

"Yes, Rick once tried to recruit me, and I laughed at him."

She nodded. "They are some of Michael's biggest supporters. I'm very scared of them. I had no idea about Rick. I didn't know he was one of those…people."

"It has caused some tension due to Rick trying to recruit inside the office. We had to shut that down, and I think it pissed him off, but I didn't care."

"Rick wouldn't tell Michael about your cabin, would he?" she asked.

"No, I don't think he would. I mean, he doesn't know where it is exactly."

THE VOICE OF REASON

Maggie pulled back to look at him. "Okay, now I'm concerned."

"Look, even if he guessed I'd bring you here, he has never been here, and there are something like three thousand vacation homes in the Whistler area. He wouldn't know how to find this place. I'm not listed in the phone book, and the property is under a primary corporation I put together because I thought about using it as a rental. Those primary corporations are like LLCs in the United States. Besides, the car is in the garage, so if he were looking for that, he wouldn't find it."

"What are we going to do?" she asked, the reality of just how trapped she was starting to take hold of her.

"Have you thought of doing an interview with the press? Ask Jack, but I think it is your next step."

"That is an intriguing idea."

They sat in silence for the next few minutes and contemplated the day.

When Maggie's eyelids were too heavy to keep them open, she said, "I'm so tired. I think it is time for bed."

Henry stood and pulled her off the couch and into his arms. She sank into his familiar warmth and sighed. How was she going to be safe? And how could she keep him safe?

CHAPTER FORTY-TWO
(Maggie)

Maggie didn't sleep well despite having Henry spoon her throughout the night. At one point, when the clock next to the bed read 2:30 a.m., she kissed him awake, and they made quiet love in the dark room. It was slow and easy, that kind of waking from one dream into another. It had been lovely, soft, slow, and very intimate. Even though they hadn't been making love for very long, they brought out the best in each other. They had from the start. And despite that first time when she doubted herself, she was blossoming when it came to this man's gentle touch and loving way.

She slipped out of bed with the early morning light, wrapped herself in one of the terrycloth robes from the closet, and went into the main room. It was foggy, almost misty, and she felt both hidden and exposed at the same time.

Finding all the things she needed, she made coffee, waiting quietly for it to percolate, her eyes gazing out the window as she waited. What did she expect to see? Michael leering in? Maybe Henry was right. Maybe he had no idea where they were. Unfortunately, she was just insecure enough not to believe in luck.

Henry quietly entered the room, wearing a matching terrycloth robe to hers. He said nothing but pulled her into his arms, where he rocked her, the only sound being the coffee in the background as it dripped slowly into the pot.

He whispered in her ear, "I love waking up to you."

She snuggled against him and said, "I could get used to this."

"Me too," he said as he kissed her temple.

She stepped away just to pour coffee into two mugs. They held hands as they quietly drank their coffee.

"What should we do today?" he asked.

"I think we should call Jack and Amber and strategize. Amber always has good ideas. It makes me wonder what she did before she got together with Jack."

"I think that is a good idea. I need to call a couple of clients and reschedule appointments. Then we will call them."

She dropped her head and then quietly said, "I've been thinking. Maybe you should drive me to the airport in Vancouver, and I should fly home to Minneapolis today. That way, your life can get back to normal."

He started shaking his head before she got the entire statement out.

"Maggie, I don't want to be away from you," he said, setting down his coffee, taking her mug, setting it on the counter next to his, and then pulling her close. "If you go back to Minneapolis, I have to go with you."

"Thank you, but—" she said. "Wait, do you think you can protect me?"

"Maybe, maybe I'd want to try. But mostly, I don't want to think of you, out there, alone. I just…can't."

"Thank you," she said. She had been alone for so long, the idea that she wasn't… She couldn't believe it.

They stayed in each other's embrace until the coffee got cold.

"I can be done with the calls in half an hour, then we can call Jack and Amber, okay?"

"Okay," she said.

"Then how about a drive around Whistler?"

She looked up at him. "I don't know if that is a good idea to go driving around Whistler."

THE VOICE OF REASON

"Okay, we can stay in today. Lay low. And when we find out that Michael is back in the US, then we take a day or two to sightsee. Okay?"

"Okay," she murmured.

"I got breakfast stuff, so why don't I make us something?"

She nodded. "That sounds good, but I don't know how hungry I am."

"You need to eat something."

"You're right."

"And if you keep talking about leaving, I'm going to mark you as a flight risk and not take my eyes off you. That means you'd have to take a shower with me."

She looked up at him. "Showering with you would be fun, but breakfast first, then we call Jack and Amber, okay?"

"Okay," he said.

They ate a veggie omelet in companionable silence until he observed, "I don't think you got a lot of sleep last night."

"How could you tell?" she asked.

"Because I didn't sleep well either. I kept waking up, and every time I did, you were awake. How are you this morning?"

"I'm scared. I don't know what he is capable of. I think he is looking for me, maybe us. I don't know what to do."

He set down his coffee cup. "Okay, how could he find us? Let's talk it through. It is probably a good idea before we talk to Jack and Amber anyway."

After the purse incident, she purchased an electronic bug detector. She ran it over everything in her luggage. Last night, they ran the device around under Henry's car and luggage. Henry lay on the floor of the garage and shined a flashlight under the car. They found nothing.

"We checked for bugs last night," she said.

"Yes," he said.

"Michael doesn't know my new phone. So, he can't track me on that."

"No," he said, but she could tell something had come to mind. He shook his head, but there was something he wasn't telling her.

"What is it?" she asked.

"It is something you said. I'm sure it is nothing to worry about," he said.

"But it is something," she replied.

"Okay, it is something, but I'm not worried."

"Tell me," she ordered.

"My cell phone can be tracked. All the partners agreed it was a good idea to be able to find each other when we upgraded our phones about a year and a half ago. I forgot that he has that ability. I'm sure he has too."

"Oh crap," she said. "Do you trust Rick not to look or not to share? I think he showed a certain loyalty to Michael yesterday that I keep reflecting on, and it is bothering me."

A concerned look crossed Henry's face. "Look, I've got a bit more to tell you. Last night, I googled The Traditionalists of Society and Vancouver, BC."

"And?" she asked.

"Rick is very involved. He's the vice president of the Vancouver chapter."

"Oh shit," she said.

He reached into his robe pocket, pulled out the cell, and put it on the counter. He pulled up a shared location device and turned it off. Then he put the phone on airplane mode.

"I should have done that last night."

"Yes. In fact, I have a feeling we are too late. If Rick is loyal to Michael, he has already shared our location," she said as the blood drained out of her face.

"I'm so sorry. This isn't a chance I want to take, especially if Rick has lined up with like-minded cronies," he said and turned off the phone.

"Now, what do we do?"

"I have several ideas, but I think they can wait until we are dressed. Come on, let's take a quick shower. Then we need to put our stuff in the car and leave."

Fifteen minutes later, everything was in the car. Five minutes after that, the cabin was secured, and they were in the car.

Henry had backed into the garage the night before, and Maggie was happy for the extra detail that he told her was called Combat Parking.

"Are you ready?" he asked, and she nodded, slipping down in her seat. When she was practically scrunched in the foot well, he covered her with a blanket.

"How is this?" she asked.

"Good, stay down," he said as he opened the garage door.

She heard the garage door lumber open, and from a corner opening in the blanket, she could see Henry's face, tense and alert.

"What do you see?" she asked as outside light flooded the car.

"Everything looks normal," he said as he slowly pulled forward and shut the garage door behind him.

Maggie was quiet as she watched Henry from where she crouched in the wheel well. He fumbled with his sunglasses and looked stressed. She felt bad for being responsible.

"How is everything?" she asked.

"Tell you in a minute," he said.

"You see something," she said.

"Yes," he said and then didn't say. "But it is okay."

The silence built in the car. She could feel the speed build as he got out of the subdivision. He adjusted the mirror, and she knew he was looking to see if they were followed.

"Tell me," she said.

"Okay, there was a black Escalade parked along the street by the cottage. It was in front of my next-door neighbor's house. I don't know if it is anything, but it had Washington State license plates. Help me to remember this." He then rattled off the plate to her.

She fumbled in her handbag, found a scrap of paper, and wrote it down.

"Got it," she said.

"I don't know if it is anything, but I know those neighbors. They are from Vancouver. And they don't rent out their cabin."

"Crap. Okay…okay," she said, her breath labored. "What now?"

"Damn it. Maggie, are you okay?" Henry asked.

"I'm just a little freaked out."

"Me too, but we are okay. Do you have your passport?"

"Yes," she said. "Do you want me to go to Minneapolis?"

"We are going to Minneapolis."

CHAPTER FORTY-THREE
(Dr. Michael Allan Drake)

Michael slept in his car like a barbarian. He was stiff, needed a shower, and really needed to brush his teeth. He didn't want to think about the other bodily needs he had. It was so common. And he was hungry. What other basic human weaknesses would he discover?

He had dozed off sometime around five that morning. He was in a luxury car, but it didn't mean it was comfortable. He'd had tent experiences as a Boy Scout that were better. Well, he was no Boy Scout now.

The night was awful. Sometime after midnight, when he was sure Margaret wouldn't suspect it, he had crept up to the cabin, the one where Margaret was staying with her little pansy boyfriend, the Sidepiece.

He'd looked into the living room through the window. They'd had a fire earlier in the night, and now there were dying embers in the fireplace, but the room was empty. There was also a trash can in the kitchen. One of those trendy tall ones with a lid. They were obvious slobs. Monsters. Not that it surprised him, knowing Margaret.

He moved quietly to the back of the house to what he thought was probably a bedroom, but the windows had curtains, so he couldn't see a thing. But he knew she was there. He could feel her. There was a wall between them, but she was only a few feet away. He definitely could feel her.

Now, this morning, he barely had a chance to duck down

when the Sidepiece drove his car out of the driveway and passed right by him. By the time he decided it was safe to sit up and started following the Sidepiece, he was overwhelmed by another idea. Margaret was probably alone in the cabin. Not that he was worried about this other guy, but why make the odds harder? He liked to have an advantage.

He grabbed the knife from the glove box, left the car, and slowly retraced his steps from the night before. A moment later, he was on the porch, the knife in his right hand, ready to strike or at least threaten. Whatever he felt in the moment. He knocked boldly on the door with his left hand. If this went how he was predicting, he'd reaquire Margaret easily and be on his way south in a matter of moments.

He tried to relax his jaw. He was so angry with her that he was scowling and trembling with rage.

He had to be careful. She wasn't worth a stroke.

He raised his fist again and pounded on the cabin door. As he waited for her to open it, he felt his anger surge. Maybe he'd drop the knife and just strangle her. That would be highly satisfying and much less messy.

It was a new idea, but not necessarily bad. He kind of liked the simplicity. Deal with her and be done. It would silence her and keep her from ruining his reputation.

There was water everywhere. He could hide her body in the woods and later tonight come back and toss her in the water. It was midweek. It wasn't like there were a lot of tourists around.

But the limp dick boyfriend, the Sidepiece, he'd be back. And what if he called the police? What if they pulled together a search party and found Margaret's body before he had a chance to toss it in the water?

Well, that would kind of suck.

He could hide her in the Escalade until it was dark, and then he could toss her in the water. Now that was an idea with some legs.

CHAPTER FORTY-FOUR
(Maggie)

"What about your job and the *GreatChef* account?" Maggie asked from the depths of the foot well.

"I hardly care about either at the moment," Henry said.

"Are you sure you want to do this?"

"Completely," he said, as he drove. "I think you can sit up now. We weren't followed."

Two hours later, Henry parked in long-term parking. A few minutes later, he bought tickets to Minneapolis and checked their bags. Thankfully, she'd remembered the knife in her purse. Henry took it and placed it in the bag he was checking in for the flight.

"That should make security much easier," he said with a wink.

Maggie felt shellshocked but just nodded and showed her passport when asked.

"Let's go to a gift shop and get a few books and magazines for the flight," he suggested when they had boarding passes in hand. "Maybe buy a touristy tote bag to haul it in."

"Okay," she said a little dreamily.

"Maggie, honey," he said, grabbing her hands in his larger ones, making sure that she was looking at him as he added, "It is going to be okay."

It was hard to believe him.

"I hope so. You know I don't have a home back in Minneapolis. I'm so nomadic. I feel at a loss."

"Jack and Amber seem very happy to have us stay with them. I'd go as far as to say they really didn't give us a choice. Besides, I want to meet Amber. She sounds kind of interesting and scary." They called the couple on their way from Whistler.

"She is really nice, but you sense there is more there than meets the eye."

Their flight was calm, and they spoke little, Maggie leaning against Henry.

"I wish we were flying off someplace else, like Fiji," she commented.

"Would you like to go to Fiji?" he asked.

"I really don't care where we go, as long as we go together," she said and felt a little shy for saying what was in her heart.

"I wish I'd gotten to know you the first time we met. I don't think it is too late, but I'm sad for the time we didn't get."

She smiled and leaned into him as she murmured, "Quality, not quantity."

Jack found them in baggage claim. He hugged Maggie for a long time and then gave Henry a brotherly hug.

They recounted their last day, and then Henry described the car he'd seen that morning.

"Do you have the license plate?"

"Yeah, but isn't it illegal to find out the owner?" Maggie asked.

"I have some connections," Jack said. He and Henry seemed to share a nod.

Amber greeted them the moment they stepped into their house in Minneapolis. She hugged Maggie for a long time.

"It is going to be okay," she said, focusing on Maggie. Then she turned to Henry, "It is so nice to meet you."

After the smiles and hugs, which included meeting Libby and Clay, Wicca and Pumpkin, they retired into the living room for cocktails.

"We ran away," Maggie said.

"It was a good idea. I think he is imploding, and I wouldn't trust him as far as I could throw him," Jack said.

"Some of the stories I've heard—" Henry said, shaking his head.

"I know it sounds unbelievable," Maggie said.

"It doesn't. I'm 100% on your side. I just can't believe someone who loved you would do that," Henry said.

"That isn't love," Amber said.

When it came time for bed, Maggie was a little worried about the sleeping arrangements. There was no way she would do anything other than sleep in the guest room bed, hopefully with Henry. She didn't want to upset her brother and sister-in-law. Ironically, when it came time for bed, nothing was discussed or mentioned. Henry just followed her into the guest room, and they fell asleep in each other's arms. The last thought Maggie had was that they must approve of her match with Henry. And that made her feel good.

CHAPTER FORTY-FIVE
(Dr. Michael Allan Drake)

Michael had to thank his new little *T Soldier*, Richard. He'd been dead on about the address of the cabin in Whistler and now Margaret's condo in Vancouver. His information was not just deemed reliable; it was almost guaranteed.

The cheap lock to his wife's apartment gave way easily, and after three shoves, he was inside the space.

He took a breath as he looked around. The bitch fled Canada with her Sidepiece yesterday. Richard knew that much. Heck, Richard had actually been resourceful by tracking Henry's company credit card activity online and then shared it with Michael. They had hopped on a plane, which meant she must have been hiding in the car that fled, driven by the Sidepiece yesterday.

The rage he felt at missing her led him to where he now was.

Michael had an idea where they were going, but at the moment, he didn't care. He was much more interested in discovering who his wayward wife had morphed into. Being in her space was far more interesting. He'd catch up with her later.

But predictably, he was disgusted by what he found inside her space. It only made his anger ratchet up a notch. Her closet was full of cheap clothes and pair after pair of shoes. Having left his knife in the Escalade, he found what he was looking for in her kitchen: a cheap knife with the brand name *GreatChef*. It felt like a toy in his hand and had a pink handle. WTF? It barely cut.

He used it in the closet to slash every piece of clothing he did not approve of, which happened to be every piece.

Damn, he was getting a headache from shaking his head. Who was she? Who had he been married to? He didn't recognize this woman.

Looking at the bed, he could almost see her in it fornicating with the Sidepiece. The projected scene made him angry. He plunged the knife into one of the pillows, or should he correct that phrase, he tried to plunge his knife into one of the pillows. It took several tries before the knife cut the pillowcase and plunged into the pillow. It finally gave way under his forceful guidance. He moved the pillow against the knife, and the end result was a feather explosion. That was more like it. He went back to the living room and treated some of that oversized, calming beige and aqua furniture to the same fate the pillow endured. Reducing things made for comfort to tattered ribbons had the desired effect. It gave him a deep sense of comfort and release. He could only imagine how he would feel when he reacquired Margaret. He really hadn't decided what to do with her when she was back. He had options, anything from sending her to be rehabilitated at an institution to sending her permanently to hell…the world was his oyster.

Back in the kitchen, the contents of the refrigerator were dumped on the kitchen floor. A lot of this food would make her fat. Hadn't he talked to her at least a dozen times about her weight? She had a garbage can. He might as well help her use it. He enjoyed shattering the dishes one by one. It was harder than it looked. When he punished her for chipping a plate in the past, he was justified. She must have really been careless to let that happen.

Most of the pots and pans were metal, and the best he could do was use them as weapons against things like artwork and hanging sconces that were not to his liking. There was, however, one clay pot that appeared fragile. He hurled it as far as he could from the entryway to the kitchen.

It sailed through the air and seemed to enjoy the experience before it bounced off the living room wall and fell to the ground with a telltale shatter. The sound it made was lovely. She wouldn't be making anything in that again.

In the bathroom, he found several tubes of whore red lipstick still in their little boxes. Exactly the kind of thing he banned her from using. Well, wasn't she the rebellious one? That ended now.

He returned to the bedroom and pulled the lid off the lipstick. A moment later, he wrote "Whore" in big letters on the bed. That felt so good, that he decided to try how it would feel to write it on a wall. That felt so good too, so he wrote it wherever he could on the walls, on the mirror, on the closet door, until he'd run out of lipstick. He returned to the bathroom, got another tube, and continued on with his work until he ran out of lipstick. Now, she'd understand how he really felt about her.

Deal with that, you ungrateful bitch…

And when he'd done all he could do, he left quietly, making sure not to encounter any of the neighbors.

CHAPTER FORTY-SIX
(Maggie)

Maggie made breakfast for everyone on the third day of their stay in Minneapolis. As a special treat, she made her famous praline French toast that she knew Jack loved, as their mother used to make it.

"Okay, this is heaven on a plate," Amber said. "I have the recipe, but mine never turns out this well."

"I've been making it since I was twelve, so it is kind of old hat to me. I don't even use a recipe," Maggie said.

"I always have issues with the praline," Amber said.

"Does it separate?" Maggie asked.

"Yes," Amber said, nodding. "That is exactly what happens."

"Your heat might be too high. Cook it lower and slower, no problem," Maggie said.

Amber gave her a little hug and thanked her for the tip.

Henry, who was sitting at the table, was examining his phone, lifted his head when Jack entered the room.

Jack picked up on Henry's pointed interest and asked, "What happened?" Drawing the attention of Maggie and Amber.

"Dr. Asshole returned to his book tour in the United States. He is in Seattle for two days, then onto Portland."

"Good, then we can go back," Maggie said.

"As long as he stays in the United States," Jack said.

"I have a few things to do in Vancouver, like deal with Rick," Henry said. "I don't like the idea of him being in charge. He isn't loyal to us any longer. I need to remove him. And I want to amp up security until I feel comfortable."

"I'm sorry it has come to this, but that is a good idea," Amber said quietly.

"I prefer to know who he really is than have him hide it. Sad but now we know. We also need to worry about the Canadian book tour he was planning for the madman," Henry said.

"All this to consider. I don't know when I will stop looking over my shoulder," Maggie said.

"I think something will give. I want you to stay vigilant for a few months," Jack said.

"Actually, she shouldn't let her guard down ever," Amber said. "It is, unfortunately, the world we live in."

"I'm concerned. I think when we get back, we should move you into my condo," Henry said.

Maggie nodded. She didn't want this constant fear, but this was her life now. She wanted to move in with Henry because he wanted to be with her romantically. Unfortunately, this move was a tactical decision. It had nothing at all to do with romance.

"I'd feel better about her safety if she was with you," Jack said.

Amber looked thoughtfully at them and nodded.

Maggie didn't take offense that they were talking about her if she wasn't there. She took this to mean that they all approved of her relationship with Henry.

They flew back to Vancouver that evening. And since it was Sunday, the airport was relatively busy.

Despite what they had been through, Maggie didn't think it was over with Michael. It was a dark foreboding she did not share with anyone. She remembered the way Michael would look at her and then punish her over the tiniest infraction. What they had just been through was not tiny. His rage must be epic. There was no way he would let this go. She just wondered what she could say to convince Henry that things weren't as positive as they might feel. This kind of fear and self-preservation didn't come easily.

Michael lost the battle of facing off with her in Vancouver, but he was far from losing the war. It took her a moment to realize that Henry was speaking to her.

"...get the car, drive to your place, start packing, and then we go to my condo. Does that sound okay to you?"

"Yes, yes, that sounds great," she said as they walked through the Vancouver airport.

Maggie kept a watch on their surroundings as they got the luggage, made their way to parking, and then drove despite Henry's assurances that they were not being followed.

Before long, they pulled into the parking lot of her rental condo and parked close to her front door. With an air of caution, they observed their surroundings as they approached her front door.

"Something is wrong," she said as she examined her front door. It wasn't locked, and the locking mechanism looked strange.

"I'm calling the police," Henry whispered as they retreated back to his car.

A few minutes later, they watched from Henry's locked car as one of the police officers who responded drew his weapon and gently pushed open the door, proving that the lock was, indeed, broken.

After what felt like an eternity, the police officer re-emerged with a serious look on his face as he walked to Henry's side of the car. Henry rolled down the window at his approach.

"It is bad. Your condo has been vandalized. Whoever did it, I think, was more interested in sending you a message than robbing the place," the police officer said.

"May I go look?" she asked the officer.

"I'd rather you let the crime techs photograph it first. They are on their way. Then you can tell us if anything is missing. A lot has been destroyed. The furniture and your clothing have been slashed. The person then took what appears to be your lipstick and wrote things on the walls, your sheets, etc."

They told him about her connection to Dr. Michael Allan Drake. The officer seemed taken aback but then said, "I've always thought the ones that have advice for others are the most messed up of them all."

There was a lot of chatter about Michael. A copy of the restraining order was produced. A report was filled out. The fact he hadn't done this in the United States would prove a problem. The least they could do was document the destruction and wait for the protocols to fall into place.

Three hours later, the crime scene techs had come and gone. They didn't find any fingerprints other than hers and Henry's. Walking through her little condo, Maggie felt the tears prick at her eyes. Michael found a way, yet again, to try and shatter her happiness. He had done this. She knew it, but she also knew he was in another country now. Based on how the food had rotted on the floor of the kitchen, it had been done several days earlier. The entire space felt touched by evil.

Maggie was numb. They were back in Henry's condo, but she hadn't remembered the short drive or even walking inside.

Henry long ago placed a mug of something warm into her hand. She grasped it tightly to her, but it was cold now. It smelled warm and appealing, but she had no idea what it was. She barely remembered him doing it. Nor had she remembered the blanket he placed around her shoulders. Had he sat next to her and put his arm around her shoulders? She thought so, but then everything since she had a look inside at the condo and witnessed the destruction firsthand had been a daze. She didn't even know the cup was in her hand until Henry removed it and asked her a question.

She glanced up from where she watched planes land on the water of Stanley Harbour, which was almost hypnotic, and said, "I'm sorry. What did you say?"

"I made a few phone calls. The owner of the condo was very decent. He called his insurance company, and they sent in a crew to start cleaning up the damage. However, I doubt you will get your cleaning deposit back. If anything of yours can be saved, they will do it."

"I'll have to get some new clothes, shoes, and more lipstick, which is too bad because I really liked my new stuff," she said as tears ran down her cheeks. "I'm so sorry I involved you in this."

Henry shook his head and smiled sadly as he said, "Maggie, darling, I'm here because I want to be. I want you to understand that we are in this together. Tomorrow afternoon, we will go shopping, okay? It hasn't been that long since you bought some of the things. Maybe they can be replaced."

His words did not convince her as she looked up from the window, met his eyes, and said, "What if Michael never stops?"

"Then we will stop him. Heck, the file the police are building on him is getting thicker by the minute. Your brother is keeping everyone informed. This isn't the end; it is the beginning of the end for him."

"What about his followers like Rick?"

"I will tell you my thoughts. I'm not going to sugarcoat this. We need to be careful of them. I know this is overwhelming, but we will find a way. Maybe we should go to Fiji for a month or two."

"This is the best thing you've said yet. I still can't believe Rick is involved."

"I will take care of Rick when I get back to the office tomorrow."

"I know that you and Rick go back a long way. What are you

going to do exactly?" she asked, wrinkling her nose. What could he do? Rick was a partner, and they had no real proof he'd tried to help *The Voice of Reason*. But how could Michael have known any of this without Rick's help?

"Rick is going to be bought out of the company and then shown the door. One of the phone calls I made was to my uncle, Theo Graystone. He and my aunt are in Scotland. They love to travel. He retired three years ago and made me a senior partner. He still shows up occasionally, but I'm basically in charge. I was added to the company after I graduated from Northwestern and proved myself. The contract we all signed is pretty straightforward, but there is a little something in the contract that I insisted on to make sure that control stays in the family. Theo liked it, Rick resented it and me for creating it. It was possibly foreshadowing. We might all be partners, but the company started as a family business, and I always wanted to make sure that I had a way out if I needed it."

"I bet you never thought you'd need it," she said.

"I prefer to keep an exit handy," he said. "I explained everything to Theo during the call, and he agreed with me."

The next morning, they cautiously went to the office. But instead of parking in their normal parking garage, Henry went to a different parking structure a couple of blocks away.

"Your sister-in-law, Amber, gave me a lecture about randomness. She made a good argument. I liked it," he said by way of explanation.

At the airport, Maggie ran her little electronic device over and under the car. Finding nothing, she repeated the process before they went to the office that morning.

"Why do you look so skeptical?" he asked.

"I just don't trust it," she said. "I still feel like we need to be concerned."

"I think your gut is right. I think we do."

Once in the office, Maggie was aware of the new security

team that flanked the front door. She didn't know what Henry said to them, but it was clear to her that they responded to her as if she was the VIP in the situation, and that they only worked for the two of them. Henry told her that Rick didn't have authority over them, and that was very okay with her.

CHAPTER FORTY-SEVEN
(Henry)

After Henry settled into his office, he called Rick to join him.

Rick was more than a little annoyed before Henry even started speaking, so Henry decided to let him speak first. He felt Rick was playing a good offense game, but Henry was about to put him on defense.

"I can't believe you just left like that. Clients are angry. Jeez, Henry, all over some woman? Do you have any idea the kind of damage control I've had to do? I'm starting to wonder if you are fit to run this company."

"You told him where we'd gone, didn't you?" Henry asked.

"What?" Rick asked.

"I know you did. I know you told Dr. Drake where he could find us. You remembered the tracker on my phone, right?"

"Paranoid much?" Rick asked, shaking his head. "I don't believe anything Margaret has told you about Dr. Drake. He is a fine man. You are delusional if you think he is anything like what Margaret told you. I'll be honest with you, Henry. I think it is time to reach out to your uncle. I think you should be replaced. I don't think you're fit to run this company."

"That would be so helpful for you, wouldn't it? If you could replace me then you could move on with this *T Society* agenda."

"What are you talking about?"

"I'm looking at the problem we have at this company. I give you credit for keeping it hidden for so long, but I know the truth now, and I'm deeply concerned. I know how you feel about women, especially women like Maggie, who are smart and equal to any man."

Rick's face turned red. He was keeping a lid on his control, but barely. "Who made you the authority on women and marriage?"

"I'm a human who has a healthy relationship with women. I come from a place of equality and partnership. You should try it."

"I'm not going to sit here and listen to this bullshit. Society is completely out of hand. We need order and structure. Families are breaking apart because they don't have structure. Women don't know their place."

Henry smiled, "Thank you for validating every dark thought I've ever had about you. I want you to leave."

"Under whose authority?"

He pulled a check and copy of the partnership agreement from under his desk blotter.

"Mine, as managing partner. I'm invoking page 35, section C of our partnership agreement. This check is yours as outlined in the buyout clause. Thank you for your service." He then hit a button on his phone, and the two security guards from the lobby appeared at his door.

"This isn't the end of the conversation," Rick said, incredulous, shaking his head.

Henry ignored him as he motioned for the security men to step into his office.

"Gentlemen, please make sure Mr. Fields has all of his personal items from his office. An empty box is sitting on his desk. Watch what he puts in it. No papers, no storyboards, and no office equipment like a laptop. Then escort him out. Rick, please hand over your company cellphone, keys, and the building pass. Your garage pass has been canceled, as have your corporate credit cards."

"Hey, you can't—"

"Oh, but I have."

"You know, I'm going to talk to Theo. Then you are going to be sorry. We worked together for a long time before you showed up. In a day or two, it is going to be you who is packing."

Henry reached under his blotter a second time and produced a printed email from Theo that gave Henry the endorsement to remove Rick. He placed it before Rick, who read it with increasing anger.

"You'll regret this. Think of all the clients I'll take with me."

"Those aren't the kinds of clients I want. Make sure to get a retainer out of Dr. Drake before he is arrested for assault on his wife and vandalism with breaking and entering," Henry said coldly.

"You're a disgrace, a pussy-whipped disgrace!" Rick yelled as the security team indicated it was time for him to go.

CHAPTER FORTY-EIGHT
(Miss Violet)

Miss Violet always loved dressing up for Halloween. Things weren't much different now, except the wig, glasses, and prosthetics that she used to transform her into a Ukrainian maid, complete with accent, were much better and more sophisticated than the costumes she had worn as a child. And really, since she'd murdered her adulterous husband and moved to Yachats, creating the Miss Violet persona, hadn't she always adapted well to a new character? Well, that time, she needed a little plastic surgery to help her before she became Miss Violet. But really, had she ever liked her nose? No. She liked the new one much better. An argument could be made that every day in Miss Violet's life was Halloween. And she was loving it.

Life became far more interesting when Amber and Jack came into her life. They sparked in her a new, vivacious energy. She was envious of Amber. That girl was not only pretty and kind, but she also knew her stuff. Even though Amber was young enough to be Miss Violet's daughter, Miss Violet wasn't too old to learn a few new tricks from such a spirited woman. Their alliance was fun and given her a new lease on life.

She walked through the long hallways of the waterfront Marriott in Portland as if she belonged there. Well, okay, today she did belong in this hotel. As for secured spaces that needed room keys to even get onto the floors, it wasn't a problem. Not like it was a challenge.

Thanks to Amber's friend Neil, Miss Violet didn't need to

swipe a master pass from an unaware person at the hotel. Neil had given her some gizmo that took care of such little annoyances. It made mincemeat of any lock it met. The best part was that it was a gift so she could keep it!

It had been three days since Michael left Canada. Now, he was in Portland visiting the big bookstores like Powell's, where he was talking his swill and signing books for the traditional housewives of America. If only they knew how he really thought of them. Miss Violet hoped they'd revolt and impale him on a spear, maybe display it publicly for all to enjoy-- but that was just wishful thinking. No one but their inner circle knew how evil he really was.

Miss Violet felt sorry for Maggie for living this nightmare. But she also felt sorry for Amber. Miss Violet could sense that Amber wanted to do this job. She missed her old life. She created the idea and then created the means to make it happen. All Miss Violet was doing was delivering the means to the end. Poor Amber, she liked to facilitate an end result. Miss Violet needed to find her another gig, one that was hands-on to help her remember who she was. Motherhood was fine, but come on, it didn't compare to vigilante justice. Changing a diaper or taking the life of an evil person, definitely one was more thrilling.

Miss Violet knocked on the hotel room door registered to Dr. Drake and announced in an accented tone, "Housekeeping!" She sounded good if she said so herself.

There was no sound. She used her gizmo, making sure the hallway stayed empty.

A moment later, she was inside Dr. Drake's room. Housekeeping already made up the room, so if he suddenly appeared, she could tell him she was a housekeeping supervisor just checking up on some new employee's work. She'd add a big toothy grin that she had been told was irresistible. She always thought it was a good idea to have a good story ready to use in any scenario which might arise. She had several prepared and ready.

Hidden in a little cleaning supply basket she carried on her arm was a plastic baggie of the sinus wash in little packages that Amber had enhanced. She intended to dump out the good stuff from his box and replace it with Amber's formula.

She stepped into the bathroom, did a quick scan, and froze.

Houston, we have a big problem…

Having ditched her hotel uniform for something a little more Portland hippie, Miss Violet walked along the Riverfront of Portland's Willamette River and looked back over her shoulder at the Waterfront Marriott.

Pulling her burner phone from her purse, she dialed the only number this phone would ever call. Amber didn't pick up, so Miss Violet left a message.

"Listen, I visited our friend. Some of his things are there, but a lot of them aren't. I don't think the room has been slept in. I think he is going to be a no-show at his Portland events. He has a signing at Powell's at 3 p.m. today. I'm going, but I'm worried. Very worried. I'll have the phone on me, so call when you can. It is time to come up with Plan B."

CHAPTER FORTY-NINE
(Maggie)

"I wrote up my thoughts on all the small *GreatChef* kitchen appliances," Maggie said. "I can't believe there haven't been injuries. Every appliance I've tried is a piece of crap. The choppers are fine on things like soft cucumbers but give them a carrot, and the machine falls apart, and you have flying shrapnel."

Maggie sat across the desk from Henry several hours after Rick's departure.

"Who wants a soft cucumber?" he asked, shaking his head.

"Exactly my point," she said and gave a little smile.

They were trying very hard to keep it to business as usual, but there were a lot of things in the air. Rick's departure was the talk of the office, and all the young employees were dealing with their personal shock or fear that they might be the next to go.

Henry sighed. Then he said, "It is just as well. We might lose the account. Rick and the owners of *GreatChef* have become close. It bothered me at the time, but I didn't do anything to stop it. Now, I'm not sure if I want to represent such a company. We have a good reputation. If we end up representing them, it could take us down. The knives were a clue, but I hoped that it was isolated to one part of their company. But it sounds like it isn't."

"What about the revenue?"

"This happens all the time in advertising. Easy come, easy go. I care more about your safety and you than any stupid account," Henry said softly and then smiled. The way he looked at her made her blush, and she knew, just knew, he would never let her go, and she didn't want him to. This was what it felt like to fall in love.

"This, between us, is the way it is supposed to feel," she said. "It is so new to me. Yet it is happening in the middle of this mess."

"You can't choose the timing. This is how it feels when it is right, and it is love."

He said love and she needed a moment for the word to sink in.

"I'm sorry it has cost you so much," she said.

"What wouldn't I do for love?" he asked. He got up from his chair, circled the desk, and pulled her into his arms, where they remained for several minutes.

Finally, she asked, "Is there any word nicer than love?"

"I don't think so," he said.

"I get giddy at the thought of coming home to you."

"Why don't you blow off the shopping, and let's go home now? It has already been one hell of a day."

"I know. I'm sorry but I can't. This is the suit I left in last week when we ran to Whistler. It is the only appropriate business outfit I have. I have nothing to wear tomorrow. I must go shopping."

"Okay, I just wished I could go with you, but despite what I said, there are a lot of fires I need to put out."

"I'll only be a couple of hours."

"Well, I think I might be counting the minutes. Be careful."

"I will," she said and enjoyed a final kiss before she left.

CHAPTER FIFTY
(Amber)

Amber chatted with the other moms at the weekly playdate in the neighborhood park as if she were a professional at this motherhood thing. Let it be known she knew she was faking it. The fact the twins were thriving under her and Jack's care was as much of a surprise to Amber as it was to Jack. They were frauds. Okay, they loved their children. They would protect and defend them until the end of time. But they didn't know the first thing about raising them other than what they'd read in books and seen on television. Okay, so Jack had the advantage because his mother was wonderful, but he couldn't remember how she'd become that way. But Amber's mother was a piece of work. Aside from being horrible at raising her only child, her next best accomplishment was grifting with Amber as bait to every pedophile she met. Amber hadn't seen her mother in years. That was okay.

"Oh, my gawd, have you tried the apricot puree by Healthy Baby?" one of the mothers asked Amber. She had forgotten the woman's name a few weeks ago, but the woman brought their dog, a golden retriever named Honey. Now that was a sweet dog.

"No, I haven't," Amber said, shaking her head. Ground-up apricots sounded disgusting.

"They are so disgusting," the woman said, mirroring Amber's thoughts. "And they give little Robbie the runs. No, thank you."

See? She didn't need to try them to know they were bad. Little Robbie didn't look like he was going to grow up to be a powerhouse adult human, anyway. Heck, only two weeks earlier, Amber watched him eating dirt from one of the flowerbeds, worms and all.

Clay and Libby sat on a gingham blanket and quietly played with their trucks and dolls while the other teacup humans ran around the park like hyenas on meth. Maybe she and Jack were doing something right after all.

Sweet Pumpkin lay nearby, doing her frog dog imitation, legs spread eagle, cooling the undercarriage, judging as she observed the crazy around her. She would catch Amber's eye occasionally as if to say, "Can you believe these little animals in human form are our future?"

Amber felt a little vibration in her pocket. Her pager went off when someone called her burner phone. She had to cut the playdate short, thankfully.

Ten minutes later, the twins were set up in the living room, and Amber dashed to her greenhouse and back again to find the twins in the same position she'd left them, playing with their toys and smiling.

With the burner phone in hand, she listened to Miss Violet's message and then swore under her breath. Libby looked at her, and Amber realized the little peepers in her life had big ears.

The phone rang while in her hand. Miss Violet.

"Hey," she said.

"I went to the 3 p.m. event. He was a no-show. The organizer said he got ill, but I'll tell you, he is out in the wind. I think you should warn your sister-in-law."

After a few more words, Amber grabbed her landline and dialed Maggie's number from memory.

Thankfully, Maggie answered on the second ring.

"Hey, I'm just trying on a few things to replace what I lost. How are you? I miss shopping with you."

THE VOICE OF REASON

Amber knew about the destruction of Maggie's rental and possessions. She was more than a little disturbed. She thought about an unplanned trip to Vancouver then, but they confirmed that Michael was back in the US. Well, now it was time to make a judgment call. She just hoped she wasn't making a mistake.

Shattering anyone's happiness always took a toll on her.

"I have something to tell you, and I want you to listen very carefully. Michael isn't in Portland. I have on very good information that his whereabouts are unknown. A friend of mine went to his signing, and he wasn't there. He isn't in his hotel room either."

"How do you—"

"We never had this conversation. Now, watch your back. I will call Jack, and you should call Henry, okay?"

"Y...yesss."

"Be careful. Have your pepper spray out and in your hand, okay?"

"Ooo...okay," Maggie managed.

CHAPTER FIFTY-ONE
(Dr. Michael Allan Drake)

Okay, so Michael could admit that Richard wasn't a complete twat waffle. The man came forth with adequate intelligence once in a while. Heck, today, he'd given Michael not only the address of the Sidepiece's condo, but the actual lock code to his front door and the alarm code. Michael was actually a little impressed by the short, pudgy little man. He had to remember never to cross Richard. The man had a vengeful streak and was a short-man syndrome weasel. I mean, heck, he turned on his supposed good friend after just a few conversations with Michael. It spoke to Michael's ability to persuade the masses. Wow! Well, at least now they had a common enemy. It was all fascinating enough to make Michael bail on part of his book tour, and really, hadn't it worked out well?

He'd been able to tell his agent, Stoner Benjamin, and the promoter of the book tour that the inadequate food led to food poisoning. It bought him enough time to do what he needed to do. A quick five hour drive up to Vancouver to deal with his problem, and then he could return only hours later and resume his tour as if recovered from his illness.

Michael looked around the well-manicured common area of the condominium where the Sidepiece lived. He could admit he liked the discipline of the gardeners. They kept a tidy and efficient outdoor space. If he could, he'd move them to Minnesota. He could use their services.

When they finished on the common area and left, and he was sure he was alone, he let himself into the Sidepiece's condo.

The interior of the Sidepiece's place was more to Michael's liking than Margaret's condo. Besides the intimacy of her, they had that in common.

There were good lines, lots of dark colors, and none of the junk that Margaret liked. No photos of the loser family. No plants. No knickknacks. Okay, a framed diploma from Northwestern in the Sidepiece's home office. Kind of ostentatious. But why, why was he slumming with Margaret? Hell, Michael knew he could do better. He bet the Sidepiece could, too.

Okay, okay, don't get distracted by sideways thoughts that are more like verbal diarrhea. He had a plan and had perfected it on the drive up from Portland. He was, however, early for the main act, the grand event. The endgame. It was a few minutes after four. He had to prepare for the arrival of Margaret and the Sidepiece. Well, he had a little time to kill, a plan already forming in his mind based on the layout of the Sidepiece's condo and a few very dark conclusions he'd come to on his five-hour drive.

In the kitchen, a neat, masculine space, he found the liquor cabinet above the refrigerator. This guy, the Sidepiece, knew how to enjoy himself. Michael poured three fingers of Blanton's green-label bourbon into a glass. It wasn't his beloved Southern Comfort, and it was beyond pretentious for his palate, but it would do.

One hour, twenty-two minutes, and three Blanton's later, he was in position when the Sidepiece came home. Surprisingly, he was alone. That was okay, Michael could adapt.

Sidepiece wasn't paying attention. He was stupid. Well, surprise, buttercup!

The Sidepiece opened the door, and Michael was waiting. Before either could speak, Michael hit him with his stun gun, the sensors flying out and hitting the Sidepiece in the chest with a sickening crackle.

The Sidepiece looked like he wanted to say something, so Michael hit him a second time. Instead of speaking, the man dropped like a sack of rocks and cried out in agony.

Michael smiled. Good. It had begun.

Michael got to work with his zip ties and the duct tape he'd thought to add.

Three minutes later, the man was trussed up like a holiday hog on a spit with a dozen zip ties. He was bleeding from the nose and trying to communicate, his eyes darting here and there and looking, well, scared. Yeah, the motor skills would be sluggish. So, no communication, not for a few minutes, buddy. *You've been taken out by a superior male,* Michael thought. *That's what you got for trying to play with another man's property.*

Damn, Michael smiled. He loved his zip ties. And he'd done good work on the Sidepiece. He hadn't exactly settled on a plan for what he would do with The Sidepiece after he'd dealt with Margaret, but the final decision would come to him. And, when it did, it would be spectacular.

CHAPTER FIFTY-TWO
(Maggie)

Maggie tried to call Henry for a third time. He always picked up for her. He never let her go to voicemail. But today, this third time, her call had gone to the lone world of voicemail, and in light of Amber's messages, she felt sick.

She felt fear like a familiar dark chill, and she knew, just knew, it was something much worse. It was a knowing. Henry was in danger. Michael had removed him from the equation. He might be injured. He might be dead. The fear sunk in, but she couldn't believe it.

How dare Michael take this beautiful man from her? She had given him six years, five months, and four days. She wouldn't give him one more minute. It ended today.

She parked in the lot of Henry's condo and considered her options. Henry's car was parked at the end of the second row, which she knew was his preferred space. Carefully, to make sure Michael wouldn't see her if he was waiting to ambush her, she passed by Henry's car and felt it. It was still warm. He hadn't been home for long.

Picking up her cell, she typed the number of one of the officers who reported to her condo and witnessed the carnage firsthand. But then she paused, finger hovering over her phone. Then, instead of hitting the dial button, she deleted the number and pocketed her phone.

She couldn't involve others. No. It was time to settle this herself. If the police came and Michael went to jail, he wouldn't stay for long, and the pattern would continue. He would terrorize her when he made bail or did his time, whatever. It wouldn't stop him. That couldn't happen. She wanted her life back. She deserved happiness. But if he had harmed Henry, her happiness was already gone. She had nothing to lose.

Her mind made up, she walked confidently toward the front door of Henry's condo. She amassed several bags from shopping that she held in her arms as she walked. She didn't need the key. Henry had given her the code to his front door. She'd never used it because she had never had to. He always pulled open the door for her as if he had been watching. But not tonight. Because she knew Michael had done something to him so that he couldn't. If he'd harmed Henry, she'd rip him limb from limb. Killing him would be too easy, too quick.

She entered the code and pushed open the door.

Showtime.

Worst fears realized. Stepping inside, she stepped over a blood smear on the marble entryway. It wasn't a lot, but for Henry to shed one drop was one drop too many.

The door shut behind her, and she stepped along the entryway. One step. Two steps. Three steps. Her heels echoed on the marble floor. A light flicked on. Michael appeared at the end of the long hallway that led to the rest of the space, and he had the audacity to smile.

"Margaret," he said. "Welcome home. You've been so bad this time I don't even know where to begin. But even knowing that you've been bad, I'm happy to see you, dear wife."

"Where is Henry?" she asked.

"Your little Sidepiece? Oh, he's twitching in the corner of the living room. I don't know, shall I toss him in the harbor or just slit his throat? After all, he made my wife break her vows to me. Did he seduce you, or did you go willingly, you wanton whore?"

In his hand, he had a taser, which he raised and pointed at her. He said nothing else, but she saw his hand flicker, defusing the trigger. When he fired, the wires shot out from the gun-like machine, searching for flesh, her flesh. Unfortunately for the prongs, they hit one of the shopping bags she held in front of herself like protective armor. It held two pairs of shoes in boxes. The prongs stuck in the sturdy cardboard and sparked.

Michael hadn't considered this. His face contorted to rage as he tried to pull the taser wires back and stepped toward Margaret.

He muttered, "You bitch."

"You made me that way. But it ends today."

When he got so close that she could smell his aftershave, something woodsy she'd come to despise, she dropped the packages in her right hand, pulled the pink *GreatChef* knife she concealed in the waist band of her new raincoat, and plunged it into Michael's torso in one, smooth movement. It felt natural, like cutting a piece of steak. Well, the *GreatChef* knife was good for something after all.

Her major in college might have been marketing, but her minor was anatomy. At one point, she wanted to be a doctor. She gave the knife a little extra upward jerk while it was still in his body, which could be explained away by his frame falling against her. She smiled as Michael stood before her, his face showing shock and then disbelief as he realized what she had done. Then, he crumpled.

She hadn't hit his sternum, which had been her fear, but she did know where she plunged wouldn't be an easy fix and was, hopefully, fatal. Doctors were good, but they couldn't reanimate someone who was already beyond dead.

She watched in fascination as his eyes went from focused on her to realization to nothing. His body fell to the floor. She felt the concussion of the fall in the heels of her shoes, then up her legs, her stomach, and finally in her consciousness. He wasn't there any longer. He wouldn't hurt her again. Not with his words, his fists, or with any weapon. It was over.

She had done it.

"You should have just let me go," she said leaning down and looking at Michael's body with the knife still in it. She silenced *The Voice of Reason*.

She pulled out her cell and dialed 911. While waiting for an answer, she whispered, "If you had just walked away, I might have retained some of my humanity. But after living with you, I changed. I'd have never thought I was capable of killing someone…but everyone can evolve, I suppose…"

EPILOGUE
*(One Year Later
Fiji)*

Amber arranged the white cattleya orchids with deep golden throats in Maggie's upswept hair and then smiled. Then she gave her sister-in-law a quick hug and said, "You look beautiful. I'm so proud of you. But I'm still sad you'll be living in Vancouver."

"Our new house is big. Even if we have kids, there will be guest rooms for you, Jack, and the twins. You know you have an open invitation. And you'd better take advantage of it!"

"Well, that's good because we will be visiting."

The sleeveless, white satin gown hugged Maggie's frame in all the right places. She especially liked the plunging neckline that showed just the right amount of cleavage. When Henry proposed in the hospital room where he'd been taken on the night of Michael's attack, she did not hesitate despite the fact she figured he was on some pretty good painkillers. By chance, they should have waited to pick another night than the night when she had killed her ex-husband, but they were in love, and the dark cloud over them finally dissipated.

"I wish everyone in the press would stop referring to me as the black widow," Maggie said.

"Wait until they read your book," Amber said, their reflections shining in the mirror as their eyes met.

"Oh, damn, they could say I silenced *The Voice of Reason*. I think it is enough how they have been all over this and exposing *The T Society* stuff."

"I think we all dodged a bullet on *The T Society*. Their rise to power was starting to gain some traction," Amber said. "I think now they will be closely watched."

"Yeah, but will anything happen, or will they go deeper underground?" Maggie asked.

"They will always have a shadow. They will have to be watched."

"Their hatred of women is staggering," Maggie said.

Amber leaned close and said, "Thankfully, not all men think like that. I think we got a couple of the good ones."

"I agree."

Michael's publisher approached Maggie a month after Michael's death was ruled a justifiable homicide due to self-defense, and Maggie was cleared. They wanted her to write the story of *The Voice of Reason*. The book was written in two months in the very office where Michael had once done his infamous podcasts and radio show. It was due to be published in six weeks, or as she liked to think of it, the week after she and Henry returned from their honeymoon. After a week in Fiji, they were going to the Cook Islands and then onto Hawaii. It would be one tropical paradise after another.

GreatChef had not enjoyed the publicity of their knife being used to murder the famous Dr. Michael Allan Drake, but when public opinion started to support Maggie, they joined the winning team and awarded the very lucrative marketing campaign to the newly-created advertising agency, *Hudson and Daniels*.

It had taken her those two months when she'd written the book to also clean out the house she shared with Michael. She stayed each night with Amber and Jack, not wishing to ever spend a night in that prison again. And down in the basement, as she always feared, Michael had been busy and was building a cage. It was a new horror and beyond frightening. Was it meant for her? No authority wanted to commit and say that it was, but she knew the truth.

She wanted to demolish it, but her new agent, sweet Ben, who had been Michael's agent despite disliking him immensely, asked her to keep it for publicity's sake. She caved but removed the door so no one could ever be held in it.

"Henry is completely, totally in love with you," Amber said. "I really like that about him. He's a nice guy too."

"I love him. For the first time in my life, I'm in love. When I think of how close I came to losing him—"

Amber patted her shoulder.

"He got a nosebleed and a mild concussion. He's fine. And the worst thing you pictured, well, it never happened. Few people understand that. When we worry, we always project the worst case scenario."

"I know, but to tell you the truth, the real truth...I wanted Michael dead," she admitted. "I wanted to kill him."

"We all did, honey. Come on, Henry is excited. He and Jack are dancing around to the Polynesian band with the twins, and your parents, as well as Henry's, are getting shnockered. Let's get you married before anyone gets injured."

The night after Maggie and Henry's wedding, Amber and Jack sat on the veranda of their condo in Fiji, entertaining special guests. The sound of waves hitting the shore just beyond their balcony was like soft tropical music in the background.

The children had an active day and were already in their bedroom, asleep.

Miss Violet and Neil were sharing their table, enjoying a late candlelit supper of Kokoda, a national dish of ceviche, featuring lime, coconut milk, and fresh fish. They were on their second pitcher of piña coladas and contemplating a third.

"I don't know what to say," Miss Violet said.

"It all worked out in the end," Neill said. "But Maggie was lucky, so was Henry."

"If I could have done it over again, I'd have just done it quickly and silently," Amber said. "It would have saved a lot of drama."

"If you'd have told me my sister was capable of murder... well, I wouldn't have believed it," Jack said. "She did some wet work and didn't hesitate."

"Maybe it runs in the family," Miss Violet said.

"Please don't say that. Can you imagine what Clay and Libby could be like one day?" Amber asked. "I don't need to be thinking about this. Especially when they start dating...Libby is already too cunning for her own good."

"I kind of feel like I'm the odd one out. I mean, I've never killed someone," Neil said.

"Do you want to?" Miss Violet asked.

"Only if they are bad. I just don't know if I could do it."

"My advice, don't start. It is overrated," Amber said. "Don't become a monster like us."

"I don't think of you as a monster," Neil said.

"Thank you, and I'm serious, it is overrated."

"Liar," Jack interjected. "You love it, and we all know it."

Amber smiled coquettishly at the rest of the group and then kissed Jack, "He knows me so well."

"May I ask you a question?" Miss Violet asked.

"Shoot," Amber said with a smile.

"Have you ever thought about maybe coming back, doing a little more than the occasional job?"

Jack placed his hand on Amber's and said, "Do you mind if I add to what Miss V is saying?"

"By all means..." Amber said.

"I agree with Miss Violet. I think you should get back to it. It is something you really enjoy. Maybe not the killing, but the justice."

Amber smiled and said, "You wouldn't mind?"

"No, I think I'd like it," he said and gave her hand a squeeze.

Amber nodded, "Mmm...maybe we could do it together. We always talked about it. Maybe it is time to put it into action."

"Exactly my thought," Jack said.

Amber laughed and then said, "Talk about an interesting family business..."

The Changing Waves Nursing Home & Memory Center

"Elinore, Michael isn't coming today," the nurse said kindly and shook her head. It was like this every day. Mrs. Drake had been told repeatedly that her son wasn't coming to visit her, but that didn't stop her from throwing everything she could get her hands on when they tried to explain he wouldn't be coming. They could only hope old age would take her soon because her son would never come again.

"Michael is a good son!" she screamed as she threw her full lunch plate to the floor.

One of the aids on duty rolled her eyes at the other aid.

"I know," the second aid said. "I'm up. It is my turn. I know she doesn't understand, but I keep trying to tell her anyway. It makes you want to cry."

"It is sad, but I have a feeling she was never a nice person to begin with," the first aid commented. "Just like her son."

"I was here once when her son and daughter-in-law visited. You know, back when she could still remember people. The stuff she said to the daughter-in-law, well, it was awful. And her son did nothing to stop his mother from seriously insulting his wife. I always had a feeling about him. He just was evil, you know?"

"Well, we know where he got it from."

"I still can't believe that sweet young woman...well..."

"Was capable of murder?" the first aid asked in a whisper.

"That is the word you are looking for. Good riddance! She did the world and womankind a favor."

"Amen to that," the second aid said.

"Margaret, I hate Margarrreeetttt!" Mrs. Drake screamed as she pounded her fist on the lunch table, then she reached for two glass bottles, one containing oil and the other containing vinegar. With surprising strength, she threw them. They shattered when tossed against the wall in perfect emulsification.

Maggie stood with her new husband on the beach in Fiji, their arms gently around each other as they watched the sunrise.

"I need to say something," she said.

"Speak away," he whispered in her ear.

"I really think the best revenge is being happy."

"Are you happy?" he asked.

"Very," she said, snuggling deeper in his arms.

"Good, because I've never been happier," Henry said.

"I finally got my happily ever after," she said as he turned her body toward his, and they kissed in the warmth of the rising sun.

Acknowledgments

Thank you to Gail and Mom, who moved me out of that house in three hours, while The Voice of Reason was unaware and otherwise oblivious.

About the Author

Mary Oldham is a celebrated author of contemporary romance and romantic suspense, with 16 published books to her name. A three-time Golden Heart Finalist with the Romance Writers of America, her compelling storytelling has earned significant acclaim, including a 2025 International Impact Book Awards Finalist for The Poison Garden and a 2023 Maggie Finalist for her novel CRUSH.

Her debut novel, The Silver Linings Wedding Dress Auction, was optioned and developed by Dooney Pictures. Mary was asked to write the screenplay, leading to her induction into the Writers Guild of America West in 2024. Readers praise her work for its engaging plots, unique writing style, and strong character development.

When she's not writing, Mary divides her time between Portland and Yachats, Oregon, where she finds inspiration from the Pacific Ocean.

Also by Mary Oldham

Don't miss any of Mary Oldham's other books, available in Print or Digital at Amazon or Barnes and Noble:

Stand Alone Titles

CRUSH, May 2022

Instant Daddy, Just Add Rum, February 2025

The Poison Garden Series

The Poison Garden, 2023

Madam Emma's Love Emporium, 2024

The Voice of Reason, 2025

The Silver Linings Series

The Silver Linings Wedding Dress Auction, October 2021

Sisters Before Misters, 2023

Enchanted, Book 3, February 2024

The Hotel Baron's Series

A Paris Affair, November 2021

A Summer Affair, December 2021

A Roman Affair, April 2022

The Aphrodite Sisters Series

Sage's Redemption, Book 1, October 2022

Toni's Secret, Book 2, November 2022

Roxie's Circus, Book 3, December 2022

Kimberly's Reckoning, Book 4, March 2023

Audiobooks

The Silver Linings Wedding Dress Auction, April 2022

Narrated by Gildart Jackson

The Poison Garden, December 2023

Narrated by Robin MacAlpine

Mary loves to hear from her readers! You can email her to sign up for her newsletter at www.maryoldham.com.